Praise for The Unknown Woman of the Seine

*The Unknown Woman of the Seine i*s a haunting and seductive marvel set in 19th century France, when the Eiffel Tower was considered a scandal. Brooks Hansen captivates the reader the way artists, writers and shopkeepers were enthralled with the mysterious woman who drowned. Hansen brilliantly imagines what has remained a mystery until now, in a fiercely dramatic and sensual world. The Unknown Woman is a gem."—Patty Dann, author of *Mermaids*

"Indelibly original, fastidiously seamed, and atmospherically mysterious, The Unknown Woman of the Seine could have only been conjured by Brooks Hansen, who writes us directly into his dreams."— Beth Kephart, award-winning author of *Wife | Daughter | Self: A Memoir in Essays*

"A fascinating, amazing true story—or is it? Brooks Hansen's dazzling weave of truth and fantasy brings us into the world of 19th century Paris, full of intrigue, scoundrels, a damsel very much in distress, and a dogged hero pursuing the truth no matter the cost. It's a masterful tale, brilliantly told—a mystery whose solution is so surprising and yet perfectly inevitable it makes you want to start reading the book all over again." — Nick Davis, author of *Competing with Idiots*

"*The Unknown Woman of the Seine* is at once a literary gem and a deeply compelling mystery. With sparkling prose and intricate plotting, Hansen creates a vibrant and haunting vision of late 19th century Paris—a complex puzzle delicately unspooled with deliciously satisfying results."—McCormick Templeman, author of *The Glass Casket*

The Unknown Woman

of the Seine

a novel by

Brooks Hansen

Delphinium Books

THE UNKNOWN WOMAN
OF THE SEINE

For information, address DELPHINIUM BOOKS, INC.,
16350 Ventura Boulevard, Suite D
PO Box 803
Encino, CA 91436

Library of Congress Cataloging-in-Publication Data is
available on request.
ISBN: 978-195300213-6
22 23 24 25 26 LSC 10 9 8 7 6 5 4 3 2 1
First Paperback Edition

This is a work of fiction. Names and characters are either the
product of the author's imagination or are used fictitiously; any
resemblance to actual persons living or dead is coincidental.

Artwork and cover design by Colin Dockrill, AIGA

"No Bhagavan, the Buddha cannot be recognized by the thirty-two signs, because the signs the Buddha speaks of have no meaning in themselves. This is why they are called the thirty-two *signs* of perfection."

—*The Diamond Sutra*

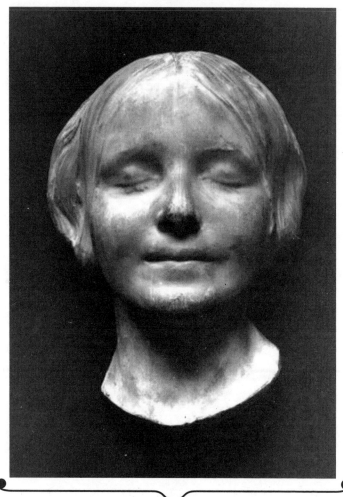

Contents

Author's Note: A Brief History of the Mask

Part One: *The Morgue, November 24, 1889*
1. *Brassard*

Part Two: *Tuesday, October 29, 1889 (or one month prior)*
2. *The Burial*
3. *Wolves*
4. *The Overnight*

Part Three: *Wednesday Evening*
5. *François Michaud and Bruno Chavarin*
6. *The Tower*
7. *The Zoo*
8. *Snakes, Pigeons, and Rats*

Part Four: *Wednesday Night*
9. *The Vault*
10. *Le Montyon*
11. *Skulls*
12. *Pennyroyal*
13. *Café de la Paix*
14. *Two More Geese*
15. *The Duel*

Part Five: *Thursday*
16. *Anonymity*
17. *The Tribunal*
18. *Entente*
19. *The Crypt*
20. *La Bijouterie*
21. *The Kliegs*
22. *The Wagon*

Part Six: *Friday*
23. *"Peg"*
24. *Sausages and Squab*
25. *The Little Bull*
26. *"Tathagata"*
27. *Mon Jésu*
28. *The River*

Author's Note:

A Brief History of the Mask

B ack in the first decade of the last century, there was a little shop on the Left Bank in Paris, halfway down the Rue Racine, that sold all kinds of plaster casts and molds. These might be of hands, busts, statuettes, or any figure really, but the most popular by far were the death masks, the molds made from the faces of the recently departed, and the most popular of these were of Napoleon, of course, this being Paris. And Ludwig van Beethoven. And Abraham Lincoln. And her.

In fact, hers was the mask that the owner of the shop, the *mouleur*, chose to hang beside the door. He did this in part because the mask was his own work, of which he was justly proud, but also because he knew it drew the passersby. Men mostly, Bohemian types with no money in their pockets and too much time on their hands.

"Who is she?" they would ask.

He pretended to be annoyed by the question. He would shoo them away like rats or pigeons, but only because he knew they'd be back—the best imaginable advertisement, standing there outside his little shop, gazing past their own reflections at her image.

And what did they see?

A young woman, rendered in chalk-white gypsum, which did well to capture the detail—each lash and little crease around the eyes and on the lips—but softly. The word "serene" often came to mind. Maybe even "beautiful," though more so in expression than in feature. Some saw innocence; others, ecstasy. The poet Rilke wrote of how she seemed to be smiling almost, but "so deceptively, as if she knew."

And though it was true that many of these "customers" were, like Rilke, content to stand outside the window and gaze, there were others, too, who paid—a full five francs—to take her away with them and do as they pleased. Treat her as a curio, an ornament, or an *objet d'art*.

To the artists, she was a study tool. It wasn't long before she could be found in almost any studio in Paris, or atelier, or academy. The masters set her by their lamps and windows to demonstrate the different types of lighting: soft, hard, and reflected; halftones; top light; under-light; split-light; *contre jour* and color bleeding. She helped teach them this in Paris. This was her first job.

To the writers, she was more muse than model. They wrote stories about her, and poems, and stories about poets. They gave her names. *Silencieux*. And *L'Inconnue*. They'd tell the stories to the women they lured up to their lairs. Afterward, flushed and drying in the chill air of their garrets, they'd rehearse the plots; it helped to hear them out loud—tales of obsession, and drowning maidens, river kings, and masks that spoke.

Eventually they'd get around to the true parts, too. The women would insist on knowing what was known—how the body had been found along the banks, all the way down at Saint-Germain apparently. The police took her back to the morgue behind Our Lady. No sign of injury or struggle. And no name either, needless to say.

She was there a month, in keeping with the city codes. They stored her in a frozen drawer at night, to make sure she didn't mold, then pulled her out each morning and put her on display with all the other *macchabées*—stiffs.

The public came to look at her. She was the most popular attraction they'd ever had at the morgue. No one had seen a face like hers. Not in death anyway. But no one came to claim her either, so what finally became of the body, the writers had no idea. An unmarked grave? Maybe the kiln in Montrouge. Whatever they did with the suicides.

"Suicides?" At this, the lovers would sit up in their beds, confused.

The writers nodded, yes. By the stove, they lit the cigarettes they'd been rolling, which flamed until they drew. "That's was what the coroner concluded."

But this made no sense. The lovers gestured to the mask again. It was hanging on the door, or leaning on the mantel. "But this is not the face of *suicide*," they'd say.

Indeed, the writers agreed, emerging from their clouds to gallantly hand over the smoke.

"Ç'est le mystère."

§

In 1925, a German publisher named Ernst Benkard heard the story, or what was known. He saw the face and had it photographed for a book he was preparing, *Das Ewige Antlitz*, an anthology of death masks. The rest of the subjects in the book were well known. Robespierre and Goethe, Lorenzo de' Medici, Wagner, Haydn, Cromwell, Pushkin. Shakespeare even.

But who do you think they put on the cover?

The collection was a success, enough that four years later, an entirely different book of death masks appeared—*Das letzte Gesicht*—which once again included her image. Two years after that came a novel, *Die Unbekannte* ("*The Unknown*"), featuring her on the cover. It was about a provincial orphan girl who meets a handsome diplomat in Paris. They fall in love, even though the man is engaged to an American woman waiting for him in Egypt. In the end the man is forced to choose.

The book became a bestseller. The Unknown Woman was better known than she had ever been, looking out (or in) from the laps of readers lounging on beach chairs, or sitting on trains, planes and porches and in beauty salons, having their hair done like hers, in a loose bob. A movie was made, based on the book. Famous actresses started to look like her as well, especially the ingénues. And the teenage girls, too— gazing up at the giant screens, or sitting before the mirrors in their bedrooms, pouching their lips, wishing them fuller, squinting their eyes, straining to see what they looked like closed.

Of course, she had her doubters, too, who said the whole thing was a hoax. She was no drowning victim. She was Italian, an heiress of some kind. She was Hungarian, but certainly never dead. No corpse could keep such an expression, the doctors said. The muscles wouldn't hold.

To which the writer's answer stood: Exactly. That was the whole point.

Nabokov wrote a poem about her—or one of his characters did. Anaïs Nin included her in a story. The philosopher Camus was said to show her off at parties. And all of this is true. Man Ray photographed her. And names of lesser note were no less devoted, and no less liberal in their inventions, their drawings, the rumors they began, the random photographs in which they claimed to have identified her. *Look at the brows. Look at the mouth.* New names emerged—Ewa, Olga—to go with the old. She was Ophelia, no? A modern Mona Lisa. Or Mary . . . either one.

§

The name that finally stuck was "Anna."

In 1958, at a conference for Scandinavian anesthesiologists, an Austrian-born physician named Peter Safar met the Swedish doctor, Bjorn Lind. Safar was living in America at the time, in Baltimore, but the two had been working independently in the field of emergency medicine, developing the procedures that would come to be known as CPR, or cardiopulmonary resuscitation: clearing the air passage, mouth-to-mouth resuscitation, and closed-chest cardiac massage. The doctors agreed, this simple sequence not only served to keep trauma victims alive, in some cases it even brought them *back* from a clinical death.

The problem was one of implementation. The sorts of situations in which CPR would be most useful tended to arise suddenly and unexpectedly, when no doctor or trained physician was around. For Lind's and Safar's methods to have impact—to save lives—there needed to be some way of educating and training the public at large. But how? Back in Baltimore, Safar had been working with medical students, living volunteers willing to practice on one another. Laymen would never agree to such a thing. Lind suggested something like a custom-designed mannequin. As it happened, he knew a Norwegian children's book publisher turned doll maker, Asmund Laerdal, who in more recent years had applied his manufacturing experience to developing prosthetic medical devices for the Red Cross. Laerdal had also almost lost his son in a near drowning incident some years before, so he was very enthusiastic when Lind and Safar came to him with their idea. He welcomed the technical challenge—of designing a kind of life-sized doll with a built-in air passage and a pliable chest cavity that would respond to compression. But he anticipated the cultural obstacles as well. Male students might be more reluctant to practice on a male dummy, for instance. On the other hand, if the subject were a too-attractive female, that could also prove distracting.

This was when Laerdal thought of the Unknown Woman of the Seine. He knew her story. He knew her face as well, enough to understand that while her looks had been appealing, there was nothing salacious about them. Or morbid. They were strangely incorrupt. The poetic appeal was not lost either, of using the image of the continent's most famous and mysterious drowning victim to help save others from the same fate. If the project was a success, the Unknown Woman would not have died in vain.

He set to work, first developing the rubber torso, making sure it was of a proper heft and responsiveness, with room for a rudimentary respiratory canal. The face he saved for last, aware that he would have to simplify, homogenize. Still, he did his best to retain the features of the original, and the expression. It was important to him that the likeness be hers.

When he showed the final product to Safar and Lind, they were pleased. They named her *Rescusci Anna*. She entered into production and was soon being shipped all over the continent, as well as to Britain and North America. Just as she'd been back at the beginning—in all the ateliers and academies of Paris—the Unknown Woman was once again a teaching tool. Classes met in school gymnasiums, conference rooms, poolsides, beaches, boat decks and piers. Lifeguards came, and security men, stewards and stewardesses, teachers, Boy Scouts, Girl Scouts, and volunteers, all to learn the lifesaving methods of Safar and Lind. Clear the wind pipe, pump the chest, tilt the chin, set mouth to mouth, and blow.

"The most kissed lips in all the world"—so it was said—which wasn't really the most accurate description, unless they meant in the Prince Charming way, of trying to awaken her from the deep and dreamless sleep. In that case, one could say that's all that *any* of them had been doing, going all the way back to the Rue Racine and those shiftless oglers outside the *mouleur*'s window, but including the storytellers, the painters, the poets, and thinkers. Their methods may have differed, but every one of them was attempting the same trick, trying to bring her back somehow, figure out who she really was. What life accounted for that face, or that expression? Even better, what death?

The writers were right. *This* has always been the mystery.

Part One

The Morgue,
November 24, 1889

Chapter 1

Brassard

Down the pew, Berenice was looking back at 'Nante-bleue with those begging eyes again. *Please.*

Again 'Nante-bleue shook her head *no*, but mostly because this was no time to be asking for such things, during the *Agnus Dei.*

Still, even 'Nante-bleue—whose name, it may bear saying, derived from the fact that she was the girls' governess, or gouver*nante*, and that her eyes, central to an otherwise paunched and dowdy appearance, had compared favorably with the eyes of their former governess, Nante-gris—'Nante-bleue had to agree, the service this afternoon seemed to be taking an awfully long time. If she'd known that Monsignor Mignolette would be presiding—Monsignor "Mini-steps," as the children called him—she might have agreed to go *before* the mass and not after, as Berenice was so desperately pleading.

It must have taken him five whole minutes to incense the altar, at the conclusion of which he seemed to just stop for a moment, as if he'd fallen asleep standing up, or as if it were now his purpose to breathe back in all the smoke he'd just dispensed. Again, Berenice leaned around to look at her. *Please?*

Again, 'Nante-bleue shook her head *no*, and *stop*, so Berenice faced front with a resigned sigh and let the bobbing of her left knee signal her protest for the remainder of the service.

What she wanted was permission to leave right after communion, which was not something 'Nante-bleue ever considered. Especially when they came all the way to Our Lady, it was her custom to stay for the *Te Deum*. Berenice knew this, but she also knew that the morgue was closing at five o'clock, and that this was the last day they would be showing the girl.

'Nante-bleue wanted to see, too, truth be told, and Berenice *was* being good. She had taken her little sister Mona's hand, and they were going through the rosary together—even now, as the family two rows ahead was getting up and leaving, all six of them. One couldn't be sure of the reason, of course, but it was a reminder that there was bound to be a rush as soon as service was over. And who knew how long the Monsignor would take with the final blessings? It could be another quarter of an hour! It was for her own sake, then, as much as for Berenice's, that 'Nante-bleue finally sent a silent prayer to the north rose window, and then another prayer to the Virgin and child, and another to St. Denis and all the saints in all the blue windows gleaming in. She hoped they would understand.

Communion was served. The cathedral was not full, but again, their line was moving slowly; the Monsignor's hands were trembling and uncertain, and he liked to bless the children. By the time Berenice approached the altar, she appeared to have resigned herself. She knelt patiently, perfectly, submitted her tongue, and crossed herself. It wasn't until she came to the top of the aisle leading back to the pew that she gave one last look around at 'Nante-bleue—*please?*

With the barest perceptible tilt of her head, 'Nante-bleue nodded yes.

Berenice bolted straight for St. Stephen's gate. She would save them a place.

Her little sister, Mona, was torn. She wanted to follow. She wanted to be loyal to 'Nante-bleue as well, and to show her thanks, so this is what she chose to do. She put her hand in 'Nante-bleue's and they made their way more slowly to the exit, 'Nante-bleue hoping that the bombast of the organ might provide them cover and that the Monsignor would not see them leave.

It was a gray day and cold outside, getting colder in the shadow of the cathedral; the wind was whisking the thin layer of snow on the ground without apparent purpose. 'Nante-bleue and Mona huddled close as they made their way around the chapter house to the morgue—a low, colorless, and windowless building, like a great stone coffin by the river. Already there was a small crowd shifting and stomping out front, in more of a loop than a line. There was only one door, a large one. People entered on the right side and left on the left, but you could go straight back on line if you wanted to see the bodies again, which was what it looked like most of the people were doing today.

Thankfully, Berenice was already there, and not too far from the door now; she cleared a space when they arrived. "She's my 'Nante, and my sister." She'd been joined by a school friend as well, Helaine, who apparently hadn't seen the girl either, which was why they *all* were there, of course. The two women just ahead were saying they might keep her another week. That was what they'd heard, at any rate, but others were shaking their heads. They'd spoken to one of the guards, and he'd been fairly sure—

"'Nante, look," said Mona, pointing over to the right side of the door. There was a dog. It looked like a cross between a husky and something smaller and more clever, like a fox. Mona gave a tug as if she might go pet it, but there was a street boy sitting right beside it, and they'd almost reached the entrance now, with the chiseled words looming over it: *liberté, égalité, fraternité*. Odd for a morgue, thought 'Nante-bleue. The first two she could almost understand, but *fraternité*? One could hope, she supposed.

But finally they were under and in and out of the wind, in with the smell of wet wool and lye, which was smeared on the large glass plates that shielded the visitors from the bodies.

The space was arranged like a gallery, or like a maternity ward, except with cadavers, not babies. The bodies were all on the other side of the giant windows—four today, set in an evenly spaced row, and all tilted up so you could see; if not for the little rails at the bottom of their pallets, they'd have slid right off. The fat man was still there, in his grubby blue smock, and two new bodies beside—a scrawny man and woman who looked like they could have been a couple. Quite elderly. The only one you couldn't see was the girl. Everyone was crowded in front of her, but Berenice and Helaine had already pushed through to the front.

'Nante-bleue decided to wait her turn with Mona, who was staring at the body of the obese man, since no one was blocking the view. He had been there awhile, too. 'Nante-bleue wished they'd put him away. He was revolting, even without that indentation in his head, which she assumed was what killed him. Mona was rapt.

"Look," said 'Nante-bleue. The dog from outside had just entered—without the boy—and was trotting through the crowd very purposefully. He went to join the young officer standing just beyond the gallery, by the Dutch door that led in to the rest of the morgue, the part that wasn't public.

But *was* he an officer? She wasn't sure why she thought so. He wasn't in uniform, but he seemed more interested in the crowd than what the crowd was looking at. He kept glancing at them sideways, skipping from face to face. His eye snagged on hers, in fact, for just a moment—held them, narrowed, confirmed, and moved on.

Perhaps it was the dog, then. The dog carried himself like an officer's dog, sitting at the man's feet like one of those Egyptian statues.

"Nice little pooch, eh?"

Mona replied with a quick tug. She had seen an opening. Another yank and 'Nante-bleue was through to where Berenice and Helaine were kneeling, gazing through the glass as if there were a saint in there—like St. Cecelia or St. Catherine, both of whom 'Nante-bleue had seen in person. Here it was the same, how quiet the people were when they looked at her.

She *was* lovely. Sad to think. Twenty years? Couldn't have been much more. In a grubby white frock—simple and thin, which would give one quite a chill in there, if one were alive, but that was the strange part. She didn't look at all bloated the way so many of the river corpses did, or have that waxy sheen; it was more as if time had somehow stopped for her, right at the moment she passed. The hair still looked wet, a bit limp, but it framed a nice round face. She had a broad forehead and wide-set eyes. A lovely girl really. That little smile.

But there was something else, too. Her eyes were closed, but it still seemed like she was looking at something. By the slanting light of the late-day sun, 'Nante-bleue could see why. The eyes were of such a size and such a nice round shape that, even though the lids were settled, you could still make out the irises underneath—an odd effect that lent her expression a certain searchingness as well.

"I think she's the most beautiful thing I've ever seen," said Berenice, but not for anyone to hear. She murmured it as if the sentence had just escaped her heart, found its way to her lips, and misted itself on the glass.

§

The gentleman standing over by the Dutch door, the one with the upright dog, was indeed a military man, former sous-lieutenant Emile Brassard, of the 3rd company of the 17th legion of the Republican Guard (aka "*La Blanche*") at Champagne-Ardenne; and more recently, by special arrangement, a squadron leader serving in the 5th column of the foreign legion in Tonkin, China.

That latter engagement accounted for his less-than-military bearing. He'd recently developed a habit of looking at people slightly sideways, to spare them the view of his left ear, eighty percent of which had been sliced from his head near the end of his captivity.

But the governess was right about his interest. It *was* the people. Specifically he wanted to know if anyone had come because they knew the victim, the young woman. It didn't seem so. He could tell by the way they were looking at her, so stilled and wondrous, that their interests fell somewhere between the religious and the lugubrious. And he was relieved.

For further confirmation, he was just about to ring the bell for a second time when the top half of the Dutch door swung open, revealing in its frame the low-jowled face of the Sunday clerk, Madame Percy.

On seeing Brassard, her eyes drifted slightly before settling into a silent, half-lidded hiss, which he ignored.

"So no one, then?"

"No. The Indian," she said—the Indian went without saying—then she glanced down. Dogs were not allowed.

He paid no mind. "But someone said they might extend another week?"

She shook her head, not that she was aware.

And he was relieved again.

Just then, however, the dog—whose name was Soter—gave a small woof, his signal woof, and no doubt the reason he'd come in. Another man had just entered from the street, and Soter was correct—they'd seen this one before.

He was very long and lean, bald-pated and pale, with a face that put one in mind of a melted candlestick. He must have been a head taller than anyone else, even though he was bent like a branch or a lamppost. The same as the last time, he was wearing a long black coat that was covered in what looked like chalk dust, only today he was carrying a sack the size of a baby in his left arm.

But it wasn't this that gave pause, or the fact of his return, or even the way he was looking at the young woman now, overtop the other visitors, as if the clock inside him had just slowed down—Brassard had been seeing that expression, in variation, for four weeks now. No, what caused actual *concern* was the glance the man sent back to the prefect in the corner, and the directness of the prefect's reply, which was to go straight for his pocket watch, confirm the time, then hoist himself up from his stool.

"Another minute then," he announced to the room, exhaustedly shuffling to the door and closing the entry side to a chorus of disappointed groans still out in the cold.

"Five o'clock," he said, as if the matter was out of his hands, then he turned much the same expression to the people inside, shepherding them on their way, snapping his fingers for them to come along and exit now, everyone except the tall man with the sack, who made no such move.

Brassard asked, "Who's he?" but Madame Percy didn't answer; the man was coming this way now. While all the other guests shuffled for the exit, craning for one last glimpse—

some even crossing themselves—the tall man walked right up to where Brassard was standing and addressed himself to Madame Percy.

"Dr. Morin." He spoke in a nasal voice. "Is he in?"

"Who may I say?"

Monsieur Larue? Lemieux? Brassard didn't hear the name exactly, but Madame Percy turned and left them, giving the two men the chance to size each other up from their respective altitudes, both with the same skeptical, and even slight resentful, expressions.

"And who are you?" asked Brassard finally.

"Who are you?" the man returned, only just then noticing the ear and failing to disguise his reaction, which was more suspicious than kind. He shifted the sack to his other arm. It was filled with chalk, it looked like, and was cradled in a stack of two ceramic bowls.

Madame Percy returned, unlatching the bottom door now and swinging it just wide enough to let the tall man through. Without a glance back at Brassard, he entered in and proceeded to the next door.

A blood relation? Brassard doubted that. Uncle by marriage? Head of the orphanage? Or perhaps he'd worked at the Order of the Midwives, *les sage-femmes*? This, he could imagine.

Either way, it was clear what he must do. Here in the face of what he hadn't really been expecting, but which in the space of a moment now seemed obvious, former sous-lieutenant Brassard experienced another of those sudden reverses that had been whiplashing him for the last month or so. As swift as a riptide, he felt compelled to go and tell the ghoulish man what he knew and what he had done, and what she had done as well; to share with him the parts he had come to understand and the parts he hadn't, and the ghoulish man would help him with the rest—where she'd come from and who her parents had been and so on and so forth. And they would fit the pieces together. They would make sense of it all, which he supposed was the right thing.

But then why did this idea seem to break his heart?

The very deliberate clearing of a throat roused him from this contemplation. The proctor was over by the exit door, waiting. Time to go. In fact, Brassard could see that someone had already come and taken her body away. The other three cadavers were all still there, displayed.

He snapped to Soter. "You go." And Soter stood. "Back to Olivier. Go on."

Soter did as he was told, gamely wagging his tail as he crossed the floor. While the proctor's attention was diverted, Brassard reached over the Dutch door and pulled the latch.

"Monsieur," the proctor objected. "You can't—"

"It's all right," he said. "I'm with Larue." And already he was gone.

This was only the second time Brassard had been back here in the main part of the building, which was even colder than the corridor, like a giant, three-story refrigerator. He passed through a kind of locker room, hanging with coarse-cloth sacks, all filled with the clothes of the unclaimed dead. The next room was hats, stacked on shelves and hanging from pegs. Bowlers and top hats, brogues, skullcaps, and millinery as well, bonnets and elaborate picture hats, one by the far door with a dead blackbird stapled on the side.

But now he came through to a much larger space, an amphitheater with six ascending benches wrapped around, for viewing lectures and demonstrations. The stage was lit principally by two wide windows facing east, looking out on the bridge of St. Louis. There were vats along the far wall filled with formaldehyde and ammonia, to judge by the smell, and a half-dozen more glass jugs afloat with organs and other severed bits and pieces.

This was where the party had assembled—the tall man, Madame Percy, and the director of the morgue, Dr. Morin. The body was there as well, flat on a rolling pallet. The tall man was over by the washstand, surrounded by a cloud of chalk-white dust, mixing up what looked like porridge in his bowl. On the counter beside him were a pair of scissors, a spoon, a spatula, the second bowl, and a pile of plaster bandages.

Brassard turned to Dr. Morin. "What's he doing?"

"Going to make a mask."

"A mask?"

Brassard was aware that the morgue was in the habit of casting masks from the faces of known degenerates—murderers and rapists and the like—for research purposes. Phrenology.

"But she's not a criminal," he said, so plaintively that the discerning ear might have heard the opposite. He said it again. "She's not a criminal."

"He asked permission." The director shrugged, now making his way over to the body. "If no one came."

The tall man—the *mouleur*—now looked over at Brassard directly. It was only for a moment, but all the distrust and unwarranted territorialism of the former exchange had been replaced by something much softer, something almost plaintive in those drooping hound-dog eyes. Brassard understood. No distant cousin, no. No clergyman or orphanage director. Just another man who'd looked at her and fell—whichever way was most natural for him to fall. But this one had a skill to offer, and after all, this was her final day. First thing in the morning they'd be taking her to the kiln. They'd give her drawer to some other cadaver, and by this time to-morrow, there'd be nothing left of her but smoke and ash.

Brassard stood back, therefore, having no jurisdiction here, and no objection, come to think of it. Or maybe one, but he was curious about that.

The director would serve as assistant. He had already applied a glob of transparent gel to her face, a preparatory solution. The *mouleur's* mixture was ready as well, a plaster of some kind. He brought it over in his bowl and set it down beside her. He blew into his dry fists, then reached down and laid his hands upon her face. And this had been Brassard's concern, in fact, that even the slightest application of pressure might disturb the expression which had been resting there. If that were lost or tampered with, that would be a kind of tragedy, it seemed to him.

Yet as the *mouleur* began to smooth the clear solution across her forehead and down into the fine thin hair of the brows, Brassard could see how firm the flesh had grown, how cold and set the features were. He even felt a tremor of jealousy as he watched, that this man should be allowed to touch her so openly. But he felt a consolation, too, at seeing the *mouleur's* expertise. There was a strange beauty to his hands, ugly as they were, with the dark hair along the tops, the inverted knuckles of his thumbs. The fingers were long, tapered, and elegant in motion; the thumbs, firm but gentle—here to preserve. Brassard could see very well the care the man was taking, in the faint breaths frosting from his nostrils and his mouth.

But timing was of the essence, and the mixture was ready. He took up the bowl and gave it a swirl to see—it moved reluctantly, like oatmeal. He held it directly above her forehead and began to tilt it. The thick white sludge leaned toward the lip, then started wedging down the shallow funnel. The young woman's expression remained unflinching, porcelain, ecstatic, even as the first length came spilling down elastically. It was just about to touch her eyelids when Brassard looked away. He preferred that his final image be of her, and of the flesh itself.

And he was quietly elated.

Part Two

Tuesday, October 29, 1889
(or one month prior)

Chapter 2

The Burial

Twice she roused, the first time much too quickly and too soon. There had been some snapping sound, not uncommon in the middle of the forest—but so sudden and so sharp, her eyes shot open before the mind was ready.

She sat up—again, much too quickly—and therefore briefly—long enough to see the bleary image of the black donkey on the far side of the water, munching away on a fern, the wagon up on the road, and the crumpled heap just upstream. It took a moment for her to remember; she didn't remember, in fact. She saw the water and the crimson ghost in it, drifting down toward her and dissolving before her eyes like smoke.

She felt a sudden crushing in her head, not as painful as it was heavy, like a dark leaden blanket being pressed against her skull, a blanket and a boulder. She lay back down beneath its weight—she had no choice—closed her eyes, and resumed unconsciousness.

§

. . . The second time was different. It wasn't quite as clear what awakened her other than a sudden heightening of the senses, though because of those heavy lids, those thick and salted lashes, her eyes would be the last to join.

The ears were first. The gentle babbling of the brook became a sudden roar, and the birdsong was everywhere—her brain became an aviary. The shushing leaves, an ocean of shells. The smells, likewise, were suddenly redolent and distinct, the same as after rain—the stone, the moss, the touch of frost, the minerals of the mud beneath her.

Those large eyes opened more slowly then, and the rest of the world came flooding in, a blinding blur at first—of green and yellow dappled sunlight. She lifted her head gingerly. Sat up, with the sticks in her hair and the print on her cheek. She looked around. Most of what was there before was still there. A donkey on the bank. A wagon up on the road. And just upstream, an apparent feast for flies and gnats. She could hear them, too.

She went there first, to see what all the buzzing was about; pushed herself up onto her feet, more fawnlike than drunk. She wasn't wearing any clothes. A young figure, slender and maybe a fraction small for the head, but soft and very fair, bearing more imprints of stick and sand on her hip and upper arm. Staggering a bit, she made her way to the dark clump in the coarse black pants and coat, with the brilliant, flashing constellation whirling above. She took a fallen branch and set its blunter end beneath the heap like a lever, and while the perching birds looked on—or didn't—she turned it over.

A man. Shaggy, light brown hair and beard. He wore a fur-trimmed coat, and he was in an oddly splayed position. One thick hand resting on his chest; the other high and outstretched, almost as if he were a tenor singing to a balcony, or to the moon.

His expression was likewise airy, with a bleary pleasantness about the mouth, accentuated by the fullness of the lips and the manipulated upturn of his mustache. This was an echo of his brows, which were distinguished by the same vertical yearning, and which further lent to the impression of his being a kind of offhand cavalier or, at the moment, a dreaming drunk.

Nothing of the kind. All a misdirection, as could clearly be detected beneath that soft brown beard, along where the jaw met the neck. Extending practically from ear to ear was a matted, nearly purple-blackness, the clotting of a deep gash clogging and clumping the unkempt whiskers. The blood, which had been ample and which the little creak had served to carry away discreetly, had almost finished oozing now; was more coagulant than liquid, thanks to the beard and to the maggots, which were already teeming and wriggling with new life. They were the truly happy ones.

The young woman looked around as if there might be others, or other bodies. There weren't, only there on the ground at her feet was a sickle with a walnut handle.

She left it there. Still slow, but steadier now, she ascended the slope, a milk-white nude.

The wagon was a small one—eight feet long, if that; five across—shaped like a large crib with a barrel roof. Along one side was a rack of tools: shovels, trowels, gloves, hoes, rakes, and a sheathed scythe. Chipping paint revealed what once had been an ornate trim of red and green, though what was left was mostly faded gray and pink.

She climbed inside. Not much more care had been taken there. It was filthy, mostly with grime. A chain lay like a snake on the plank floor. And men's underclothes. But there on a palette bed was a coarse-cloth frock, off white, with a square collar. She put this on, then she took a small shovel from the outside rack and descended the slope again, not all the way to the water. She chose a spot midway between the creek and the road, as free from roots and stones as she could find, and while the birds above looked on chirpingly and flittingly, she began to dig. One spade. Two spades. No trace of anger on her face, or sorrow, or remorse. Only focus on the task at hand, and patience. Soon enough the rasp of the blade in the dirt joined in comfortably with the other murmurs and shifts and crackles—as compatibly as the *rat-ta-tat* of a woodpecker.

She didn't pause, other than to tuck a loose strand of blondish but otherwise nondescript hair behind her ear, and to shake out her hands and wrists, which apparently weren't used to such labor. She dug and dug until the ditch was three feet deep and wet at the bottom and she was hitting more stones than dirt. She set down the shovel and returned to the body. She wrapped the head and neck in one of the spare shirts from the wagon. Then she dragged him by the feet—there was no other way, his being a fairly large body. She rolled him into the ditch. She had to scooch the legs up just to make him fit. She tossed in all the clothes and the tools, including the shovel she'd used to dig the hole, and finally the scythe with the walnut handle.

She shoved the dirt back on top with her arms and her hands, and eventually packed it down with her feet. No prayers, no curses, no tears. Nothing but the doing of it, and then a moment's silence once it was done and the earth was as flat as she could manage. She needed to catch her breath. Her chest was heaving, and she was damp with sweat.

Next, she moved to the wagon. With a bucket she found inside, she drew water from the creek, hauled it back up the slope, tore up one last shirt, then got down on her hands and knees to scrub the floor. The birds and the squirrels could see the wagon shimmy at the force of her arm inside.

There was a rag rug. She rolled it up and set it aside; she would beat it later. For now, the silted water splattered and foamed, soaked and sopped and seeped down between the cracks in the floor. She didn't seem to care, but there was a trapdoor there.

When she was satisfied that the inside of the wagon was clean, she finally attended to herself. She climbed back down to the water and bathed in the deepest part of the creek. She washed her dress. She wrung it and set it on the largest, sunniest rock she could find. While the birds and insects and worms and petals all continued with their various observances, she dipped her head baptismally, and the light bouncing off the surface of the water reflected on the leaves of the overhanging willow, creating another rippling effect overtop the gentle billow of the breeze.

The sun had just begun its early descent and was passing behind the tree line. She put the frock back on and climbed the slope again, which was entirely in shadow now, the freshly packed dirt of the gravesite like a healing scar. The donkey was standing by the wagon. She harnessed it while noting the sky; clouds were moving in. She latched the donkey to the rails. Wind, too. The poplars shivered and hissed. She took the driver's seat and considered her choice:

Behind, the road led to a black tunnel beneath a stone bridge.

Ahead was a turn.

That way, then.

She tapped the donkey, who replied with an absent swat of her tail just as the first fat flecks of rain began to patter down.

Chapter 3

Wolves

The shower had long since passed, but puddles remained. A party of three slopped its way along the same road, the same way—a prick-eared dog, a listing horse, and an officer. Or a man who appeared to be an officer.

He was wearing a dark blue uniform coat with brass buttons, though a closer inspection would reveal that the tunic, which was in sore need of a pressing, lacked any rank insignia or thread badge on either the shoulder or the collar; the brass buttons, too, could have used a shine. The rider maintained a military posture nonetheless, slackened only slightly by the demands of riding at this mildly sullen pace, which owed to the fact that he was also reading. Or scanning, really. He had a page of blue stationery in his ungloved hand, addressed to the office of the Directorate-General of the National Gendarmerie, in Paris.

The opening paragraph was more or less set, stating plainly that, as the director general's office had already been apprised, and as had been discussed in accordance with the terms of his suspension, the author and signatory was hereby submitting the following dossier as his formal request for reinstatement to active duty in the Departmental Gendarmerie.

There followed a brief detail of the various duties and assignments that he had performed in the eighteen months since the suspension, all of which were further certified in the materials of the dossier, including his service with the third foreign infantry regiment in Tonkin, China; the seven missions on which he acted as squadron leader up until his capture in Panhou; the captivity; the release, and the subsequent declaration of "duty served." All was presented in a fittingly bureaucratic digest, as prelude to the *"great eagerness"* with which he anticipated resuming his place with La Blanche, *"in whatever capacity and in whichever district your office sees fit to assign."*

Brassard had no problem with any of that.

It was the next paragraph that he'd been struggling with, the one meant to express his contrition and gratitude, even going so far as to suggest that the experience of the last eighteen months, including the district office's investigation into his misconduct, had been *"for the better."*

Not that Brassard did *not* feel these things. He did—on some level—but in a vaguely perverse way that likely lay beyond the capacity of clerical language to capture (and if any such language could be found, he would be wise to keep it to himself). What was here instead—talk of *"strengthened resolve"* and a *"clarified sense of purpose"*—felt generic by comparison, and therefore obsequious. As the horse continued on beneath him, he muttered and grumbled his way over the words, uttering nothing really discernible until coming to the bit about his father:

"My father served for thirteen years—" he stopped. "That's a bit *de trop,* don't you think?"

He said this to the dog, Soter, with whom he had been reunited only four days prior—and at no small cost, as it turned out. A Finnish Spitz of evident but inscrutable intelligence, Soter thought better than to reply.

Brassard tried again: *"My father served for thirteen years. My grandfather before him for thirty-three—"*

Again, he made a sour face, and at just that moment the

page seemed to blush in his hand—or to darken. He glanced at the sky. Another of those windblown clouds was passing between him and the sun, casting its shadow not only across the questionable paragraph, but across the road, and the wood, and—so it would seem—his peace of mind, for a stillness had descended, too. Tucked away beneath the high-born wind, a sudden calm seemed to have surrounded the three of them, which, in combination with the sifted light, visited Brassard with a sense of apprehension that in retrospect he would deem to have been presentiment—no question—but which at the moment he still took to be misgiving.

He folded the stationery, tucked it in a small brown book, and traded it for the watch in his pocket. Three thirty. At this pace, he could get to Coulommieres by nightfall, then Paris by noon at least, which would give him a full day to settle in and prepare for his meeting with the—

"Whoa, there, whoa."

He jolted forward slightly. The horse had suddenly stopped and was rearing a bit, as if she'd felt it, too, now, that same disquiet. He did not know the horse so well. She was a loan from the same man who'd sold him back his dog. But she was digging in, twisting her head this way and that, refusing to go another step.

It was Soter, then—to whom all fear was an unknown—who scented the actual cause of their unease. He was turned to the right side of the road, peering through into the descending forest. Brassard watched keenly as the dog crept down a cunning step or two, then paused, his front paw gently lifted—the left, as always.

By his own estimation, Brassard's courage lay somewhere between the horse's and the dog's, but as he was closer in spirit to the latter and considered Soter to be the angel of his better nature, he did dismount and settle the horse, briefly noting the wheel tracks on the road. Too many to read clearly. Out of instinct, he donned the black-visored cap of the gendarmerie and reached for his gun, only to remember that his holster was empty.

He proceeded nonetheless, following his partner down the embankment on quiet, cautious steps until he could see Soter poised, high shouldered and light on his pads. Brassard could hear as well now, a small chorale of drunken gargles. He took another step and the drape of the oak tree lifted just enough for him to see a pack of wolves. Four of them, at roughly thirty paces. One, the guard, stood facing them directly, showing its teeth and ice-blue eyes. The other three were gnawing at a body they appeared to have dragged from a ditch. Judging by its condition—a barely identifiable pile of rags and guts—they'd been at it awhile; there may have been red on the muzzle of the guard, and it was this that most concerned Brassard. The pack had acquired a taste.

Soter, ever-brave, was not thinking along these lines— only that he was friend to man, and that some remnant of a man was under brutal assault over there. He took a step farther in. Two of the feeding wolves responded by lifting their heads and effecting the same menacing mask as their sentry. One snapped, then the other—snapped and drooled—but Soter did not back down until his master spoke. Quietly.

"That's all right, boy. We can fight another day."

He took a step back up the incline. Soter, peripherally aware, did the same, still crouching.

"Here we go," Brassard intoned, and to the wolves this time. "As you were."

They seemed to take his meaning. One of the feeders had just stripped a nice piece of meat; a new flank exposed. The others gathered round, creatures of instinct returning to the easier meal, and not wanting to miss out.

Only when he and Soter had reached the road again did Brassard note the buzzards in the sky. Had they been there the whole time? He and Soter walked the horse another hundred yards or so along the road before stopping again. Once more he removed the pocket watch and also a compass from his saddle bag, and prepared to note his position on a small pad.

"*Un corps mâle . . .*" he began, while Soter stood watch.

§

Some miles ahead and sometime later—the numbers here are subject to dispute—the maiden emerged from the thick of the wood, her wagon trundling contentedly beneath the open sky, which was still seasonably crisp and scattered with cottony clouds. The road speared a meadow of tall grass and fern. Birds sang in answer to her squeaky wheel, the sparrows practicing their whistles and triplets, a mockingbird defending her nest. The maiden knew none of them by name, nor this now—the rolling snare of a grouse, and the thumping drum that followed. She took them all to be the voice of the forest, and joining these from up ahead were a clip-clop and a rattle. A moment later, the bend revealed another carriage coming in the opposite direction. Very large, driven by one coachman and two horses. The maiden made way. The well-appointed wagon and its driver passed haughtily and without a glance.

The maiden gave a tap to the donkey, but now she saw that *another* carriage was headed this way, even bigger and more opulent than the first, with gilded lanterns on each corner. She let it pass as well. Four horses this time, and again not a glance from the drivers. There were two.

She took no offense. On the contrary, she seemed to find

some satisfaction in their snubbing. However, in heaving back up onto the lane, there was another groaning sound, followed by a loud snap. The donkey staggered. The wagon slumped and tilted, nearly tumbling the maiden from the driver's seat. Her hip ground against the rail, but she caught herself, pushed off, then managed to climb down.

Her inspection revealed the left-side hind wheel was bent like the brim of a hat, and underneath, the axle appeared to have split.

She tried lifting the wagon to see better, but it was much too heavy. She looked back up the road, this way and that, but the carriages were long gone, and no more were coming.

She was stranded, but in no discernible way upset. Farther down the incline from the road she saw willows and moving water. The donkey looked like it could use a drink, so she took the bucket and made her way.

Again, the autumn flowers—golden, orange, and crimson with yellow trim—seemed to welcome her with nods. The white butterflies, too; they waved. The limbs and leaves responded to the afternoon breeze with a kind of lolling, reassuring gesture. She would be provided for. A prickly bush offered small red berries. She plucked one and tasted it: true.

She looked back at the trees, the oak here and the birch back upstream. Some of the limbs were shedding. Even now, the highest, brittlest leaves were descending. A sudden gust coaxed more to come, and they scattered, and she looked to the water to see if any had landed there. A few came floating by. She followed with her eye as they passed, turning gently on their backs as they headed on downstream, except for this one here, which hit upon an eddy, only to spin off and find itself trapped by the rock beneath her foot.

Not long after, she was gathering berries, filling her kerchief, when she heard a voice call down from the road.

"Hello?" A trim gentleman in a light gray suit. "Hello. Is this your carriage here?" he asked, pointing back at the wagon. "Do you need some help?"

She gathered together her fruit and her jug and took them up. She joined him on the road where he had parked a two-horse carriage. He said his name was Professor Samsa. He had silver hair, with silver-rimmed glasses perched lightly on his nose, which was long and ornate with age, but handsomely so, shading a mustache that might have been just as silvery, except that the wax at the tips gave it a faintly yellow tinge. He was smartly dressed in a pearl-gray suit that contrasted nicely with his complexion, which was smooth and apricot but reddened along the cheek by capillaries. And he had very kind eyes, gelatinous and blue and intent upon catching hers as he explained to her what had happened to her wheel.

"Do you see here? You lost a spoke somewhere along the way. No way of knowing how far back, but the problem there is that the spokes are what distribute the tension. If the tension's off, the wheel rim knows. The axle knows, and it's only a matter of time before the whole thing gives way."

She offered a nod of understanding, at which point another man, younger, equally gentle but of a fuller, softer figure and face, emerged from behind their carriage with a toolbox.

"Ah, this is my son, Eric," said the professor.

The young man bowed awkwardly.

"He doesn't speak," the professor explained. "He doesn't hear"—he tapped his ear—"but he is going to fix the wheel for you: a new spoke; see if we can straighten out the rim a bit; and he'll splint the axle until you can get a replacement. He's good at this sort of thing."

The maiden offered a bow of appreciation, which the professor's son blushingly accepted.

"Come," said the professor, and he led her, following another exchange of bows between Eric and the maiden, back to their carriage—a black Berline that they appeared to have modified and expanded. From the trunk he retrieved two folding chairs, a stool, and a small wooden chess table. On this, he proceeded to set up a little roadside tea party. They had a fine porcelain service, with cups and saucers, a sugar shell, a creamer, and silver spoons. The maiden offered her berries, which the professor accepted, and bowled.

"How delicious. How pleasant and unexpected." His jaw worked the berries aggressively. "Thank you. Do you know what they are?"

She didn't, but she agreed they were quite tart and delicious. With cream especially. She sipped her tea, while he watched her thoughtfully and with waxing concern.

Finally he gave it words: "I feel I should ask. Is there really no one with you? Father? Husband? Brother?"

"No."

"Doesn't seem quite safe. These roads. How far have you to go?"

"I'm not sure."

"Well, but *where* are you going? Perhaps we could escort you."

Again she hesitated, which the professor took to be an expression of understandable wariness about trusting her lot to a pair of strangers. He moved to reassure her with the tenderness of his eyes. And the humor. He removed a seed from his mouth and deposited it in the dish he'd set there for that purpose. "Are you coming from the city or going?"

"Which way is the city?" she asked.

And now he *was* concerned, as they were on the only road to or from.

"That way," he said, pointing behind. "Are you sure you're all right?"

She nodded most definitely.

"Because if you're in any kind of trouble," he said, "or if something has happened . . ."

It was at this moment they heard the distinctive triplet clop of hooves at trotting pace, coming from the far end of the road, the same end the maiden had come from—a horse and rider, and a grinning prick-eared dog doing well to keep up, although now, upon spotting the wagon, the carriage, and the roadside party, the rider slowed.

He was wearing a gendarme's coat and hat, and his manner upon approaching was decorous. The professor's son, still working on the wheel in shirtsleeves, had felt the rhythm and the motion, and stood from his work to acknowledge the passing, which the officer acknowledged in turn with a tip of his cap.

He took a good long look at the wagon itself and its hobbled condition, craning his head as his mount continued on toward the tea party. The officer then turned and engaged the two members with an equally solicitous demi-bow, removing his cap entirely for the young maiden, then finishing on the professor, whose first welcome was nonetheless to the dog.

"Well, what have we here? Good day, Officer. I know this dog. Finnish, yes?"

"Very good." The officer swung his leg and dismounted.

"Smart," said the professor. "Loyal."

"Very." The officer now removed his gloves.

He had a certain élan, which extended from the almost balletic line of his various limbs to the contours of his face, whose centerpiece was a nose just long enough to give the head as a whole the aspect of a weather vane. In that respect, he looked more like the professor's son than the professor's son, though for all of this, the maiden seemed most taken with the height of his black, mud-splattered boots. And the prick-eared dog, of course, who seemed equally fetched by her.

"Would you join us for tea?" asked the professor

"Thank you, no. I'm on duty."

The professor subtly scanned Brassard's coat, the bare left breast, the empty holster . . . and doubted this.

"Which way are you headed?" asked Brassard.

"East," said the professor. "Geneva, eventually."

"You might want to take the north fork. There's an inn if you need lodging. Two miles or so."

"Is there a problem? Did something happen?"

The officer shook his head, not so much to deny the suggestion as to characterize its severity. "We're just trying to keep the woods clear." He looked down at the young maiden and offered, by way of explanation: "Wolves."

She held his eye. Brassard's first thought was that he recognized her from somewhere. He wasn't sure where or why, but there was a confidence about her—the way she held his eye, as solid and composed as a river stone.

He turned back to the professor, then, pleasantly. "So all the way to Switzerland. Quite a trek."

"Yes. We're coming from the Exposition."

The dog had locked in on the young woman as well.

"Have you been?" asked the professor.

"Not yet, no."

"How can that be? And so close. What region do you serve? I have a cousin up in Bourgogne."

This was a test; Brassard remained gracious. "Champagne-Ardenne most recently."

He had gestured with his head when he said this, inadvertently exposing his left ear, the one that had been brutalized, albeit in a curiously artful way. The professor and the young woman both saw: The outer helix and lobe were gone, but the inner remained, so that what was there looked like a much smaller ear, almost elfin in size and shape, but with a wider aperture.

The professor's brow curdled when he saw; hers did not.

"Well, you must make the time before it closes," said the professor, speaking of the Exposition again. "They really have managed to bring the whole world into one place—like a little globe. Here—"

He reached into a leather case he had beside him, and Brassard looked back at the young woman, who still seemed to be wondering about him and his ear. It was an expression one encountered more often in children—deeply curious, but absent any note of revulsion. Or sympathy. But again, it was the familiarity that struck him. Where had he seen her before?

"Are you sure you didn't want a cup?" asked the professor, now setting the various cards and pamphlets out on the table.

Brassard answered, "Quite."

Most were from the Exposition. One boasted of the "World's largest diamond!!!" Another bore the image of a great black train engine looking more like a bull. There was one advertising the "Galérie des Machines"; another, more genteelly, "Le Jardin Zoologique." There was a photograph of the professor and his son standing in a parlor of some kind, or a library. And finally, on top, was the most popular image. Brassard had seen this one: "Exposition Universelle de 1889," featuring a high, vista view of the city and the fair, with the grand new tower standing dead center. *la tour Eiffel.*

"There it is. My son and I, we're engineers, you see. That's why we came." He tapped the picture.

"And what did you make of it?" asked Brassard. "I've heard some people complain."

"Well, it's quite a view, I'll say that. You go all the way to the top, you can see everything. You could see us right now, I expect."

He gestured back behind them as if the crow's nest might be peeking over the treetops at them. The maiden continued looking at the photograph of the professor and his son; the tower was perfectly, centrally framed in the window between them.

"A real marvel, as far the engineering goes," the professor went on. "My hat is off."

"But . . ." said Brassard, sensing critique.

"Well, yes," the professor conceded. "The problem for a man such as myself, you see, is that it has no purpose. At least that I can tell. My son says I am wrong." He gestured and all three looked back down the road where Eric seemed to have finished shaving the new wheel post. "He says the purpose is perfectly clear: To be." The professor smiled. "Youth." He directed this at the maiden for some reason.

She was still examining the cards and photographs. She'd taken one in her left hand, the grip side of which was clearly pink and raw. Brassard saw. In addition to there being no ring—which he had noted from the first—there was a split in the skin on the pad of her thumb, and a stubborn line of dirt beneath her fingernails. Five telltale black moons, which caused him to revise his initial assessment. *I have mistaken recognition for instinct*, he thought. It wasn't that he knew who this woman was; it was that he knew what she had done.

"And would this be your daughter?" he asked.

"My daughter? No."

The professor consulted with her first—with his eyes. She offered no encouragement either way, but the professor clearly did not trust Brassard, this supposed officer, with the truth.

". . . My niece," he said finally. "We felt we might need a civilizing influence."

Brassard looked her way and nodded as though he understood. "And what did the mademoiselle think?"

"Of what, monsieur?" she replied.

"Of the tower. Does it have . . . sufficient purpose?"

She looked down at the card again to consider, while the professor—made plainly nervous by this improvisation—gently cleared his throat.

"It is . . ." she finally answered, still searching for the word—what word? "Attractive."

The professor offered a gentle laugh. "Yes, I hadn't thought of that." He smiled, much relieved. "A giant iron magnet."

Brassard pressed no further; he couldn't place her accent, though. Maybe a Picard tinge? Rouchi? Back by the wagon, the son appeared to have reset the spoke.

"It looks like he might need some help."

"He may," said the professor.

Brassard excused himself, but the dog stayed put, still intent upon the young maiden, who drank her tea with a steady hand, eyes focused on the leaves at the bottom of her cup.

"Do you need some help with that?"

The professor's son, Eric, was rolling the wheel to the wagon. He didn't seem to have heard.

Brassard tried again. "Help?"

The son turned suddenly this time, startled but polite. He accepted with a bow. Brassard lifted the axle with two hands and held it as steadily as he could while Eric slid the wheel on. He surveyed the tracks on the road as well. Still too scrambled to read, but he did detect the slight warp in the wheel they were setting, and the fact that the wagon—in addition to bearing no resemblance to the customized Berline on the other side of the road—was pointed in the opposite direction.

The wheel was on. "And whose wagon is this, by the way?" Brassard asked.

The son didn't reply. He was fastening the cap to the hub. Brassard tried again and more clearly.

"Is. This. Your. Wagon?"

Oh. No. The son pointed back down to the young woman still sipping her tea, still under Soter's watch. The professor, however, seeing the wheel in place, gestured for Eric to come. Pinky high, he turned his wrist; his cup was waiting.

"Tea?" asked Eric, and Brassard's assumption was confirmed—by the Indian softness of the consonant, and the throaty quality of the vowel—Eric was stone deaf, not remotely dumb.

"No, thank you." He indicated that he had to relieve himself and would be doing so on the blind side of the road. Understanding, Eric left him with a bow and made his way down to the party on the near side.

Brassard did not need to relieve himself. Rather, he waited a moment on the down slope, then crept back to the wagon and entered it stealthily, detectable from the vantage of the tea party only as a slight shudder of the carriage.

Once inside, Brassard conducted a lightning survey, first with his eye, zipping from corner to corner, from beam to lathe to drawer—all was curiously Spartan. The bed shelf, just so. The floor, scrubbed clean. The only thing out of place, an anchor chain, clasped to a cleat beside the shelf, with a brass ring at the other end, maybe three inches in diameter.

There was a rag rug as well. He slid it to the side and right away located a seam in the floor. A trapdoor. He used his jackknife to pry it open, and right there, as if he'd planted it himself, he did find plunder: a pair of two-tined silver candlesticks standing guard, one on each side of a cast-iron safe, precisely the kind in which a family, say, might be expected to keep its most valuable jewels, bonds, certificates, coins, etc. Given the space, it lay on its back, and had been wrapped in another long chain, lengthwise and widthwise in the manner of gift ribbon.

He tugged once at the chain to make sure. The thing was very much in place, very much locked. He could hear the professor's voice, the convivial raconteur, but with his new ear, he couldn't *place* sounds the way he used to; he couldn't tell if the professor might be coming near, so he recovered the trapdoor and replaced the rug. There was a headscarf in the open drawer of the one bureau. He held it to his nose, pocketed it, then made his exit as nimbly as he was able.

As before, it was the professor who welcomed his return to the party. The cups were empty. "I suppose I didn't realize it was so late. You said the inn was two miles from here?"

"Along the north road," Brassard confirmed. "Small but safe."

"Sounds just right, thank you. Did we get your name, Officer?"

Another challenge. Brassard didn't blink.

"Dimanche," he said. "I'll write down my information."

While he and the professor exchanged names in writing, the young maiden remained silent, focused now on the texture of the lace of the cloth they'd laid on the table. At least for the moment, she appeared to have entered the soundless world of the professor's son.

Brassard broke the spell with a quick whistle, calling Soter from his watch.

"Here we go, then."

They started for the horse while the others looked on, the professor only too happy to see him go.

The maiden gave no such indication. She observed his mount. She could not see his ear—it was his right-side profile he was presenting, and mostly in silhouette. The sun had hit the farther treetops behind him, so that he and the light did a kind of dance as he took saddle—a brief tango—then parted, the man and his horse and his dog continuing along the road at the same pace as they'd come.

As soon as they were safely away, the professor turned to her and spoke quietly but emphatically. "You will join us, then," he said, "what with all the wolves."

Chapter 4

The Overnight

The party Duplessy were well enough into their celebration to happily sacrifice their own accommodations, tripling and quadrupling up in order that the pilgrim three—Professor Samsa, his son, and his now "niece"—could have the *two* rooms on the second floor of what had formally been the Moranville barn.

In exchange, the pilgrims were merely asked to join the revelers awhile in their revelry, which they graciously did. Food was ample. Ham featured, though the formally seated portion of the evening was well behind them. There were musicians among the party, two fiddlers and an accordionist and what ended up being two dozen percussionists who gamely played their hands and feet.

That the pilgrims should join in and dance with them was another requirement of the bond, this according to the father of the bride, a rosy, mutton-chopped, and delightful man—this evening at least. Large-armed, large-handed, barrel-chested, and literally bursting from his clothes—he lost three buttons before the evening was through—he was also well into his cups by the time our party arrived, and apparently impossible to refuse. Not only was he adamant that all three pilgrims join them on the floor—including, Eric, whose deafness was never mentioned—he was equally insistent on mistaking the cousins—Eric and the young woman, that is—for a couple. Fiancés, specifically. He made at least two awkward toasts on their behalf, and sent countless knowing and approving glances the way of the professor, whose reaction softened over the course of several refilled glasses.

He treated himself to the notion that the bride's father might be on to something, and that she—the woman they had rescued from the roadside and that lying officer—might indeed be his daughter some day, be the one to love his poor son, Eric. And why not? Did he not think his son would have been a fortunate man in that case? True, the professor was having trouble determining her station. Nothing in her comportment identified her by class, or even by region, so far as he could tell (though he was no expert in that regard, being Swiss-Magyar). But just look at her, dancing there with the father of the bride, in his massive embrace, while he whispered in her ear. Whispered a great deal in her ear, in fact. Whispered so much, it made the professor uncomfortable. What could he be saying at such length? Typical slobberings about age and beauty, he supposed, about life and the gatherings of rosebuds, inspired by the presence of something so evidently in bloom. The professor didn't blame him; he envied the man his boldness, and his embrace. And whatever he was saying into her ear, she was polite, nodding and smiling indulgently, giving him back his hands, demurring drink, very ladylike. Sipping water. He was proud of her. He beamed, and Monsieur Duplessy saw him beaming. And maybe he was right.

And better this—more pleasant this, this fancy—than the deeper and more abiding concern that such fancies (and the wine, don't forget) were designed to distract him from: that she was in some kind of peril; that she was lost and not saying so; that she needed to see a doctor. These thoughts were like the trees outside—black and shifting and very real—waiting out there, but for the moment fended off by the golden light of the Moranvilles' musical parlor.

Then he lost track of her, got caught up in a conversation

with one of the Duplessy cousins about tulips, and then with Moranville the Innkeeper, who might have been an imbecile, the professor wasn't sure—clinically, that is, or maybe just drunk—but who was kind enough to recommend a local doctor. There was one in Esternay, he said, and only one, but he was good. Moranville showed him the scar on his arm and the stitches he'd received last spring.

"Smart man," he kept saying. "Smart."

But no seamstress apparently.

Then at some point the professor looked for her and could not find her and was told that she had excused herself. Gone to her room, the one they'd been shown earlier.

He followed not long after. He couldn't find Eric either. He staggered unaided through the moonlight to the barn. He ascended the slinking, rubbery stairs to find the light was still on in her room, a golden, wavering bar beneath the door. And again, for just a moment, he fancied the idea that they were in there, the young woman and his son. Out of decency, he went to his room through the catty-corner door and there found Eric, alas, asleep in the double bed, rosy cheeked as always, ever since he was a boy.

He returned to the hall and stood awhile before the door, wobbling and for no good reason. He listened to the party in the house. He listened to the forest outside, and to the hooting of the owl, until it occurred to him that she could probably see his shoes, and might be wondering at his intentions. He removed his shoes right there, and went to his room and to bed. The light could still be seen beneath her door when he fell asleep.

In the morning both he and Eric awakened late. When they emerged from their room—Eric first, to use the outhouse down below—he unwittingly kicked the bowl, her bowl, which had been set at the foot of their door. Some water spilled, but not the nosegay, tied at the stems. And not the berries.

These were her thanks, she having left some hours before, for reasons the doctor gleaned right away—or one of them at least—which was that she had heard him speaking to Monsieur Moranville the night before, and that she had no intention of seeing any doctor.

§

Brassard spent the night about three miles farther along the road from where he had come, in a tiny hut made of interlocking logs and a sod roof, one of several dozen such dwellings that the Gendarmerie had set out some twenty years before to provide refuge for traveling officers. Deeply flawed in concept, the huts had proved a better design for confrontation than peacekeeping—between man and man, and man and bear, and man and wolf—but Brassard nonetheless counted himself fortunate this evening, and well served.

It hadn't been so late when he came upon it. He could, in fact, have probably gotten all the way to Coulommiers, but he didn't want to stray too far from the party he'd just left behind, and in fact the little cabin—the back of which even had an eaved pen for his horse—furnished him with the perfectly adequate means for completing his other most pressing order of business, which was to compose, to certify, and then send off an official dispatch to the station in Sézanne—first making clear that he was acting in his capacity as a private citizen but former officer, then detailing his discovery of the body in the woods some seven miles back.

He made no mention of his encounter with Professor Samsa or his "niece." On that subject, he was still operating in the realm of surmise. Also, he had been expressly forbidden from participating in any law enforcement activities until such time as the director general reinstated him. That was why he had not acted more preemptively back at the tea party—that, and his admitted preference for seeing where threads led.

To state the obvious, though: Not for one second did he believe that the young woman back there was the niece of Professor Samsa. Nor did he believe she was a "civilizing influence." (Nor, for that matter, did he blame the professor for wanting him to think so. Samsa had only lied on her behalf because he had recognized Brassard to be without credential and therefore did not trust him. Rightly so. And he had taken pity on her because she was young and attractive and apparently in distress.) But clearly *she* was the one who had buried the body in the woods back there. Most likely she had killed the man she'd buried, and was now headed to Paris with whatever was in that cast-iron safe, which was why Brassard had stationed himself here for the night, on the only passable road between the inn and the city.

The next eastbound mail coach came by about an hour after he'd arrived. Brassard handed over his dispatch and returned to the hut. He made a fire in the little stove. He and Soter shared beans and bread. He treated himself to a jar of smoked oysters and crackers as well, and the rest of his flask of brandy.

As his last task of the long day, he took the dossier from his saddlebag, as well as his own statement, the one on the blue stationery. He lit the one provided lamp, sat at the one provided chair—a straight back with armrests. Across these, he set the one provided shelf—which he had removed from the brackets on the wall—and used the surface as a desk. There he spent the next hour or so going over the contents of his application one last time, while Soter lay at his feet, nuzzling the head scarf of the young woman with the wagon. Specifically, the contents included:

—The full transcript of his record as a student at the Lycée Henri-IV, which he attended for two years (first in class)

—The full transcript of his record at St. Cyr (second in class)

—The full transcript of his record as a cadet in both Paris and Amiens

—A complete record of his first two years of service as an officer and sous-lieutenant in Champagne-Ardenne

—Three citations for exceptional work in the area of criminal investigation

—Two citations for exceptional work in the area of surveillance and intervention

—One letter from his former captain in Champagne-Ardenne, Monsaingeon (the one who'd arranged for his special commission)

—One certificate of honorable discharge from his tour in Tonkin

—One letter of commendation from his former commander in Tonkin, Admiral Bouvard, citing him for his courage under fire

—One letter of commendation from Marcel Robert, commander of the entire seventh legion, recognizing his extraordinary valor and sacrifice

—One certificate recognizing the same

—One hospital record certifying the nature of injuries he had received and his recovery therefrom

—One medal recognizing the same

A collection of endorsements and testimonials more than adequate to satisfy the requirements of his current application, one would think. The lingering question had been whether the dossier should somewhere include mention of the disciplinary action that occasioned it. Early drafts of his cover letter had been explicit on the matter, but subsequent revisions had all tended in the same clear direction—of discretion—and this was probably wise. Best to let his record speak for itself, resist the urge to relitigate, to further explain, to justify, or to defend. The time for that had passed, and this latest draft, the one he was currently reviewing, reflected that opinion absolutely. Or almost. As a *pro forma* gesture of respect, he decided to keep the obsequious expressions of gratitude. Otherwise, there was really only one word in the summary that could be interpreted as remotely snipe-ish or corrective—"presumably." But seeing as that word could be so construed, and seeing as he had nothing better to do while he was waiting, he took out his pen and his inkwell and set about composing what he was determined should be his last, and by far most cosmetic, revision.

At issue—and by these efforts consigned once and for all to the subtext of any and all dealings with the Departmental Gendarmerie—were a series of technical violations peripheral to an investigation that Brassard had participated in the spring before last, aimed at a local cadre of ethnic nationalists, the "Gallic Front," who had been raiding Gypsy camps along the Rhine and openly provoking hostilities with the German speakers just across the border in Alsace. Sous-Lieutenant Brassard was found to have been accepting bribes—which was true, he had—but only so as not to call attention to himself or to rouse suspicion. As it turned out, he was guarding the wrong shore. The reason he was singled out for graft, as would eventually be made clear, was the fear among certain superior parties that his efforts were beginning to expose other members of the department who were supportive of—and in certain cases, directly supervising—said cadre of jingoistic and usually inebriated thugs. To discourage any further or more meaningful investigation into the front, Brassard had been made an example of. There was no doubt of this—the *point* was to be clear—which was why, on the advice of his most loyal champion in the department, Captain Monsaingeon, Brassard eventually chose the course he did: Plead guilty to the lesser charge of conduct unbecoming, accept the year's suspension, and use that time to burnish his credential in the foreign service—as he had surely done—on the tacit but still fairly explicit understanding that he would receive a new assignment upon his return, most likely in a new district, *with* the promotion he'd fully expected to receive just prior to the disciplinary action.

This, at any rate, was the expectation that had sustained him through the various drudgeries and trials of the last year, and which lent this last task of the day a more or less clerical quality.

Or should have, but for the fact that the evening hours treated him differently than the daylight, especially of late. If the sun said, *All is well, all will turn out in due time,* the moon knew better. The moon said, *Beware.* The moon shed light on the darker and more difficult truths, and he could feel them this evening as he wrote—the low clouds of doubt drifting into his brain, or lurking like wolves just behind the tree line, grinning and shimmering with the knowledge that his confidence was without ground; he was fooling himself;

the matter of his reinstatement was not nearly as simple or assured as he liked to think. There had been no assurance, no agreement, nothing was signed or promised. There were men out there who doubted him, and who made it their business to undermine him. Who was to say that Larive, for instance—his nemesis up in Champagne-Ardenne—hadn't written more letters against him? Or that bastard Dimanche in Tonkin? The whole trip back, in fact, since leaving Saigon, he'd been needled by the idea that he was racing against some secret communiqué, telling of who-knew-what—how his capture had cost them Luong Zhou, or that he had given information. This idea existed. Who was to say it would not follow him to Paris? Or meet him there? Who was to say that hadn't been the plan all along, to send him off on an errand so foolish—so absurd—that he would never return, or only return a more damaged good?

The letter was done now—again and for the last time, he vowed. He was tired, but fitful, too, in his mind. Fog-fed, wolf-hounded, he took to the bunk, aware he would probably need some further help to sleep. More brandy, and maybe some reading, too. A buffer of words. He had just the one book with him, *L'Élevage de Chiens*, about breeding dogs. He started reading by the lantern, but only for the purpose it provided, to lull him, which it succeeded at. Five or so pages, mostly unretained, and it fell to his chest, still open.

He closed his eyes. His breathing slowed. But he did not really rest. Here and there a little dream perhaps, but for the better part of the evening, he drifted in a dreadful hinterland, stuck upon a stubborn reverie that this little hut was not a hut—or not *only* a hut—but another version of his cell in Panhou, which it did resemble in dimension, if not material.

So Quan, his keeper, was there as well, but not in his usual place out in the passageway. He was farther down, crouched outside the mouth of the cave, or the maze—whatever it was, Brassard was never entirely sure—just that Quan was there now, keeping watch in case any messengers should pass by, bearing lies that might be used against him.

Why, even now, Quan was lifting his head. He heard one, the tread of an unseen underminer coming this way. But how would he warn you?

He had the jar beside him, plucked from the lap of the stone Buddha that sat in the passageway, perched in its own little carved-out niche. Quan had taken the jar and was dumping its contents out onto the ground at the mouth of the cave. They looked like mushrooms tumbling, or dried fruit. He picked one up, held it to his mouth, and spoke. Or his lips moved, but Brassard couldn't hear what he was saying. The sound was distant and muffled. Quan tried another, brown and shriveled. He spoke into it as he did the first, and now Brassard understood. It wasn't a mushroom or an apricot. It was an ear. This was Quan's collection—of all the ears he'd claimed over the years—but which one was Brassard's? Quan's fingers kept rummaging through the pile while the messenger came nearer. One by one he tried them, shaking them like rattles, blowing on them and speaking, but Brassard couldn't hear the warning until—aha, this one? With the torn-off lobe? Quan held it to his mouth and the word exploded in Brassard's brain—*Tuk zai!* Wake up! So loud he clasped the side of his head. *Tuk zai!* He bolted upright in his bed with such a gasp that Soter lifted his head as well.

The sky outside the window was still night blue, but not for too much longer. There was a note of lavender down low.

"Up," he said, sitting up. "Come on, boy. Up, up."

He swung his legs; he stood. He gathered together all the letters. He shoved them in his saddlebag. He needed to get to Paris. Stopping here had been a mistake. He snapped his finger. "We have to go." He took the shelf from the chair and returned it to its bracket on the wall. He pulled on his boots, his tunic, his belt. The blue in the wall square was paler now. The fire in the stove was nearly out. He used his spoon to chop at the coals. He had to go. He slung the saddlebag over his shoulder. He would wake the horse. Again he snapped his finger, but Soter was standing at the window now, facing it square and straight, ears turned like saucers. Brassard could hear it, too—the first tweedling squeaks of her wheel.

A low growl issued from Soter's throat, *rrrrr*—

"Sh-sh."

Brassard drew back beside the little stove to where he could see but not be seen, and there it was: the wagon, like an apparition passing through the frame, a cool blue ghost in the morning mist, undulating almost snakelike behind the flows of glass.

He even thought he saw her turn and look his way, though not at him. Her gaze seemed to follow the whisper of smoke rising up from the stove pipe, and she was smiling again—that cold and certain grin—both aware and unaware of the gently serpentine trail that her left hind wheel was leaving in its wake.

Part Three

Wednesday Evening

Chapter 5

François Michaud
and
Bruno Chavarin

Outside the window and through the black iron bars that fended off both intruders and escape artists, the tower could be seen—if one was willing to lean. Half the tower, at any rate, looking almost beige in the distance, and a thumb shorter than the window casement of the adjoining wall.

And there were better things to look at in here, softer and more supple things—namely, and at the moment, the smooth black line where the rounder flesh of Mam'selle Odette's left thigh (radically foreshortened by the direct angle at which Michaud was facing her) met the pelvis, a perfectly delineated spoonlike curve that contrasted nicely with the frantic scribble of her distinctively golden-orange tuft, Mam'selle Odette's being one of the more generous, and therefore picturesque, offerings in the *maison*.

Michaud's pastel danced observantly above the page, freely, swiftly. To give each separate element its own line—this was the challenge. Though capturing the colors, too, since the orange wasn't quite right. Perhaps a hint more marigold. He reached into his pouch with a small but exquisite hand, counterpart to a face that likewise showed flashes of refinement—a thin beard framed lips that were delicately bowed and red. He had unusually long eyelashes as well, on account of which the ladies of Le Montyon had taken to comparing him to a horse. Not the optimal reason, but there it was. He squinted with them often and keenly and shamelessly—now, for instance, past the black stockings and underneath the eyelet embroidery of Odette's hiked petticoat.

"How much longer?" she asked.

"I said I'm paying."

"With what? Not that." She eyed the drawing, as he'd been known to try this, hand over the product as reimbursement. He didn't answer. He finished blacking in the stocking now, as flat as he was able, to give the shape a more abstract quality.

"... I'm bored," she sighed.

He was as well—of her impatience. He closed the book. "We're losing the light anyway."

She lowered her dress and started removing her stockings—he'd had her put them on for the sitting—while he packed up his art pouch, a grubby collection of charcoals, pencils, and pastels, bound by a broken strap

"Have you ever been south?" he asked, winding it around.

"I want to go. To Biarritz. I want to get out of here."

"Out of Paris?" said Odette, her professional name. "You'd last two days."

"I want to see the sea," he replied as if he hadn't heard. "There's a house I know about, a bungalow right on the beach. Are you interested?"

"Are you paying?"

His expression, wholly disingenuous, seemed to say *why not*? "Room and board."

She didn't believe him.

"Come on. Soon as the Expo is over."

"Why wait?" She was putting up her hair again, and he wondered if this was the pose he should have drawn. The underside of her arm.

"I told you," he said, still gazing. "I have some pieces showing."

"'Some pieces.'"

"A piece. But that could be enough. I want to go and stay. I don't want to have to worry about money. And I want to take someone with me."

Still gathering her hair, she quickly turned her wrist—charmed—but he didn't see this either. He was flipping through his sketchbook, past more images of hiked petticoats, languorous arms, splayed legs, and casual self-stimulation.

"Well, you let me know, Michelangelo. Soon as that painting sells."

This was the first of her jibes that caught his attention, for reasons not so complicated. She said it as she was passing, her hip swinging close, and the floral scent of her perfume. He grabbed hold of her arm.

"Hands off," she said. A flash of anger, on both their parts. He gripped too hard, and she spat. She spat and he smacked her with the back of his hand—harder than he had meant to. He was wearing a ring, the ring struck her tooth. He hadn't meant that either. He had meant to strike flush, and deservedly, on the round of her cheek, but now she was holding her mouth and calling him a bastard.

"You broke my toof!"

"*You* broke your tooth."

But he had not meant to do this, and he felt a fondness for her. Suddenly contrite, he pulled the gold cap off his own incisor and flung it at her. "There."

He took up his wilted wide-brim hat and left, and she recovered fairly quickly, considering. She inspected the cap, found it surprisingly to her satisfaction, and tucked it into her cleavage.

§

"Now, now, what seems to be the problem?" Bruno Chavarin's celebrated charm was running a stride or so ahead of his actual person, which was still a bit flushed, and required two or three comb-swipes through his hair—to retame it and set it in its proper place.

"The problem is I have to breathe!" the new girl was saying, hiding her embarrassment behind a thin veil of hostility. "A person has to breathe!" She sniffed, sitting upright on the faux marble slab.

"Yes, we understand," replied Duchamps, the director. "But there are ways—"

"—that do not *work* for me!" she barked.

It was for this, apparently, that Chavarin had been summoned from his office, the smaller of the two he kept here at the Folies Nouvelle. The new girl—the "Hourglass," whom he had personally suggested for the part after meeting her at the Tuileries the day before—was finding herself unable to perform its only real requirement, of seeming not to breathe. Ironically, the heaving bosom which had recommended her to Chavarin's attention was turning out to be a major obstacle, the part being better suited to a slenderer, flatter figure. But surely the problem was surmountable, and he *had* promised.

"Have you shown her how?" he asked Duchamps.

"Of course. It's very simple. You count—"

"I know, I know," said the Hourglass, kicking her feet. "But this is not the way a person breathes!"

At this moment, two more members joined the circle from opposite sides—Chavarin's valet, Monsieur Singh, came from the lobby, while Mademoiselle Eschette seemed to have come from the general direction of Chavarin's smaller office, albeit a sufficiently discreet moment after him, her hair pinned and in place.

Mademoiselle Eschette was, in fact, the featured player of the revue now in its final rehearsals—"Le Plus Belle Femme du Monde," the latest edition of the "extravaganza" that Chavarin had been producing for the last three years, which in that time had proven a highly successful vehicle for both attracting and introducing new talent to the city and the continent. The new star was an apt choice—of the raven-haired variety. Pale skinned, blue eyed, widow's peaked, and porcelain featured—with a small, shapely mouth and very slender but highly dramatic brows that at the moment seemed to be indicating a fast-dwindling patience.

"What about a corset?" she suggested.

"I can't," said the Hourglass. "Then I can't lie down."

"Monsieur," the valet tried, as they had to go, in fact. Chavarin only raised his hand, *another moment.*

"Try," he said to the Hourglass, smiling at her in that deeply dimpled, very dashing way he had. "For me." He patted the slab. "Show us you can do this."

She complied, not just because he was the producer of the review, but because he was so very handsome, so very persuasive and reassuring—though it had been observed by those who'd known him longer, that the crest of Monsieur Chavarin's still considerable handsomeness was a few years behind him, as result of which he was, by way of compensation, operating at an almost constant surfeit of surface charm. The Hourglass, not having known him so long, simply blushed, and agreed to give it one more try. She scooted herself up onto the faux marble slab, while the others gathered round, the Indian valet included. She drew the sheet up over her face. She gently kicked her feet to settle the fabric and to expend any excess energy; the drape gently descended and went still above her.

Somewhat. There was, even from the first moment, a tremor to the tent, and up about her face a perceptible rising and falling. Chavarin permitted his hand to slip behind Mademoiselle Eschette and slide very delicately—and then not so delicately—up between her legs to stroke the spot where all roads meet, as he put it. She, being a somewhat more accomplished actress than the Hourglass, offered no reaction.

"I am going to lower the sheet now," said Duchamps, gently taking it by the hem and sliding it down to the waist of the Hourglass. The jury watched and waited—while over to the side, the chorus girls stretched their arms and legs and the prop man blew his nose. The circle leaned in closer, all eyes fixed upon the round white bosom, which held commendably still for a moment, but only a moment. Then it began to tremble, very subtly at first—like a bowl of aspic with the trolley passing—but the young woman's effort to stop this and calm herself only took the opposite effect, of causing her to breathe more heavily. The bosom wriggled and jiggled, and the surrounding party could all see the thin wet trails trickling down the sides of her face. A moment later she burst into tears.

"I can't!" she hyperventilated, and all eyes rolled to varying degrees. Chavarin went to console her.

"It's all right," he said soothingly, taking her hand, but turning to the others. "We'll find someone."

"Quickly," murmured Eschette.

At this, it seemed, the church bells outside began to chime. Six o'clock.

"Monsieur—" This was the valet again, Monsieur Singh, underlining the point. "If you still want the baron to see the tower."

"Of course I do."

"But *before* the opera—"

"But you said my wife is here as well?"

He hadn't, but yes, she was also waiting in the carriage.

"Then I should think the opera will wait."

He kissed the hand of the Hourglass, who seemed resigned to the fact that her career in show business had just ended. With a sniffle, she accepted his best wishes, then he hooked the arm of Mademoiselle Eschette and they proceeded out, unhurried, with the valet following.

Chapter 6

The Tower

The same church bells could be heard inside the wagon, clanging out some song the maiden did not know. She did not mind. Whatever the tune was, it roused the eyes beneath those lids—awakened them like children beneath their blankets—though she had not been asleep. She had not slept or dreamt for more than two days now, but rather this: the sort of breathing that Duchamps had been trying to teach the Hourglass; the sort of breathing that takes its lesson from the candle flame or the flame of an oil lamp—steady, even, constant; the sort of breathing that, even in proximity to such a flame, as hers was now, does not move it, so smooth are the transitions from in to out. Such breathing seeds a stillness in the breast, and a silence in the heart that replenishes far better than sleep. And much more safely. If we fall asleep, we can never be sure who will wake up.

But the bell song was all dying echoes now, and dissonance. The expectation of another verse dying out as well, she opened her eyes to the unwavering light and turned it down. She would need more oil soon.

The shift of the carriage was noted from the outside, so the opening of the door was noted as well, and the emergence of the maiden—for one, by the boy in the limb of the tree just above. A *gamin* who sadly looked the part, in a flat cap, rolled pants, and a tattered coat too large for him, stuffed with newspapers. He appeared to be nine or so.

He watched the woman descend the step and go to the

donkey, which was tied to the very tree that he was perched in. She whispered in its ear, something about bringing it food, then she made her way across the boulevard, the Quai d'Orsay. It looked like she was headed to the tower, which wasn't so far—closer in distance than its own height.

The other observer of this—of both the woman and the boy—was Brassard, of course, who was seated on a bench just opposite the wagon but down a bit. Thanks to a natural gift for stealth, as well as that waffling left wheel, he had tracked the young woman all the way from the roadside hut. He had dropped off the horse at an exposition stable just beyond Les Invalides and then pursued on foot. He was in civilian clothes, a black sack coat and dark wool pants. His uniform hat and tunic were tucked inside his saddlebag, which was under the bench, partially hidden by Soter, who was seated beside him.

He had been in his present position for the last hour, principally to surveil, but also (apparently) to be reminded of the mixed feelings that Paris always roused in him. He had been a cadet here, and spent several years as a boy here as well. This was after his mother died of typhus, and before the siege in '70. His father, who served in the XII army corps, had sent him to Mont-Saint-Michel that year to live with his uncle. A month later his father was killed by a Prussian sniper at Chevilly. Brassard was twelve.

But it wasn't any of this that disturbed him about the place. His father's death had been an act of heroism, after all, defending the city against the invading army; that was why one wore a uniform. The disturbing part was the juxtapositions one encountered here. That ragged boy on the limb, for instance, and the ridiculous tower behind. It was much larger than he'd expected, even having seen the posters—an awkward colossus planted there for no other purpose than to overwhelm, to awe, and to divert attention from the children roosting in the trees.

He'd heard the church bells, too—though, again, he couldn't tell where they were. He'd seen the maiden emerge in the same plain white frock as before, with a light gray sweater overtop—coarse, square, unbuttoned. He wasn't sure what to make of her empty-handedness, or of the queer, near abandonment of the wagon in the middle of a well-trafficked thoroughfare. He assumed she wasn't going far, or for long. Still, it was a strange enough decision—on her part—to force another one on his: whether to stay here and keep an eye on the wagon, or to follow her to wherever she was headed now. It was a choice he had to make quickly, too, as she was already crossing the boulevard, either headed for the tower or some other rendezvous at the Expo.

Boldly, then, and with a certainty of purpose that effectively deflected all attention (save for the boy's, which was fast upon him), Brassard crossed to the wagon and entered. The door was open. The rug was in place. He slid it aside to see the trapdoor, which once again he pried open with his jackknife, so to confirm the presence of the cast-iron safe and the candlesticks, neither of which appeared to have been touched since he last saw them.

He stepped back down and closed the door.

So a drop-off, then?

The boy was still looking down at him like a little macaque on his limb. Brassard reached into his pocket and removed six coins.

"Do you want these?"

The boy descended quickly. A bit dull in veneer, he gave nothing away by expression. Olive-skinned, with bulbous, slightly gaping eyes, a straight Grecian nose, and an unruly mop of dark brown hair that Brassard well remembered.

"I will give you one now," he said. "You get the rest if you follow the young woman who just left."

The boy turned to look. She could still be seen, but barely, with all the people crossing back and forth between them. The white of her frock distinguished her, as did the strange imperturbability of her gait and direction.

"I want to know where she goes, whom she sees, and everything she does until she comes back."

The boy took the coin. "What if she doesn't come back?"

"Then I want to know where she spends the night. I'll find you, don't worry. What's your name?"

"Olivier."

"Hold out your hand, Olivier."

Olivier did. Brassard snapped his fingers and Soter responded by giving the boy's hand a sniff and a lick.

"You live here in the park?"

The boy nodded, but barely, in the direction of the Trocadéro.

"He will come with you."

"What's his name?" the boy asked, enjoying the attention the dog was paying his hand, purposeful though it was.

"To you? 'Sir,'" said Brassard. "And if for some reason I'm not here when you get back, I'll meet you at the Barracks. La Caserne. You know where that is?"

He didn't seem to.

"He'll show you." Brassard consulted Soter to make sure he understood. He did. "All right, go."

Olivier and the dog were quick to close the gap between themselves and the maiden, who wasn't moving so quickly, her progress slowed both by the scattered swarm of people buzzing around the base of the tower and by her wonder at the sheer size of the thing. It was a good twenty times taller than any structure surrounding, and only seemed to grow the closer you came.

Olivier even felt a certain pride at her seeing it, as on some level he felt that the tower was his. They'd started building it around the time he'd come to live at the gardens in front of the Trocadéro. He'd watched it grow from the great base up. He still felt a kind of awe whenever he looked at it, how tall, how delicate it appeared from across the river, like a blunt needle pushing its way through a web, and how those filaments transformed into girders of steel as you crossed the bridge, how the needle grew into a tower, swooping up into the spire, spearing the sky, and making the weather. He had seen it do this, sprout clouds and storms and lightning and thunder.

But now the woman was entering under and into the space created by the four great arches, leaning in toward one another like giants huddled in conference. He could tell by the way she was looking up and all around, this was her first time. The base alone was broader and wider than a whole city block, so large and cavernous there was a strange kind of half-light underneath, where you couldn't really tell if you were indoors or out-, because you weren't either. And there were always lots of people because the tower was the entrance to the Expo; it was the gate, so there were always performers as well—jugglers and dancers, street musicians, puppeteers and animals. The monkey and the organ grinder were his favorite, always having to run and hide from the officers. But he liked looking at the people, too—the ladies in pairs with their hats and parasols, walking arm in arm while the men stood watching them, pretending not to. Olivier did the same, though he didn't really pretend. He looked straight at them usually, because whenever he dreamt that he saw his mother—of whom he had no memory—it was here.

The young woman in the frock kept moving through and

cutting between the people. She had seen the lifts swinging up and sliding down past each other like pulleys. Only two of them were working, both in the northeast stanchion. *If she goes there*, thought Olivier, *we can't follow.* It cost money and they wouldn't let a dog in.

The one touched down now and the people came out, and that did seem to be where she was headed. She'd have gotten straight on if the ticket man hadn't stopped her. He touched her shoulder. He showed her there was a line. He showed her the sign: 2 FRANCS. But she mustn't have had any money, because then she pointed to the stairs and the people walking up. The ticket man said that was fine, walking was free, so she went to that gate instead and got in that line, which was shorter.

Olivier stayed put. He still wouldn't have been allowed with the dog, and it wasn't as if she was going anywhere. Also, the mime was here, making fun of the people—the German man who looked like a walrus, or the Nanny with the great big bustle. The mime kept setting an invisible cup of tea on it, and having to run after her to take his next sip. The dog didn't notice. The dog didn't even turn. Just kept his eye on the lady the whole time, as if she were a squirrel, slowly, slowly, slowly spiraling up the tree. They would wait here. And anyway, the monkey had just arrived with the organ grinder, and all the ladies with all their different faces.

§

Brassard, meanwhile, had resumed his seat across from the wagon and down a ways. He had the book in his lap, the one on dog breeding, and he was periodically turning the page, but his focus was on the human traffic.

He had already identified a potential contact, in fact—a

loitering rag-and-bone man. Gray, grizzled, and wooly, he carried a sack on his back, and his coat was covered with grease, stained slick with the fat of the bones he spent all day collecting. This was already the third pass he'd taken at the gypsy wagon, although he pointedly did *not* look at it, glancing about instead to see who might be watching. Brassard turned the page of his book, and the rag-and-bone man continued on his way. Or rather, he stopped this time and took a seat on one of the benches. He began rooting through his sack.

Why? A gendarme, a current member of the Guard, was passing. With his boot, Brassard slid his saddlebag farther beneath the bench, just in case his hat or coat might be showing, but the gendarme had other things to think about. Farther up the Quai, some commotion was turning heads. Pedestrians could be heard yelping and hollering. A carriage was careening this way. Nursemaids swerved their perambulators, parasols shook in anger, a bicyclist teetered and tilted, while others stood back and watched in open admiration as the very stately gray horse cantered by, bearing an equally stately carriage. It was open, but rode so high above the wheel that none could quite see the passengers. Only that champagne glasses were out, and spilling.

They were headed for the tower. They swerved left to make their entrance, and now all the scandalized pedestrians turned to the gendarme, wondering if he was going to do anything. He offered a show of concern. He picked up his pace a bit, but it was not a convincing display.

More to the point, the rag-and-bone man used the diversion to go find cover under one of the elm trees. Brassard assumed he'd be back. He kept his place on the bench, therefore, and returned to the book in his lap.

§

Monkey or no monkey, the speed and grandeur of the in-coming carriage was more than enough to turn both Olivier's and Soter's heads. It was coming straight their way, bypassing all checkpoints and pulling directly up to the elevator gate.

The line was still long and restless, but was likewise di-verted by the arrival, especially now as the passengers de-scended: a countess of some stripe (most thought this because they'd heard someone else say so, but also because of her hat, cocked and raven feathered); the very dashing gentleman who helped her down; the strikingly beautiful younger wom-an who followed (whom he also helped); a spry dandy with a monocle, walking stick, and lavender spats; an Indian (one presumed from his complexion and the cut of his coat); and finally a more portly and Germanic gentleman whom most took to be the countess's counterpart, the count.

Not so.

The guards at least seemed to recognize the older wom-an. With the carriage of a military general, she led the par-ty straight to the head of the line, not without apology. The dashing man explained to the couple at the head that his friends were in a hurry, which seemed gallant of him. Even more, his offer to pay the cost of the next ten tickets. "Make it twelve." He handed over a bill to the ticket man, to mild applause as space was made in the waiting elevator.

The lift itself was like a little chapel, with ten or so bench-es seating ten passengers each, hip to hip. In this instance, the arrangement posed a diplomatic challenge. At the entrance of the countess, a family of four—son in sailor suit and older daughter in sun hat—all stood up to give their seats, which her ladyship duly accepted. Then came the tricky part, which was simplified somewhat by Chavarin's decision to stand. Monsieur Singh did the same, which helped determine the rest. This evening's special guest, the Viennese financier Baron von Dorn, sat beside the countess, then their friend Montesquiou in the lavender spats, then—with all sufficient buffers provided—Mademoiselle Eschette. So arranged, and at the behest of the operator's polished brass crank, up they went.

The mood inside the elevator was still chilly, for reasons even the casual observer, apprised of the legal pairings up front, might have gleaned. The countess was a good deal older than her husband—twelve years—and while one might like to suppose that she had once been beautiful, one would be wrong. The jaw had always been lantern-like, the lips thin and flat, the brow square. She was, in age, a more formidable specimen than she had ever been in youth, having grown into what had always been a commanding bearing and temperament. She held herself like her grandfather (the general), and was built like him, too: barrel-chestedly. She was an expert pistol shot, and an equally expert handler of her own estate, which had taken on Bruno Chavarin as an asset some three years ago, he being famously attractive, socially gifted, coveted, supportive of her philanthropic, political, and cultural ventures, and suitably ambitious in his own more popular sphere. Also, he was legitimately appreciative of the various advantages that she provided him. For the most part. And even there, his penchant for dalliance had seemed to be an accepted part of the contract. All of which was to say that it could not be assumed what found the countess so disgruntled this evening, or even—given the natural set of her features—whether she was disgruntled at all.

Baron von Dorn, who was looking a little pale, ventured one possibility. "You don't like the tower?"

"Oh, I can't wait for them to take it down," she said. She looked out as the iron latticework flicked by, and let several more phrases of contempt drift murmurously from her lips: "Monstrous . . . tasteless . . ." and, most audibly, ". . . nothing but a giant prick."

Chavarin had taken note, and smiled lovingly.

"You may have to get used to it," he said, now leaning down to the younger child of the standing family, the boy in a blue sailor suit. "I bet you like it, don't you? The tower."

The boy nodded, very much so.

"You see?" said Chavarin. "The people have spoken." And the congregation in the pews now grinned and nodded and looked out proudly at the receding world below. The baron swallowed greenly.

Several moments of communal silence ensued, presumably to let the cables have their say, and to let Chavarin pose a bit—though, in his defense, it was difficult for such a handsome man in evening dress, in an open and ascending lift at sunset, *not* to pose. The question was who enjoyed the show the most. The sailor boy's mother, who was holding her daughter's hand, seemed off-put. The countess was indifferent. Of all, Mademoiselle Eschette was probably the most evidently entertained, not that she was fooled or failed to see his vanity, just that she found it charming in its way— because *he* was aware of it as well—so she indulged it with several knowing glances that were returned in kind, and rather openly, though again, whether the countess even saw was anyone's guess.

"First level," said the operator, pivoting the crank. The elevator slowed and stopped on cue. The gate screeched open, and roughly half the passengers stood to get off, to see the view from here. The countess was among them, much to Chavarin's surprise.

"I thought we didn't have time to make two stops."

"We don't," she said. "But once to the top is enough for

me. You can stay." She offered a thin smile to the baron. "I'll be in the carriage. Don't dally." She directed this last to the valet, Monsieur Singh, who assured her with a bow that he would see to it.

If Mademoiselle Eschette took any satisfaction at the countess's departure, it was short-lived. The lift was refilling with passengers from the first level, but out on the platform now there appeared a young woman in a sweater and a plain white frock. Having just reached the level by stairs, she was flushed, and took a moment to catch her breath by the rail. That was all, though as she was looking west, the low sun cast her face in glowing hues of rose and amber, at the same time lighting the outermost strands of her hair a brilliant blond-white—the lashes, too, and the finer down of her cheek—which had the effect of hallowing her as she stood there. Even in the midst of all the traffic, it was an image not to be missed, least of all by Bruno Chavarin—"the man with the eye." He reacted at once. "We've room for one more." He signaled to the operator. "This one. Come. She shouldn't have to climb all the way."

For a folded bill, the operator obliged, and the countess saw all this. She had yet to leave the platform herself, still waiting for the down-bound elevator to fill. She had seen the hallowed young woman and her husband's reflex, and she saw the young woman now boarding the lift and taking the very same seat that she, the countess, had been sitting in. And her husband saw that she saw and he showed no shame.

"We'll see you at the bottom!" he called and waved. With that, the gates closed and the two elevators went their separate ways.

In the one headed up, another round of musical chairs. Chavarin remained standing, so Monsieur Singh did, too. The family of four had taken new seats, all in a row. And the new passenger, the young woman who hadn't paid, was seated between Baron von Dorn and Montesquiou, though she still didn't seem to know why she'd been offered the place, or by whom. She sent a searching smile to Montesquiou, who replied with more of a sidelong grin and, remarkably, a pat upon his knee. Baron von Dorn more than ever looked as if he might have preferred getting off with the countess, while for her part, Mademoiselle Eschette didn't understand why any of this had been necessary, taking pity on the young woman, who looked to her like a laundress.

"I still want to see the diamond, though," said the sailor boy's sister. She was wearing a sun hat with a dark blue ribbon that matched her waistband.

"We will," her mother said. "Don't worry."

"But what about the feeding?" asked her brother, looking to his father now.

The father replied through his mustache, "Maybe." He was wearing a top hat and tails, and the downward tilt at the outer edges of his eyes lent his expression a permanent long-suffering quality. "We don't all have to do the same thing."

He turned this to his wife—it wasn't clear if he'd meant this as a question or a statement—but just then the whole lift seemed to swoop, eliciting swoons and gasps throughout the little chapel. They were coming vertical, headed straight up, and more than one in the congregation thought to themselves, *This is what it must feel like to go to heaven.* There were some embarrassed chuckles and sighs of relief, and finally Chavarin caught his new guest's eye long enough to wink, though again it wasn't clear that she knew what to make of this. She turned away.

Still hovering was the matter of "the feeding."

"Does anyone know if the baby has arrived?" asked a

woman's voice, several rows back.

No one answered at first. The children looked at the operator as if he might have been told, but he shook his head.

"I didn't even know there *was* a baby," said Chavarin.

"I want to see it, too," the sailor boy whispered to his father intensely.

"If it's here," his mustache replied. "I suspect we'd know if it were."

More latticework flickered by, making the seashell sky behind look like the projection of a giant magic lantern.

"But why is it taking so long?" the sister asked.

"Tall tower," her father replied.

"No, I mean the baby."

"Oh," the father shrugged. "Maybe different . . . what's the word?"

"'Gestations'?" Baron von Dorn wiped his brow again.

"Yes, 'gestations,' thank you—"

A few more heads nodded vaguely. Too bad, though. One would want to see the baby, after all. Probably adorable.

The lift continued up, and the city spanned and sprawled beneath them all, and abstracted, and more than one passenger thought it strange that the city wasn't *supposed* to be seen this way—so neatly and geometrically arranged. One would think that was the purpose.

Chavarin saw the young woman looking out, saw her eyes dancing and darting. He managed to catch them again. "Is this your first time?" he twinkled.

Again it wasn't clear she understood, or even heard (in retrospect, Monsieur Singh would assume that she had clearly *mis*understood). In any case, she replied, "I don't believe so."

A moment later, the elevator came to a lurching halt, which, to judge by the sounds of the congregation, caught several stomachs by surprise. The gate opened, but again most of the passengers were furtive, excepting the sailor boy, who had to be restrained by his father. Ladies first. Mademoiselle Eschette obliged, then the mother and the sister. Then the boy bolted, heading straight for a small cannon pointed east.

While most of the rest were still slow to make their way, the young woman—the one who'd boarded at the first level—crossed directly to the southern vantage, moving with an even stride. She gripped the rail with her hands, more for the cool than the security, and began a slow survey of the surrounding panorama with an evenness of purpose that might be compared to a seconds hand of a watchface.

To the west, the sunset was in full bloom—a radiant peach dissolving in a watercolor sky. The pink and gold of its refracted light was coating all the western faces of the city below, including the cathedral. Beneath them, the Champs de Mars had taken on an emerald glow in the general loaming. The great glass roofs of the long buildings reflected the sky like mother-of-pearl. The flags waved briskly, while at the far end the same crisp wind was sweeping away the smoke from the two great stacks—dissolving charcoal ribbons, beneath which the giant Ferris wheel was the perfect cog, generating everything: the smoke, the lights, the people, the dogs, the carriages, and the slow but, from here, seemingly perceptible turning of the earth.

Despite all this, Monsieur Chavarin was practically having to drag his guests out onto the platform.

"Come. Come. Did I not tell you?"

"You didn't tell me it was going to be so windy." Mademoiselle Eschette scowled.

"Well, obviously," he replied, refusing to credit the effort that had been put into styling her hair this evening, and that the pins and combs and compound would be no match for the flurries sweeping through the platform.

He finally gave up on her and went to join Baron von Dorn and Montesquiou, whom he often invited along on such occasions, he being not only the premier poet-dandy in all of Paris, but also a raconteur of the first order, and very adept at greasing the wheels of conversation when moneyed interests came to town.

He and the baron were themselves standing a cautious distance from the rail, not so much from fear of heights or dishevelment—Montesquiou's hair was under sufficient control of Macassar oil—but to have a better view of the young woman who'd joined them on the elevator.

"Yes, who is this girl?" said Chavarin. He lit himself a cigarette—or tried. Montesquiou provided screen. "Doesn't she just restore your faith?"

Montesquiou agreed, not taking his eye from her. "But in what?"

"This is the question."

They continued to observe, though perhaps not with the same level of attention as Chavarin's valet, Monsieur Singh, who also had been watching the young woman—from the moment she boarded the lift, in fact—partly because she was his master's guest, but also because of her expression, a peculiar yet familiar combination of engagement and disinterest. It was there when she had been listening to the conversation in the elevator. It was here again as she looked out upon the city. For though she had been among the first to reach the railing and start drinking in the view, she did so with nothing like the overt wonder of the others, who seemed to enjoy showing when their breath was taken, who pointed and sighed, comparing what they saw to what they knew it to be. ("Like ants," they would invariably say. "Like a little colony of ants!")

The young woman's face reflected no such fascination with height, or size, or depth, or distance. Hers was an expression that would have been equally appropriate to the survey of a yarn shop window, it seemed to Singh, or to a tuning orchestra. Indeed, the way her eyes kept glancing from perch to perch, alighting from gable to treetop to hedgerow, from passing cloud to a passing carriage ("Like a beetle!" the others would say), gave the sense that her attention was being guided more by the ear than by the eye; and that she was listening not just to the sounds they *all* could hear—the bells, the pigeons, the gentle ruffle of the wind against their ears, or whistling through the girders of the tower—but the *less* evident sounds as well. The organ in the cathedral, for instance, or the prayers of the people in the pews. The muttering baker. The snoring dog. The whitecaps on the river. All the sounds that must have been, but went unheard.

Monsieur Singh was of mixed descent—and persuasion. Though born in Bombay and raised according to Hindu custom, his mother had been Chinese—and Buddhist—and she had told him stories when he was young, stories she had been told by *her* father, a captain in the South China Sea, about a goddess to whom all the sailors prayed. The goddess was called Miaoshan, and there were many legends attached to her name: of how her father had tried to kill her for not marrying the man he chose; how she was saved from hanging and by a giant tiger; how later, as "one without anger," she had offered her arm and her eye to the potion that saved her father's life. But the most memorable story by far was about the day that Miaoshan was set to leave this world. She had come to the gate. She was just about to enter the Land of the Pure when out of nowhere she heard the cries of all the suffering people on earth. Her ears could not bear the sound, so Buddha took pity and gave her eleven heads. Hearing the people's anguish more clearly, she wanted to help them, but she could not reach them with just one arm, so Buddha took pity again and gave her a thousand more.

Monsieur Singh had not thought of Miaoshan in years, but she was who came to mind when he looked at the young woman at the top of the tower, even now as Monsieur Chavarin approached her from behind, cigarette in hand

§

"So? Did you ever think you'd see the world from such a height?" He leaned against the rail beside her. They were looking east along the river, back in the direction of the palace.

He offered her a cigarette from his case. She demurred, but in a way that caused him to look back at his friend Montesquiou, who replied by coaxing him further with a nod.

"I should tell you, though," he said. "My friend and I are having a little disagreement. You see, he has a theory about you. He thinks that you might be asleep right now, and he is worried. Is that possible, do you think, that you are asleep right now?"

His look was one of both humor and concern, and she seemed to give the question weight. Finally, she replied, "Then you would be a dream?"

It wasn't completely clear whether, by this, she was answering or joking or seeking clarification, so for a moment Chavarin wasn't sure how to respond. "Well . . . no," he finally said, and then on second thought. "Though that might explain a few things." He laughed, a single shout of self-delight so loud that others on the platform turned, excepting Mademoiselle Eschette, who had been observing the whole exchange from within the shelter of the platform, and therefore could not hear a word.

"But you see I disagree with my friend here," said Chavarin. "I think you are wide awake. I do. I'm not concerned about you in the least. But how do we prove which of us is correct?"

The young woman looked bewildered by the question, understandably, so he moved in even closer, to a range of confidence and intimacy that turned Mam'selle Eschette's distant shiver into a bristle. His voice was low, in tone and volume. "I was told by a doctor friend one time—who knows if it's true?—but he said that in our dreams, we cannot adjust the light. We cannot turn on lamps or light candles or things like that. Have you heard this? That if you can adjust the light, then you know you are awake?"

The young woman had not heard this. Nor, to judge from her expression—the judge here being Monsieur Singh—was she quite certain whether she was being asked to *test* the theory. Either way, it happened that at this very moment, far below and to their left, in the deepening blue of the Trocadéro gardens, with all its spires and onion domes, the lights of the reflecting pool just now flickered on. And the lanterns along the bridge as well—*blink, blink, blink.* The lamplighters were on their ladders all throughout the park and the surrounding gardens, so that in a matter of moments, and as if by magic, the world beneath their feet began to glitter.

From their high vantage, it was an effect so brilliant— and so brilliantly timed—that Chavarin's own eyes lit up. He laughed out loud and turned back to his friend Montesquiou. "I think you owe me ten francs!" He laughed again and returned to the young woman, bowing his head in a courtly and reverent way. "Which I would happily share with our—"

"Monsieur," Monsieur Singh stepped in. "The time." The streetlamps were both a signal and an excuse. Also, the elevator was sliding into view.

"Oh. Yes." Chavarin drooped. "I am called." He took her hand, and bowed as if to kiss it. He did not go as far as that, but he did press something into her palm. A card.

"Monsieur," Singh tried again.

"All right, all right," said Chavarin, pulling away. "Down we go." He turned and began collecting all his guests, starting with Montesquiou, then the baron, who was taking shelter with Mam'selle Eschette inside. Grudgingly she accepted Chavarin's arm, while letting it be known that she had appreciated no part of the foregoing exchange out on the platform. This was conveyed by the extreme arch of her painted left brow, to which Monsieur Chavarin replied with an equally extreme, but still playful, furrow: She had herself to blame. *Windy.*

All members of the party returned to the elevator and resumed their places inside. The maiden remained at the rail, looking back to receive one final bow and beaming glance from the dashing man's dark-skinned servant—he with the obsidian hair, combed high on top to look like an ocean wave—just before the gate closed and the company dropped from view.

§

The sister in the sun hat stamps her foot. *But it's not working!* She is standing by the telescope not far to the maiden's left. The girl's mother bustles over and they argue like twins—all frowns and scowls—about one of the exhibits down below, with a diamond. The girl is saying she thinks it's closed already when out of nowhere her little brother dashes up and throws something over the side. It flashes and drops. A coin.

He knows right away he has done something wrong.

I didn't.

His mother swats him on the rear and tells him it could lodge in someone's skull! *It could split them in half!*

For a moment, the boy's eyes well at the thought, but he quickly reverts to anger. He says he wants to see the zoo. *I want to see the feeding.*

The mother at this point turns to the maiden. *What are you smiling at?* she snaps. She says she should mind her own "onions." Then she takes the boy's hand and yanks him away.

The maiden was not aware that she was smiling. Nor, for that matter, had it occurred to her that all of this might be a dream. She does not think it is. She looks east. The lights below are even clearer now, the little lampposts that much more pronounced in the deepening blue. There are so many surrounding the tower, they cast a golden glow on the gardens and the boulevards and the buildings, the riverbanks, the statues and the carriages. Every detail, every leaf and carving, present and accounted for. But the farther out she looks, the fewer lights there are, and the smaller they become, their little orbs like the heads of dandelions. They hang like necklaces along the distant streets and overtop the churches. And farther on toward the city's edge they scatter and make constellations, a reflecting lake, beyond which everything goes dark as if a blanket had been thrown.

Though not completely dark. Squint and she can see a few more candles flickering in the folds. Homes? Little villages? She knows there is a winding road out there that one can follow here; she knows that alongside that road there is a meadow where one can have tea with the professor and his son; she knows that farther along there is an inn where one can dance with the man with such large hands; and that there is a forest beyond that; and that within that forest there is a grave; and within that grave there is a body . . .

Only she does not think this really. There is no body in the grave. That is why the officer looked at her the way he did, the one with the little ear—because she did not dig it deep—

Enough! The gate screeches open behind her. The next elevator has arrived. It coughs out its passengers. They straggle their ways to the rails, leaving the little chapel and all the benches empty.

§

Down along the river, the same dusk was descending, and Brassard was still sitting, reading by the light of the nearby streetlamp. Or he was pretending to, when the rag-and-bone man returned, a gray rat from hiding. He had brought a gift this time—an apple for his friend the donkey. He treated her very openly, and the beast yielded to his ministrations, offering no objection as he casually harnessed her to the rails, speaking to her all the while, scratching her neck, telling her she was a good girl. While the tourists and the city folk passed this way and that, he gently led her out onto the boulevard, turning a wide circle, then starting away in an easterly direction along the riverbank.

He was taking the wagon.

Once again Brassard had to choose. Stay and wait for the woman to return, or pursue the wagon and its contents?

He looked back at the tower to see if she might be coming, or the boy, or Soter. But no. Strangers all, and the wagon was headed away with its cast-iron safe inside. If there was a deeper root here, the rag-and-bone man might well be leading him to it. So Brassard stuffed his book back into his saddlebag, stood, stretched, then casually strolled off in the same easterly direction.

Chapter 7
The Zoo

She feels the push of the chapel floor beneath her, the tension in her knees. They have reached the ground again, but the family is still squabbling. They have been the whole way down.

Don't get too close, though, the mother warns the father. *I don't want him up against the fence.*

He tells her they don't bite.

Do you know that? Her eyes are wide and glaring. *Have you seen the teeth?* She is calling him a fool.

The gate screeches. The passengers rise. The son stays where he is, with his chin on his chest, his lower lip jutting out. His father coaxes gently, *Come along, Mathieu.* He leans all the way down to whisper in his ear. *I won't let them bite you, I promise.*

But the boy is not afraid they'll bite. He is afraid that he has split someone in half.

There are many more people out beneath the stanchions now, all heading in different directions—back toward the river and the bridge, and a park across the bridge. She enters into the eddy; it is difficult to know which way to go. Someone offers her a flower—a man with a white-painted face. He clasps his hands to his heart; it throbs; he is in love. The people laugh, but she sees the father and son now, and she feels the current. She lets it carry her away from the river, out from underneath the tower and in toward the fairground and the esplanade with the great wheel at the far end, and the two smokestacks. It's a long green field, crisscrossed by paths and bounded by great glass halls, divided one from the next by golden-domed porticoes with flags. There are flags all along the rooftops, too, whipping and stiff.

A shudder of light and a hollow *pop* within a long low tent: CARTES DE VISITE! says the sign. HAVE YOUR PIC-TURE TAKEN! The poster in front is of a man and wife standing in a parlor with the tower framed in the window. It's the same room where the professor and his son were standing in their photograph. This is where they must have taken it, even though the perspective makes no sense. Farther along the path, there's the gate from another of the professor's cards: square brick columns and the words in iron letters arching overtop—JARDIN ZOOLOGIQUE.

And now she sees Mathieu pulling his father along. *Ga-dong ga-dong.* There's man with a handbell and a bucket, and a crowd gathering behind him already. *Ga-dong ga-dong . . .*

The feeding.

She lets herself be drawn. Through the gate, she enters into a more canopied space of tree limbs and strung lights, exotic bird calls, tiki torches and totem poles carved up and down with wild faces—snarling, ogling, laughing, yawning. This one's crowned by a real live cockatoo. Another pole stands just beyond, posted with arrow signs all cockeyed and akimbo—AFRIQUE! ARABIE! INDE! POLYNÉSIE! They point to the branching paths ahead, divided by holding pens and fences. A male peacock strolls by, the turquoise eyes of its tail feathers winking at her as she passes.

Ga-dong ga-dong—the feeder has come to the nearest of the pens. A driftwood plaque has been mounted to the fencepost. MALAWI. He sets down his bucket, and the visitors behind him crane to see. ("Yam. Yech!" "They love it, though." "There are some greens as well." "But are they even cooked?") More people gather and push, Mathieu and his father included. The maiden weaves her way.

The pen is a dirt patch mostly, with a strange-looking wheelbarrow in the middle, but on the far side is a little grotto made of boulders rolled together. One woman covers her nose, then another, then several of the children; they smell nothing foul, or off. But look, they point. Something just moved above the cave. A shadow—it looked like a snake almost, or maybe a panther. "Did you see? There! It moved again!"

Ga-donga . . . ga-donga.

The slower, slightly altered rhythm of the bell shushes them. It is a signal. All eyes turn to the mouth of the grotto, and they wait. A moment passes, then another shadow silently emerges. As one, the crowd draws its breath. The figure stays low at first, but then stand uprights like a bear. One of the women in front turns away; she cannot look. But the maiden is rapt. It's too lean for a bear, too long for a monkey, too dark to be sure. It isn't until the Malawi has reached the barrow that the light makes clear: He's wearing a cloth around his waist and tucked underneath, and a lion pelt on his shoulder, and he's carrying a large bowl in his hand.

It is a man.

But she has never seen one so dark.

The feeder sets his bucket down inside the pen and steps back. All the visitors step back, too, to watch in silence, wide-eyed.

His skin is almost blue-black and it shines smooth, and his mouth goes farther out than his nose, because his nose is flat and his teeth protrude. They buck even. His eyes are deep and flashing, and his hair is like black wool.

He takes the yams from the bucket. His hands and fingers are long and slender, and as he starts filling his bowl, which is wooden, a *swish-swish* turns several heads. Behind them, in the pen on the other side of the path, another man has stepped out from a small circus tent. He is dark, too, but not as dark as this one. He is wearing a turban and swishy balloon pants, a grimy purple and white, and he is wielding a sword that looks like a bat's wing. He rolls his wrist, but nothing glints; the sword is made of papier-mâché.

One of the children asks, "Are we allowed to feed them?" A little girl in a pinafore. She is holding out a biscuit to the Black man. The feeder clucks his tongue, no, and she takes it back quickly, as if she'd burned her hand. The Black man doesn't respond, but as he turns with his bowl and starts back to the grotto, the little girl calls after him, "Did the baby come?"

He stops, his shoulders high and broad and slender. He looks at her.

"BAY-BE," says the girl, trying to explain. "*Waah-waaah.*" She makes a cradle of her arms. The people outside the fence all smile; they want to know, too. Is there a baby now? They wait, but the black man stays grim. He scans their faces; the whites of his eyes are a milky yellow, the pupils like black marbles. They meet hers only briefly, but when they do, something flares inside her so sudden and so hot, she feels that she must smother it at once.

Finally he looks down at the girl in the pinafore and shakes his head impassively, *no. No baby.*

He takes his bowl, then, and walks back across the patch on long, bowed legs. He has to duck to reenter the grotto. The other one—the younger and more panther-like—drops down from the top of the rocks and follows him in. But how many more are in there, the maiden cannot see. A family? Two? And is there even room for the mother to lie down?

A great blast cracks the sky overhead, so sudden and loud that several of the visitors gasp. The sailor boy's father smiles.

"Eight o'clock," he says casually. He points to the tower. It's still puffing smoke, and sending out a beam of light, a white column high into the sky. As it tilts down and swings over their heads, a second shot fires, re-startling the crowd and sparking a second column of light—this one red; it swings and scissors with the white like two long stilts. The visitors crane, enchanted, even as the phantom shell still howls overhead, tearing through the sky as if it were a sheet of paper. And now a third blast sounds, as they all knew it would—blue—joining with the red and the white to scan and weave about the clouds and the grounds.

The father smiles to his cringing son, *That's it, that's all. And listen now*, he points to his ear. Drums! They're coming from farther up the path. Another child cries, "The Pygmies! The Pygmies are out! They are going to dance!" In shiny buckled shoes the children all scramble around the bend to the next exhibit, their parents trailing.

The feeder seems to have made his way as well, leaving the young woman alone. She steps up to the fence and peers. There's a light on inside the grotto now. Very faint. A small lamp, or maybe just a candle—but shedding enough to reveal the glimmers and shadows of the figures within. She still can't see how many, or where the mother would be. They're all huddled together and eating from bowls with their hands; their fingers look like beaks—

"*Pardon.*"

—but where is the mother?

"*. . . Excusez-moi.*"

She turns. There is a little rumpled man standing next to her. Young, with pale skin and a soft beard, and holding out an open book to her.

"It's a courtesy." He removes his hat; his hair is long, thick, and greasy. "When we draw, we show."

She's not sure who he means by "we," but he wants her to see the drawing he has made. It's very scribbly.

"Do you know about the mother?" she asks. She points back to the grotto. "Is she in there?"

The man shrugs, he wouldn't know, but he shows the drawing again. Playfully his eyes keep shifting between her and the image and back to her—the one *is* the other, he means to say—but she still doesn't see because of what's over the young man's shoulder now. It's only a glimpse at first—more people pass between—but then yes, there it is again:

On the far side of the totem pole, it's the prick-eared dog. The officer's dog from the roadside, and it's staring straight back at her.

"Have you ever modeled?" the man asks. "Sat, I mean."

Again, she shakes her head, she isn't sure. *But then who is that grubby boy?* she thinks. *And where is the officer with the little ear?*

"Because you should," the man is saying. He emphasizes the word "*you,*" and he insists he's not being forward. He says he "sees these things." But even as he speaks, she is looking for the officer, and now she can hear the voices of the Malawi as well, coming from inside the grotto. It sounds like they're moaning, or it could be a prayer.

"Don't worry about them," says the man. "It's all for show. Half the Arabs are Gypsy." He picks up a framed painting that's been leaning against his leg. "Let me show you." He points back in the direction of the gate. He wants to take her somewhere. It isn't far.

And she doesn't *want* to go with him, but the dog is still looking at her, and if it's the same dog—the officer's dog—and if they've followed her all the way here, then this is not where she wants to lead them—to the Malawi or to the mother. This is the *last* place.

So she accepts the artist's invitation. While the drums keep thumping up the path, and the visitors *ooh* and *aah* at the Pygmies, and laugh—and while the voices of the Malawi continue murmuring inside the grotto, mournfully—she and the artist start walking back toward the gate. His jacket smells like tobacco. And turpentine.

He asks if she lives in Paris. She says no. He asks if she has family, and they pass the peacock again. The man is leading her to the long tent with the flashing lights inside.

He asks again about her family, and she says, "I have an uncle. And a cousin."

"Perfect," he says. "So you can send your picture to them."

The dog and the boy are moving now. The visitors glide back and forth like schools of fish, but they are coming this way, the dog's nose still pointing at her like the scope of a rifle.

The artist directs her to the entrance flap of the tent. He says he will buy. "I owe you," he smiles; he has a chipped front tooth.

What has she to fear? She smiles gently in reply and enters the tent.

Chapter 8

Snakes, Pigeons, and Rats

Up to a point, Brassard's pursuit of the wagon was a simple matter, owing to the fact that the rag-and-bone man continued along the Quai d'Orsay, which was still official Expo grounds, at least up until the palace. This meant that it was better lit, tree-lined, and most important of all, well-trafficked. Had the rag-and-bone man chosen a less-beaten path, Brassard might have had to conceal his pursuit. As it was, he was one of countless others enjoying the evening air, the view, the boats, the book bins, and the smaller stalls, choosing between little tokens and picture postcards.

All this ended at the palace, however, which the donkey and the rag-and-bone man were presently passing, wagon safely in tow. One could tell by the suddenly diminished lighting just beyond—as if the donkey were exiting the stage into a shroud of darkness—and more pointedly by the presence of two last officers, Republican Guards.

These were not the first that Brassard had seen along the way, but inasmuch as they might be the last, the thought did occur that he might let them know about the pursuit in which he was currently engaged; identify himself and say, "I have reason to believe that that wagon up ahead has either been absconded from—or delivered by—the suspect in a probable murder . . ." and so on and so forth.

He didn't particularly want to, though. He was quite sure tomorrow's committee would frown upon the actions he'd been taking (and *not* taking) the last twenty-four hours or so. Also, the length of this pursuit—the deliberate pace and the route of the suspect—all indicated there being some *particular* destination up ahead. The more particular the destination, the more particular the purpose. The point being, that to intervene now—as these officers here surely would have done, or found some other clumsy way to give up the game entirely—would deprive them all of further and more telling discoveries, which was something Brassard was constitutionally loath to do.

Were there any lingering doubt as to whether he should or should not reveal his present interest, these were erased as he came within earshot of the two officers, the taller of whom—the one sporting the Souvarov—could be heard saying the word "*romanische*." This was reference to the wagon, of course, offered casually—and Brassard, it should be said, was no champion of the Gypsy people—but the word alone, as issued from the overly decorated lips of this officer, was born from a bed of such sneering contempt, such presumption, such transparent and pathetic self-aggrandizement, that Brassard was, at least for that crucial moment, swayed to silence.

Six strides later, he himself stepped out beyond the farthest reach of the Exposition's last lamppost, and was swallowed up into a much darker shadow than he had expected, yet it was a strange sensation. He had no idea how much longer this trail would lead. He could be walking all night, for all he knew, and as there were fewer pedestrians here, he'd have to give the wagon a longer leash. It was as much by sound as sight that he followed now—thankful for that squeaky wheel. It led him past the Pont Royal, then the Pont du Carrousel, by which point he had resigned himself to not seeing either Soter or the boy again this evening. He was not overly concerned, however. He felt a kind of freedom, in fact, as if he were plunging down. But voluntarily.

The wagon continued along the right bank of the river until it reached the Pont Neuf, whereupon it turned left to make its way across to the island, Île de la Cité. This was a short crossing, so Brassard let the wagon finish before following, still not wanting to call attention to himself.

It was from the crest of the bridge, then, that he observed the wagon—which once again had turned east along the river—now pause at the head of a shallow ramp that led back down toward the lower embankment. There, either by chance or by arrangement, the rag-and-bone man met with another vagrant type. This one looked more like a Russian monk, hooded and long bearded. In low tones the two spoke while the rag-and-bone man unhitched the donkey and tied it to the lamppost. Then they parted. The starets made his way, while the rag-and-bone man now *reversed* the wagon, holding on to the rails himself—or to a strap he'd fastened between them—in order to slowly and carefully roll the caravan *down* the shallow ramp and into the unseen recess where the bridge rejoined the land.

Brassard held his position, relying on his ear to determine what followed. No sooner had the squeaking, groaning wagon left his view than it went silent. There followed the unmistakable rasp and clang of an iron gate. Then the wheel could be heard again, seeming to enter an interior space—a tunnel—which at first echoed and then set about swallowing the telltale tweedle.

Quickly Brassard resumed pursuit, dashing around to where the donkey was hitched and the ramp led down. All was black beneath the bridge, so on careful, quiet feet he descended, very much wishing he had his gun now. He entered into the deeper shadow where bridge met bank and found there was indeed an iron gate, but that it was locked by chain. The tunnel beyond was pitch, but from its depths he could hear the diminishing birdcall of the wheel growing ever fainter and more muffled. He stepped back out into the moonlight to look for some alternate entry. There was none, but just beyond the overhang was a smaller opening in the stonewall—the mouth of a gutter, it looked like, barely large enough for a man to crawl inside.

So that is what he did. He stashed his saddlebag in the darkest corner he could find, then climbed head first into the narrow blackness, like a snake into a hole.

§

"They are very clever this way," said Michaud, speaking of the café people and the photographer, who was another acquaintance of his. "He says twenty minutes. What else is there to do? You must sit and wait. Have a drink. Are you hungry? Have you eaten?"

They had found a table nearby, Michaud and the young woman—out beneath the open sky, where drinks and small plates of cheese and charcuterie were served.

All she wanted was some bread. He was drinking Pernod, and slurring just a bit, though he hadn't had much. He felt light-headed. He felt a swelling in his breast; he wasn't exactly sure why. He *was* sure why. The woman, with whom he was already convinced he was in love. Granted, he was rash in such matters, but never in quite this way. The others always made him want to lie, to conceal, and to exaggerate. But he felt strangely liberated by her, to say the things he truly felt. He told her so:

"So much in life goes unexpressed," he said. "A person thinks he is being heard, but he does not say. He expects people to know. He expects them to respond when he does not *speak*. And he becomes angry when they do not understand him."

He was saying this to her, aloud. He was speaking directly, confiding and confessing the things he told no one else but always assumed they knew.

"It's important to be *able* to be in the presence of something beautiful, without wanting to possess it." He said this to her! And that this was not easy for a man. "You know, a man sees a beautiful woman"—he gestured simply in her direction, because she was—"he feels pain. It's true. Or a beautiful woman standing over there, if he sees her from behind?" He showed her what a man felt; he winced. She smiled. He went on:

"But then if she turns around and maybe she is not so beautiful from the other side—maybe she has a mushroom nose, or no chin, or she is simply plain, yes—do you know what a man feels when he sees this? Do you think he is disappointed? No. He is *relieved*. 'Thank God.' It's true. Because then this beauty he *thought* he saw—that he thought might be out there—it isn't there, after all, so this is not something *else* he cannot have."

He drank. He set his glass back down with an enthusiastic crack against the tabletop. She jolted, but she kept looking at him, too, understandingly, agreeing. He was thrilled.

"And this is why I draw, more than any other reason, this is why I paint. To teach myself. To restrain myself. To be in front of something beautiful"—again he gestured to her— "and not to want to *have* it."

The waiter came, more bread.

"Do you want more? It's all right."

"Just water, please."

"You're sure?"

She was.

He looked down at the coins on the table. Why did he want to tell her . . . everything? To be so honest?

"You see this money? Do you want to know how I got it? I stole it. Tonight. Not so long before I saw you. I stole it from the pocket of the man who threw this out."

His painting, still leaning up against his knee.

"And that's why I did it. Not because I wanted the money, but out of spite. Out of wounded pride. Because he set my painting out on the sidewalk, I took his money." He smiled, embarrassed.

She nodded.

"I am not a good man," he continued. "I confess this. I do bad things. Often. But I look at you now, I don't feel bad. I'm not professing love, don't worry. Maybe I am, but I don't feel this looking at you: bad. I see clearly. Do you have this effect? Have you been told this?"

She shook her head. Apparently not.

"Well, I like that, then," he said. "I want to ask you who you are, but then I don't. Because it's the same problem: If I *know* something, I want to keep it, and I don't want that. With you, whoever you are. I want to draw you. Do you mind my *not* asking . . . who you are?"

No, she did not mind, though again her eye did drift over his shoulder, as it had been doing the whole while he was speaking. There was the dog there. And the street boy. They'd been there since she and the artist sat down, over by a low brick wall. Michaud paid no mind, he was too excited.

"Ah, here we are," he said. The waiter had returned with a stiff envelope. The photographs. Michaud looked back in the direction of the tent and offered a wave, though his friend the photographer was nowhere to be seen. He went ahead and opened the envelope for her. He removed two of the cards.

"Look at that."

They both did together. She'd chosen the backdrop with

the tower in the window of the parlor. But rather than look directly at the camera, she had focused on the stuffed bird in the corner, the yellow finch. Maybe this was why her expression seemed more sorrowful in the picture than in person.

"You should model," he said. "Look at your eyes. How relaxed your mouth is. And your hands. This isn't easy. But these are for you. To keep."

He slipped her card back in the envelope with all the rest, but he kept the other for himself. "I hope you don't mind." He slid it into the pages of his little sketchbook; a man must do. But again he saw her looking over his shoulder. Finally he turned around.

"You there."

He spoke directly to the boy on the wall, who was not expecting this. Michaud waved him over, him and his dog. He had to wait, as it was a walk of some twenty paces and the boy seemed to be in no hurry, but finally he was standing before them, looking dull and unapologetic.

"Now, you must stop this," said Michaud. "Do you understand? You must stop following people and begging this way. It makes them uncomfortable, and you're going to get chased off. Here." He handed the boy a piece of bread, to show that he himself was not opposed to generosity. "But you have to go now. It isn't fair to the people, to have children moping around like pigeons. Do you have somewhere?"

After some thought, the boy did nod, but Michaud didn't seem to notice.

"Then here." He gave the boy three francs. "Have you been on the Ferris wheel?"

No, the boy shook his head.

"All right then. You have more than enough. For that and a sausage." He looked down at the dog. "What's his name?"

The boy shook his head, he didn't know.

Michaud ignored this, though it made no sense. "Now go," he said. "Please leave us."

The boy took the money and the bread, and he and the dog started back in the direction of the low brick wall.

"Now, tell me." Michaud stood to help pull out her chair. He was overwhelmed by gallantry. "You haven't far to go, I hope."

She said no. "I'm by the river. I have a wagon."

"A wagon?" He stood back. "Tell me this isn't true. It's dangerous. Believe me, I know. I'm why it's dangerous. Will you show me?"

The cool of the evening had set in. He offered her his jacket, but she refused, and he kept talking as they made their way.

"Have you ever been south?" he asked. "Is that where you've come from?"

She didn't answer, and he realized he was breaking his own rule; he didn't want to know. "I have a friend who has a house," he said. "In Biarritz. An acquaintance. He's never there, and I haven't seen it myself. He says it's just a bunga-low, but it's right on the beach. He says you step out the door, your toes are in the sand. And there are fruit trees in back. I've been wanting to go there." He let the thought hang. "Do you believe me?"

She nodded. Why wouldn't she believe him?

"Exactly. Exactly," he said. "You see? *You* believe I am go-ing there. That's all I ask."

And he was going to ask if she wanted to come. He was going to tell her that she should feel free, that she could come and go as she pleased, of course, but now she stopped.

"What?" he asked.

She pointed across the boulevard. "It was right there."

Her wagon. He could see where it might have been, in

the space next to the linden tree. He understood just as well that it had been taken. Of course it had.

"Too many rats in this town," he said. "You left out a biscuit."

They crossed to the very place, as if it might appear again on closer view. She touched the tree, but didn't seem so upset. More disoriented.

There was a row of hansom cabs standing by. Michaud asked one of the drivers if he had seen anyone. "She parked a wagon here." He turned back to her. "What did it look like?"

"Old," she said. She spoke of it with no affection. "It had a roof. And there was a donkey."

She drifted. The cabby shrugged.

Michaud asked her, "Do you know anyone? In Paris?"

She shook her head absently. "I am worried about the donkey."

"Of course," he replied, though he wasn't worried about the donkey. He was thrilled, in fact. Upset, too, of course. For her sake. And ashamed of the city, his city, for having treated her so poorly, but he had never been more grateful either. Tonight, Paris was his partner.

"Listen to me," he said. "I think I may know where your wagon is. Let me put you somewhere. For tonight. Not my flat. But somewhere safe. And clean. You can sleep."

He checked his wallet. He still had plenty.

"You can sleep, and I will find it."

"I'm worried about the donkey," she said again.

"Well, I may find the donkey, too." He looked at her. "Will you trust me?"

She gave one more glance back in the direction of the tower and the Expo. It was clear she had nowhere else, but there was the boy again—the pigeon boy—and his dog.

"I should have known," said Michaud. "You feed them,

they come back. This is how you train them."

But she was nodding now. Yes, she would go. They both got in the cab right there.

Part Four

Wednesday Night

Chapter 9

The Vault

As Brassard emerged from the crawl space, there was almost no light at all, though the fact that there was any—creeping in from crannies and grates up ahead—was encouragement enough to continue on.

The problem was, he had entered by a different route than the rag-and-bone man. The best he could do was keep the wagon within earshot, but there again, he'd been having trouble locating sounds ever since the injury to his ear. He could *hear* the wheel. He just couldn't quite tell where the sound was coming from, so following it now was like trying to find a cricket in a barn.

The other problem—or maybe just a feature of the space—was the smell. It smelled like death. Not fresh or foul, but old and settled, and heaps of it, which made sense. There were Roman ruins underneath the cathedral. There must have been old tombs as well, the same as underneath Montparnasse. What he hadn't been quite prepared for was how vividly the dank air put him in mind of Tonkin, again, and his little cell in Panhou. That, too, had been a tunneled space, not quite as stone-*built* as this—more stone-*hewn*—but it was the air. A connoisseur could perhaps have told the difference, the subtle notes of rice versus grape that distinguished the ancient dust and bones of Chinamen as opposed to Gauls. Still, the overwhelming impression was of sameness. And strangely he was not repelled by this, but rather reassured—maybe because of the integrity it implied, that even in such wildly disparate locations, the same conditions should yield more or less the same effect; as when the left shoelace snaps soon after the right. This a good thing. It says there is coherence.

But again, the more immediate concern was keeping up with the wagon. Certain passageways he couldn't see at all. He had to feel along the stone, treading as lightly as he could on what felt, and sounded, like shells beneath his heels. And the thought did flutter through his mind that he might lose the chase, lose the wagon, find himself trapped down here. Would he be able to retrace his path?

He stopped. The tweedling had stopped as well, but there were voices coming from somewhere up ahead. Quietly he crept past a gated duct and met with a choice: down into the shadow, or up into another crawl space where there was light?

He chose the latter and was quickly forced by the low ceiling down onto his hands and knees. There was an open grate just ahead, which let him see these were not shells beneath him, but vertebrae—or bones of some type. But the voices were nearer now. He inched his way forward, lay down as flat as he could, and looked through the iron bars into what appeared to be a vault—or a former carriage house perhaps, now being used as a junk shop for the dismantling of stolen coaches and the like.

The maiden's wagon was right there in the middle. The rag-and-bone man stood beside it, waiting, surrounded by stacks of wheels, axles, frames, and lumber. Detached walls and doors and lantern fixtures. There was furniture as well, likely pried from carriages, and smaller furnishings—lamps, chests, pillows, wallets, and scarves. He could see two exits: the more open corridor from which the rag-and-bone man had come, then on the far side, a smaller gate-door, chain-locked. There were locks and chains everywhere, in fact, lying about in buckets and hanging from hooks, but also in use. Everything that could be locked down was—by bolt, rope, pad, or manacle.

The rag-and-bone man was examining a pair of these, in fact—handcuffs—when out from behind an open icebox emerged the junkman himself. A troll, as might have been imagined. He was pendulously jowled, loose-lipped, and un-shaven. He had black scrambled hair with some gray entering in, but his most defining feature by far was his size. He was both immense and obese, so much so he had forgone more "normal" clothing, opting instead for a long artist's smock. It was a filthy, wilted-hydrangea blue, and failed utterly to disguise the hovering rotundity of his belly, which echoed his every gesture and expression.

He set down his bowl on a small school desk, the more easily to count his paper money. He thumbed through less than half and handed it over, a sum which the rag-and-bone man clearly judged to be inadequate. He mumbled as much. The junkman grumbled back something to the effect that the rag-and-bone man should be paying *him* for taking on such garbage, which was concerning—to Brassard's hunch, that is; even more so, the fact that the rag-and-bone man, after some head scratching, seemed to accept the terms and make his way. A long haul for not much profit.

Unmoved—and apparently more hungry than curious about his new item in stock—the junkman returned to the disproportionately small chair behind the school desk, where waited a soup bowl, a hunk of bread, a Lefaucheux military revolver, and the latest edition of *Le Charivari*. There he sat, improbably, tore some bread to swipe himself a mouthful of whatever soup or sauce was in the bowl, then very daintily opened the magazine.

In addition to being confused, Brassard was also trapped.

So much as a stir would reveal him, so he waited in his blind and continued to watch while the junkman chewed his bread like cud, ruminatively scanning the comic on the page in front of him—spending, by Brassard's unofficial calculation, as much as a minute per frame—before finally letting out a faint chuckle, then turning to the next page.

Chapter 10

Le Montyon

Le Montyon was over in the 2nd Arrondissement, in what was called the "boulevard area," about a ten-minute ride by cab from the Expo. It was a typical four-story building that stood out from its neighbors more for its history than its appearance, having once been an orphanage, then a finishing school, then a boardinghouse, and now this—a respectable but not particularly respected non-luxury brothel for non-luxury clientele. Its heyday past, the house had no pretensions other than to be reasonably clean, disease-free, and "affordable."

Tonight was a slow night. The house had not experienced quite the boom in business that the other, higher-end maisons had enjoyed during the Exposition, and most of that business was gone anyway. When Michaud and the young woman entered, there were no customers being entertained in the front parlor, other (perhaps) than the old man slung low in an easy chair, bent more in the spine than the waist, asleep with a cat on his lap. Otherwise, there were only the women—one reading over there, and then a small circle here by the bar, dressed in robes. They were playing a game of loto.

Among these was Mam'selle Odette, whose tooth Michaud had chipped earlier in the day. She was first to note his entrance, with guest. She signaled the house mistress, Madame Renée, who was playing cards alone at a roll-top desk. Older than her stable, Madame Renée was more decorously attired, in a dark velveteen robe and a variety of necklaces.

Most striking was her hair, a shock so frizzy and red, it looked like a cloud of brick dust had exploded just above her head—this, to frame a very bold, chin-first face, home to a gap-toothed grin with which she was normally quite generous, but which here dissolved the moment she saw who had just entered her house. She went to greet him nonetheless.

"Some nerve."

"I'll say," put in Odette, who'd joined.

Michaud ignored all this. "Do you have a room? My friend needs a place for the night."

"Who?"

He pointed.

The young woman had seated herself in the foyer, but was looking into the parlor, too fascinated to be quite demure. The parlor was an ornamental feast, what with all the fabrics and tassels, the drapes and stained glass shades on the flickering gas lamps. One suspected that a blast of sunlight would have revealed a sobering presence of must and dust, including stains across the various carpets and cushions and floorboards—wine prints and sweat stains and various other oily blemishes of undetermined but no less disturbing origin.

At the moment, however, she was most taken by the gathering along the bar, and in particular by the fullness of the arms and breasts of the women as they set down their chips and chirped, the amplest now claiming victory. "Again?" said the others. While they dumped their scorecards, the winner poured herself another glass and lifted it, the white flesh wagging gleefully beneath her upper arm like dough.

"Pretty," said the mistress, noting the young one's smile. "But this isn't a boardinghouse."

"It's a house with rooms for let," said Michaud. "She's alone. She's new. She has nothing."

The mistress sniffed. Pity did not work with her.

"I'll pay," he said.

"With what? Not that." She indicated the painting. Michaud still had the rejected painting in his hand.

"No, I have money." He went to his pocket to show her—wadded bills—seeing which, Odette left. She returned to the parlor, but paused in passing by the young woman, who was still sitting on the settee in the foyer. She had her her hands in her lap, knees together, ankles crossed. Odette admired the pose. It seemed quite elegant to her. Their eyes met and she smiled—but briefly. Her tooth.

"She have a card?" asked the mistress.

"No," said Michaud. "I don't think so. No."

"She'll need a card."

"She's not here for that."

The mistress sniffed again.

"And I won't even be here," said Michaud. "I'll come get her in the morning."

"You're not hiding her from someone?"

"No. Look." He extended the cash again. "Do you want this?"

She looked. "Seven's open."

Seven was the only room Michaud ever used, because it was cheaper, because it was small—a laundry room at one time. These days the girls mostly used it for naps. It was on the first floor, at the end of the short hall beyond the parlor. Michaud snatched a handful of flowers from a vase on the way, pricking his finger. He was still sucking it when they entered.

There wasn't even a bed. Just a covered divan with a wooden chest at the foot, and a dresser with a standing mirror.

"Air."

He opened the only window, which was barred and brick-facing. He turned and assessed the painting on the wall. A still-life of flowers. He removed it and hung his own instead.

"I'll be right back." He exited.

Alone, she continued her own survey. There was an unlit candle on the dresser. She checked the drawers and found them locked, except for the top-right, in which there was a box of matches. She took this out just as Michaud re-entered with an armful of blankets. He set them on the divan.

"These are all I could find." He gave his finger another suck. The blood.

She thanked him and told him that these would be fine.

" . . . So I'll come for you in the morning," he said. "Sorry about the view."

She said she didn't mind.

"And there's a towel if you want a bath. Do you want a bath? I don't mean that you need one, but . . . I could ask."

She nodded, that would be fine.

"But I'll find your wagon. I will. What does it look like? I'll find it."

"You don't need to go to any trouble," she said, but he looked back at her as if of course he did.

"That's your home," he said. "And you can't stay here."

He seemed ashamed of the room all of a sudden. Then he paused a moment, looking at her. He wanted to kiss her.

"You make me greedy. This is the problem."

So he left, a knight in threadbare armor.

§

Alone for a second time, she sits on the divan. She runs her hand over the quilting and her eyes drift, tired. She gathers the fabric in her fist. She would like to close her eyes, but she mustn't sleep. She rises instead. She goes to the matchbox on the bureau and lights the candle, which illuminates the painting on the wall, the one the artist put there.

For the first time she looks at it, but the candlelight is shining on the paint. She cannot see unless she looks at an angle, and even then a flurry of brushstrokes is all she can make out, pinks and brown and reds, with blue and white sparks. From up close it looks like exploding fireworks.

She remembers the drawing that he gave her. She takes it from the pocket of her frock, holds it to the light, and it is the same confusion of lines, only in dark charcoal. She holds it at arm's length and the image emerges again. The figure of a woman in a dress.

Her, apparently.

She takes the rest of what's in her pocket, all her ballast, and sets it out on the dresser top beside the candle:

The flower the clown gave her.

A calling card, the one the dashing man slipped into her hand at the top of the tower. The words in the middle are typeset, and curvilinear. *Café de la Paix*. What's underneath has been written in pen.

Ce soir . . . 10 heures?

B. Chavarin

She sets this in the bowl beside the flower.

Finally she removes all the cards with her picture on them. Twelve—or no, eleven. She splays them like a fan. She squints at the topmost to see the grain of the paper, how the softness of the edges is made by the grain, but again how a mere adjustment of her focus can turn this edge into her cheek. This little ashen smudge into her right eye.

She turns to the mirror, which tilts on a hinge. She sees

her skin. She looks at the creases and the puckered flesh of her lips. She wonders when these first appeared. She looks into her eyes. It's almost too dark, but if she leans in close to the flame, she can see the iris. A sunburst of golden-green feathers, hazel and nutmeg, and yet the center, the pupil—the part that sees out—is a pure-black veil.

A heavy tread sounds somewhere near; there's a surprising yield to the floor. The candle flame answers with a little dance, which is answered in turn by a much louder thump coming from the next room. The flame shivers and there's laughter behind the wall. A woman's voice. "*Clumsy,*" she says. More laughter, then such a loud thud, the painting rattles. A moment more of fumbling, then the thumping resumes—not as loud, but rhythmic—and something quickens in her. She knows this rhythm, the stilted, stabbing pulse. There's a grunt, and something seizes in her. The room sways as if it's floating, adrift on the sea of some other world. It's about to come flooding in when *knock, knock, knock,* there's someone at the door—a woman standing with her feet square, instantly steadying the floor. She has flowing ringlet hair—all honeys and auburns—and she's wearing nothing but bloomers and a camisole, smiling a tilted smile.

"Odette," she introduces herself. The younger woman from the parlor. "So you're gonna need a card," she says. "And the doctor is here, turns out. He's down—hey, you all right? You look kinda green." She reaches out to feel her forehead, and the thumping starts up again next door, playing the room like a snare drum. Odette shakes her head. "These walls are paper. But c'mon, he might be about to leave."

She leads her out and down a narrow set of back stairs to another long hall. "So how do you know Michaud?" she asks. "Because you might want to be careful with that one."

Halfway along, two women in bathrobes emerge from a

sudden cloud of steam. Odette asks, "Is Doc still here?" The women shrug and pass. Odette knocks on the opposite door and the strap drops from her shoulder. "Doc? You there?" There's writing on her skin, underneath her arm. "P.L.V."

A man's voice answers, "Just a moment"—brusque and distracted.

"That's Doc." She lifts the strap. "He'll give you a number, too. What's your name, by the way?"

The door opens and another woman steps out, much larger and covered with freckles.

"I get it," says Odette. "We can give you a new one. Zel, what's her name? Zel's good at this."

Zel with the freckles scrunches her face to think. " . . . '*Modeste*'?"

"I like that," says Odette. "'*Modeste*.' See?" She steps aside, ladies first.

The room is twice the size of No. 7, but there are no windows, and there is a strange chair in the middle—it looks like a giant insect—beyond which stands a Japanese screen featuring a flat flock of geese flying in a migratory V. Odette shows her around to find a little man seated on a foot-stool, filling out a certificate. He is in shirtsleeves and a vest, and his head is barely covered by wisps of black hair that he has arranged into a shape that resembles a treble clef.

"New girl," says Odette. "Name's '*Modeste*.'" She gives her a nod to go ahead.

Gingerly the maiden steps into his little office behind the screen. There is a higher chair directly in front of him, and on the floor at his feet is a black leather case.

"That's it?" He barely glances up. "'*Modeste*?'"

She nods vaguely, more focused on the leather case. The end looks like the nose of a bull, but it might be an open fire, or a coiled serpent for the sudden repulsion and attraction it excites in her. Her heart begins to thump. Before she knows it, she is speaking:

"What medicines do you have?"

The doctor stops his pen. "Why, are you not feeling well?" He leans forward to check her eyes. "I can give you aspirin."

"What else?" she asks.

"This isn't an office," he says. "But you seem all right." He wants to see her tongue. "Ahh," he demonstrates.

Aaaah, she repeats. He looks into her mouth.

She asks, "Do you have oil?"

He frowns. "Oil?"

"Or ether?"

He straightens, annoyed now. "You are speaking to the wrong man, I think." He shakes his head. "There is another. Savarese, yes?"

Odette nods, that's the one.

"He can get you these sorts of things. I am here to make sure that you're clean. Do you understand?"

She nods, but she doesn't—quite.

He resumes his position on the stool. He looks at her knees and waits.

"... If you would ..."

She hesitates. She's not sure what he's asking.

"Open, please."

She opens her mouth again.

"No. Knees. Please."

He waits.

"... Mademoiselle, if you want the card, I have to see ..."

Oh. She parts her knees—only slightly at first—but she is starting to feel the tightness in her chest again, and her breath is growing shallow. She looks at the geese on the screen.

"She okay? You okay?" Odette has come behind the screen as well. "Don't be bashful, hon." Odette is touching her softly, patting her head. "It's just Doc." But the man is clenching his jaw. He needs her to do as she's told.

She looks at the screen again and spreads her legs farther. The hem of her frock inches up her thighs.

"There's a girl," says Odette.

The geese are flying left to right, toward a setting sun. There are seven. They are alike, but none are quite the same. The leader's beak is—*cold*. Her breath catches in her throat. Something metal has touched her—there—like a cold, cold spoon. She looks down. The man is studying her beneath her frock, his forehead all furrows of concern—and as if by a poison she is suddenly shot through with dread at what he'll find, what he *won't* find, what she has done. The cold sinks deeper and the room begins to drift and teeter again in the sea of the other world, the prior life.

"Please hold her still," the doctor says, but she sees the black of his eye and knows it isn't him in there. This doctor is only a mask. The maggot-bearded man is looking out, sneering at the idea that she would try to escape him, fool him, or bury him so clumsily. With stones and mud. He knows what she has done—

She tries to close her legs again but catches his arm between her knees.

"Mademoiselle, I must—"

"No!" she says out loud, but her voice is strange to her, and hoarse.

"You feelin' all right?" Odette is still behind her, still stroking her hair to try to calm her, but even this feels strange and unwelcome, and now the older woman—with the red cloud of hair—is standing at the door, arms crossed. Again, the maiden's eyes begin to drift. A glimmer invades her mind—a sharp pain, and then a sudden flash of light, the same as struck her at the tower, and here in the room upstairs. There is another life behind this one, swarming and prowling and peering at her, coming after her. And she is not the only one who knows. First the officer, then his dog, and now the maggot-bearded man has sniffed her out, is down between her legs, wedging her apart—

She clamps them shut. "No!" She grabs the doctor by his wispy hair and yanks him away, toppling the screen and all the geese.

"Hey!" says Odette. "What's going on? Are you all right?"

She cannot answer. She is afraid of the voice that will come out. She staggers by the Madame with her folded arms. She lurches down the groaning, undulating hall and barely manages to clamber up the stairs.

§

Olivier and Soter were seated outside the maison this whole time. They'd managed to follow the cab, thanks to a snarl on the Pont Carrousel and an unwitting coal cart whose hind runner they rode for five blocks.

They were sitting on a stoop directly across from the entrance, where another cab had just now pulled up to let off two passengers. Men of no remarkable feature. This they saw, but just then the great wooden door behind them barked open, releasing an extremely aged female tenant and her oddly youthful dog, both of whom, on seeing Olivier and Soter, started growling and snapping.

"Shoo now, shoo! You can't sit here." The old lady took a swipe at them with her cane while her ratlike terrier strained against its leash, a kite in raging wind.

Soter and Olivier remained admirably composed even so, standing back and out of range. However, it was as a result of this interruption that they failed to see the small figure exiting the maison across the way and entering directly into the waiting cab.

To be fair, Soter did—while the old lady's dog shifted from yapping to snarling—turn back to the maison, out of nosed suspicion that something significant might just have occurred, but the cab had pulled away by then. There was another young woman in the doorway now, shawled, peeking her head out, seeing just the scrap across the street, and pulling back in. She smelled of lilac.

Chapter 11

Skulls

This week's edition of *Le Charivari* was evidently quite amusing, and in parts worth keeping. The junkman, with a far more delicate hand than Brassard would have credited him, tore out at least five separate cartoons from the pages, all remarkably square, and posted them, by tack, on the side of a bookshelf he had presumably filched from another carriage but chosen not to trade

He proved to be as slow and relishing an eater as he was a reader, casually shredding his way through the whole of his baguette, sopping his broth and stuffing the sponge into his mouth, licking his fingertips and chewing slowly, luxuriously, and with cheerily whistling nostrils.

Finally the bowl was clean and dry, and the magazine had been plundered of its best humor, which seemed to have left the junkman in a good humor as well. And a patient one. It was with a tortoise-like interest that he finally shifted focus to his newest acquisition, rising from his little chair—actually having to wriggle it from his backside before taking up a canvas tool belt, extended by a rope, tying this around his equatorial middle, and lumbering over to the wagon.

Still watching from the crawl space above the ceiling grate, Brassard could see the wagon strain and sag at his entrance; could hear him whistling, with puckered lips this time. He was clearing out everything inside, which wasn't much. The bucket. A few tin cups and saucers. The palette bed. Each of these required its own trip, and its own strain upon the poor frame. Brassard heard the sound of screwing or unscrewing, and a moment later, the junkman emerged with the empty bureau. Before re-entering this time, he briefly paused to lean down and examine the axle. He saw the splint. He saw the waffling wheel. He clucked his tongue and climbed back in. The rag rug shot out, rolled. A moment passed, then a very low chuckle followed by the word "AllooOO."

He had discovered the trapdoor. A moment later he exited the wagon with the two silver candlesticks and a definite skip in his step. He rooted through a pile of tools, whistling tunelessly, then emerged with the largest set of shears Brassard had ever seen.

He climbed back into the wagon. Again a moment passed, followed by a tremendous ringing snap and the slackening of a chain. Then out he came with the chain over his shoulder and the safe tucked beneath his beefy arm. A beast he was.

He brought this to his workbench and set straight to cracking, first clamping the whole of the safe in a large vise to keep it still and firm. He let finesse have the first go, leaning his ear up against the casement and listening while, with those same deceptively dexterous and delicate fingers, he began spinning the dial—a standard inset combination lock—first right, then left a few turns, then right again. Something about what he heard in the tumblers convinced him that this was not a fruitful path, so he resorted to brute force—a shamefully simple matter of hammer-and-chiseling his way into the seams of the safe, creating a wide enough gap for his crowbar, then using that crowbar with what Brassard could only imagine was an oxen's strength to physically pry the thing open. He needed only two breaches—one on the top side, the other on the "bolt" side—but in a matter of maybe three determined minutes, the safe door was swinging wide like a medicine cabinet.

Brassard couldn't see inside from his angle, only that the junkman—breathing more heavily, and maybe even drooling—removed a rolled velvet cloth, light blue. He looked confused, but now he turned his head.

Brassard heard it, too. Footsteps, coming from within the tunnel. Quickly, the junkman flung the rag rug over the safe and took up his revolver.

A furtive voice called in, "Hello?" and then a figure emerged from the nearside shadow. A very slight, almost willowy man in a Borsalino hat that looked as if it had been caught in the rain a few dozen times and never reblocked.

The junkman put down the revolver. They seemed to know each other, but not in a friendly way.

"What do you want?"

The wilted Borsalino pointed to the wagon. "When did this come in?" His voice was thin, and high, at least in comparison to the junkman's, which was only a few notches above a belch.

"None of your business."

"How much do you want for it?"

"For the wagon?"

"And what's inside."

The junkman was amused. "More than you have."

"How much?"

"I'm taking inventory. I'm not selling—"

The smaller man looked around. He had the beard of a young disciple, and the pallor of someone either very sickly or glowing, it was hard to tell. "Was there a donkey?"

"A donkey?" The junkman looked at him dryly. "Yes. I ate it. I'm sorry, if I'd known you were coming—"

"I'll give three hundred francs."

This was more than the junkman was expecting. "Show me."

"I'll bring it tomorrow."

"Go away."

"I'll bring it. I'm not asking for any favors. We'll set a price—"

Here the junkman lost patience. His face, a fist of features at its most pleasant, became a scowling contortion of fat and grease. He stood up to make his point, and to establish that he was two or three times the size of his guest.

"In the first place," he said, "I don't like the fact that you came down here. This is not a place of business. You're not invited. So I'm going to ask you to leave, and you're going to forget—"

"Five hundred francs."

"Okay, now you're irritating me. I don't want to see you again. I don't want your stories, and I don't want your promises. Go." He leaned in closer until his forehead bumped the brim of the little man's hat and very slowly pushed right off his head and onto the floor.

The smaller man looked like he was about to say something, but the junkman stopped him short. *Not another word.* He made a little whisking motion with his hands, and the smaller man replied—pathetically—by turning, taking up his hat, and skulking back into the shadows from whence he'd come, albeit haltingly and with misgiving.

The junkman didn't even watch him go. He turned and resumed his seat, muttering, unaware that the cadence of the little man's shuffling retreat—rather than fading off into the distance—had, in fact, discernibly slowed and then stopped.

Why? Because there in the shadows of the island catacombs, and as witnessed by the three skulls on the ledge, François Michaud had come to a personal threshold. A sort of critical mass of humiliation and failure had been reached, the pressure of which Michaud felt not so much as result of the force applied—that being the smug dismissal of the junkman—as from the force against which that dismissal was now pressing, which was, to put it much too vaguely, Michaud's smittenness with the young woman he had just met at the Exposition. Under normal circumstances, there was no end to the abuse he might have taken from the junkman and his like, pushing as it usually did against nothing so much, no ground against which he might have dug his heels. But this evening—and now—there was a very firm ground. There was she. There was her face. There was what she had brought out in him—all that honesty, and clarity, and the willingness to say out loud what he had always kept to himself.

It took a moment for him to remember it all—the truths he had spoken and felt, and the promises he had made. It took the darkness of the tunnel and the three hilarious skulls gaping at him, reminding him that he really didn't have that much to lose anyway. No one did, because what was life, what was dignity, what was consequence in the face of the mysterious elation he had felt beside her, from the moment he had first seen her, in fact, standing there outside the pen of the Malawi. Was it love? He still wasn't sure, but whatever it was, it cast aside all strategy and doubt. He must return to her with the wagon—it was as simple as that—because he had *said* he would, and because it was *right there behind him*. The three skulls agreed entirely. He grabbed the middle one by its eye sockets.

What happened next Brassard still had a fairly good view of from his blind, coming only a moment after the suspicious *ritardando* of footsteps. There was a beat of silence, then a quicker tread returning, then from out of the shadow, a figure—the willowy little man in the Borsalino—moving with a catlike swiftness, dashed up and, before the junkman could react, clubbed him over the head with something. Brassard couldn't tell what it was at first, except that it was hard and hollow. The junkman responded by flailing his arms and trying to stand, but the chair was attached to his rear end like the wiring of a champagne cork. He staggered back into a sitting potion. The Borsalino took advantage, striking him again with his weapon, again directly on the head, only this time the weapon shattered, revealing itself to be, by the sudden scattering of teeth and bone splinters, a skull. The junkman covered his face, blinded and howling. In a panic that he might lose this advantage, the Borsalino grabbed the crowbar and started to beat the junkman until he toppled onto the floor, still plugged to his chair, but with a pool of blood expanding beneath him at an alarming, and clearly lethal, rate.

There was little that Brassard could do. He had no weapon of his own, as he was reminded again when he reached for his empty holster. He could have cried out, he supposed, but that would only have alerted the assailant, most likely have caused him to run, and Brassard was in no position to pursue.

He looked once again to the small gate behind the junkman. It was chain-locked, and that the man in the Borsalino had now located the junkman's revolver. With that as protection against any intruders, he knelt down to check his victim for breathing. Careful to avoid the pool of blood, he leaned his ear against the mouth.

"*Merde*," he muttered.

Winded and frantic, he began putting things back in the wagon. The tools and then the rug. He didn't seem much interested in the safe. Of greater concern was the body of the junkman and what to do with it.

Finally he decided—for reasons unclear—that he couldn't

just leave it. He went to some pains to disengage the rump from the tiny chair, then started dragging the body over to the wagon, a process requiring so much strain and effort that Brassard finally took the chance of removing himself from his cramped position, shimmying back down to where there was standing room, and then feeling his way around the outside of the vault wall, slowly and gropingly, to what he hoped would be that gated door—all while the little man could be heard grunting and huffing and puffing and generally cursing his task.

It *was* the gated door, in fact, but by the time Brassard reached it, the little man had succeeded in heaving the junk-man's body up into the back of the wagon. One of the arms could be seen still wedged in the door as the assailant hoisted the wooden rails up onto his shoulders—another Herculean task, given the general spindliness of his frame and legs— and began pulling the caravan behind him, freight and all, knocking over a chiffonnier and a hat-stand in the process. The mission was seen to completion, however, as the shadow of the far corridor swallowed all: the man, the wagon, the squeaky wheel, and—lastly—the hand of the victim, his fingers dangling like sausages.

Brassard allowed three beats before trying the lock on the gate, which held firm, no surprise. The revolver was still there on the ground, but out of reach. He could see the safe as well, but not anything inside, and there wasn't time to dwell. The man—the killer, the thief—was getting away.

With no better alternative, Brassard headed back along the path he'd come, to see if maybe there was some tunnel that intercepted the assailant's. But again, the passages were dark and byzantine—up steps, down steps. Striking matches all the way, he came upon another lower corridor flooded with water. He didn't like to think . . . *Splash, splash.*

Then another fork. He stopped to listen, but couldn't be sure if he was hearing the wagon or rats or the echo of dripping water. He chose left, quickly found himself in a much drier passageway, and followed this—for that reason—for far too long, 'round and around on an inward spiral (he was much too late in recognizing) that led him finally to the deadest of ends.

The lone match flickering against his breath was barely adequate to light the space, but he could see it was not large, the size of a toolshed maybe. At the center stood a slender fluted pillar with a stone collar halfway up. Chest high, it looked almost like a baptismal basin. Most remarkable, though, was the wall surrounding, a perfectly rounded panel made entirely of human bones—femurs and vertebrae stacked like brick columns, here and there relieved by ornamental patterns, diagonals and diamonds mostly, formed from the round white tops of human skulls.

"Damn."

His fingertips felt the sudden burning heat. Instinctively he let go, and all fell black.

Chapter 12

Pennyroyal

The ride over was a matter of ten or so blocks—a mile, if that, along Montmarte and then the Boulevard des Italiens—but the incident at the maison had left her even more exhausted than before, and the inside of the carriage had felt oddly comforting, and warm, like a potbelly stove almost. There was even a wool blanket for her knees.

Add to this the dancing glare of the lantern just outside the window. The smeariness of the glass gave the light a flashing and prismatic quality, so much so she closed her eyes, though she knew that she should not have. She felt the rhythm of the wheels on the cobblestone, heard the hollow clopping of the horse hooves out front, flecking the dirt and the pebbles against the folding knee-high door. A faint swerve and the darkness took hold, sweeping her away like a great black river—one bend and then another, then down into an even deeper, stiller, and more quiet place, a suspended realm in the distant elsewhere in which muffled voices could be heard, of children coming near, running up and laughing, setting their hands upon the soft, surrounding globe—and their ears and red round cheeks.

"Kick," the younger voice was saying. *Coup, coup.*

She wants to reply, but feeling herself unable, she wells with an unbearable sadness. She doesn't know why, only that it seems to rise from the same black reservoir inside her (*Allez, petit. Allez!*) higher and higher until, with a sudden cold smothering, it takes her breath. She thrashes. Her foot thuds against the carriage door. (The children laugh. "I felt it! I felt it!" *Je l'ai senti!*) Then a sudden blast sounds—the first of the shots—and a heartbeat starts thumping all around as if she were trapped inside a giant drum—

ba-dum ba-DUM BA-DUM!

She tries twisting free, but the river takes hold again and pulls her away so fast she can barely hear the second shot in the distance. Another voice enters instead—much lower and closer. "Comenium," it says, and the river slows again to listen because it's him, sitting directly across from her, pulling the oars, slurring words she doesn't understand, to passengers she cannot see. "She keeps trying," he mutters, shaking his head. "Calumny and Runaway and Fornicant—she denies and it's on both our hands." He's talking about her, and the bodies. They're all surrounding them like lily pads, floating facedown, faceup. A little girl, she can't be more than three—forever now—dark-haired and moon-white. It's about to come to her, who, when the third shot shocks the air so loud and so near that everything shatters into a mist, a gray-brown fog suffused with all the matter of the prior moment, but no shape, no motion. No memory . . .

. . . except for one more maybe.

Deep inside the stagnant gloom there can be heard the faintest piping of a shore bird—or two—bringing one last image to light. Their back-and-forth burns through the haze, clearing the air until it's like polished glass, and she is there again, sitting on the stoop of the wagon. She has a mug in her hand and a foul taste in her mouth—of metallic stale-sweetness and bile. She should be shelling peas but she's feeling too sick, peering through a copse of trees beyond which lies a marsh. It's sunset, with flamingoes and workers in a field, bent and striking at the grasses. He is among them. She forces another sip because he's standing straight again, looking back at her: *You drink up now. Get you better*, he nods, with the grasses in one hand, and the sickle in the other.

He thinks it's medicine in her mug, not this vile blend of warm red wine, pennyroyal, and turpentine.

She swallows and another wave of nausea heaves inside her. Another deep and stabbing pain is just about to strike when the jolt of an upturned cobblestone claps her teeth. Her foot hits the carriage door, and she's awake again inside the little cab, suddenly restored to the chill-damp air of the Parisian night, the trundling rhythm of the wheels and the smeary lantern light erasing all the nightmares, swipe by merciful swipe.

The city street scrolls from left to right through the black window frame, though even now it seems to be slowing: the trident lamp post . . . the creeping vine . . . the gated door, all gliding by at a more and more dwindling pace . . . the tall black alley glowering down, and finally the long green awning with all the little tables underneath, sliding up to the corner, then easing to a stop along with the clop of the hooves. There's movement within—of well-dressed men and women crossing back and forth in front of the bulbs and blobs of glowing light—while above, the ornate iron balcony displays the golden letters in a row: C-A-F-É D-E L-A P-A-I-X.

The Café of Peace.

Chapter 13

Café de la Paix

"Of course you will. Of course she will." Chavarin assured the others in the circle that of course this evening's contralto, Madame Parisot, would grace them with a song. "One song is all." She just needed a little coaxing

Which was true, and she would. Bruno Chavarin was a persuasive man, after all, and very much in his element here at the café, an hour or so after curtain. There were at least two hundred guests in attendance, not all of whom had come from the Massenet, but all of whom could be useful in one way or another. Monsieur Zidler, for instance, who already owned the Olympia but who was about to open a new theater over on Boulevard de Clichy.

That is what they had been discussing, in fact, before Madame Parisot joined. Zidler now resumed.

"And what about your show?" he asked kindly—or maybe not so. "Is everything in place?"

"Some T's to cross," said Chavarin, "but everything that matters, yes." His glance referred them all to Mademoiselle Eschette, who was over by the bar, chatting with Montesquiou and the flush-cheeked baron.

"And looking every bit the part," said Zidler. "You'll have to introduce us."

Of course, smiled Chavarin.

"Where is your wife, by the way?" asked Madame Parisot.

"Tired." Chavarin tilted wistfully. "You know the countess. Always more interested in the show than the tell."

They agreed with this, and it was at this moment, as they all were quietly appreciating the countess's substance, that the maître d' of the café, who had been standing by for much of the foregoing, finally leaned in to inform Monsieur Chavarin in whispers. Monsieur Singh, also attending, couldn't hear what it was, and Chavarin himself seemed not to understand until he turned to look at the door. His face lit, then burst into a devilishly dimpled grin. He excused himself at once and went to her. He could not have been more delighted. He extended his arm, turned his wrist, and splayed his fingers like a bird's wing.

"I must admit"—he took the young woman's hand, the girl from the tower—"I didn't expect you." He noted that her frock was the same as before, and much too plain for the occasion. "You have come from the Exposition?"

As she shook her head, the maître d'—who had followed apace—once again spoke into Chavarin's ear. "Did you want me to take care of this, monsieur?"

The cab was still waiting.

"No, no. You stay." He said this to the young woman and stepped outside to confer with the driver. He took his money from a silver clip.

"She had nothing then?"

The driver shook his head.

"And where did you pick her up?"

"Rue de Temple." The driver scowled. "Le Montyon."

Chavarin frowned. This he found hard to believe, and apparently upsetting. He tipped the man well and returned to his new guest just inside the door, once again transforming his expression in the time it took to receive her hand in his, the right. He set the left upon the low curve of her back, and by this firm but gentle guide, escorted her back into the main space of the café.

An ornate setting. Gilded, chandeliered, mirrored, sconced, and yet for some reason—maybe just the sheer extent of the detail—she was reminded of the forest again. Something about the plumage of all the dresses, the foliage sewn into the cuffs and fabrics. The pillars for trees. The sky painted on the ceiling, and the ornate vines and garlands carved into all the frames and casements and cornices. Even the sounds—the swishes of fabric, the clinks and dings of silver and crystal, combined with all the chatter, the innuendo, and polite laughter—were very like the steady warble of the woods to which she had awakened.

The difference—aside from the geometry underlying all this ornament—was the way in which the woods had seemed to take her in, as one more creature come to make temporary home. Here, the fauna all turned to see and to greet—politely, yes, but also to wonder at the image of the dashing man arm in arm with this waif of a thing. For the first time she was made aware of the inadequacy of her frock, just from the way they all were looking at her.

Except for this one, who had been up on the tower as well. She was glad to see him, with the beaming eyes so large and pronounced; and the caramel, furrowless skin; the round full lips; and the jet-black hair swept up into that remarkable wave. He bowed in greeting.

"It is a bit chilly in here," said Chavarin. "Maybe we could see about getting her a wrap." He made a swirling motion with his hand, directed at his torso. Maybe more than a wrap.

Monsieur Singh understood and went to confer with the maître d'.

"So tell me again." Chavarin had to lean down to speak to her, and to hear. "Where have you come from?"

She told him she didn't know the name of the place. He asked her how she had found it, and she said that a man had brought her. An artist.

"An artist?" He sounded a note combining humor and irritation, then drew her aside behind a column. His face became suddenly severe. "Listen to me. You will spend the night here at the hotel, do you understand? This is not a problem, but you must promise me. You will never, *never* talk to this man again, the one who took you to that place. That man was not your friend."

She did not agree or disagree. She only remarked the speed and amplitude with which his expressions swung. Here again the quick smile to welcome his helper.

"This is Monsieur Singh. He will take care of the room, and he can get you anything you wish. He has my absolute trust."

"If the mademoiselle would come with me," said Singh.

She did, and Chavarin returned to Mademoiselle Eschette, who had been watching all this from a distance.

"You've made a friend. Who is she?"

"Just a girl," said Chavarin. "New in town. It seems she may need some help."

"Aren't you an angel?" Her brows were arched; her tone, flat.

§

Monsieur Singh led their newest guest back into the hotel's own boutique, which the maître d' had to open for them. It was also the maître d' who took the lead in preparing her ensemble. He lit a standing lamp and began sizing up her figure.

"White. Off-white. Petite."

Monsieur Singh agreed.

"And I assume we have no time to do anything about the hair."

"No," said Singh. "But shoes."

The maître d' looked down at what she was wearing—a pair of handmade leather sabots—and went off to find what he could.

Monsieur Singh turned back to her, though he demurred from meeting her eye, by training and by instinct.

"We will arrange a room here at the hotel. Is there anything the mademoiselle would require?"

She looked at him. She did not understand at first what he was saying.

"Is there anything that we could provide that would make the mademoiselle's stay more comfortable?"

She noted the indirection of his gaze, and the tilt of his posture—slightly bent at the waist with one hand behind his back.

She took two things from this. First, that Monsieur Singh sought nothing in return. Second, that by averting his eyes in this way, he meant to protect her from any incursion of the kind that had entered through the eyes of the doctor at the other house, Le Montyon.

"Do you have tea?" she asked.

"But of course," he said, his eye still cast down and to the side. "Is there a kind of tea that the mademoiselle would prefer?"

She likewise felt assured by the way that he referred to her—as someone else. It seemed more apt than the direct address of the others.

"Yes," she said. "Raspberry leaf, if that would be possible."

"Of course," he replied. "And to be clear, the mademoiselle would prefer this presently, or when she goes to her room?"

"Oh, later," she said. "Not now."

"Of course. Will there be anything else?"

He waited, still smiling, almost as if he were talking to an invisible child at her side. She looked in the mirror to see there were only two of them.

"Oil," she said.

"Of course," he replied, and if he was at all surprised by this request, he made no outward show. He sought only to be clear. "... Does the mademoiselle mean such as ... olive oil?"

"Or linseed," she said. "Or castor, if that would be possible."

"I can get you any of these."

"Castor, then. Thank you."

"Very good, mademoiselle." He waited again; would that be all?

She thought. "And some nettle, if you please ... And ginger."

Monsieur Singh nodded, adding these to the list in his head. "They will be waiting for the mademoiselle."

"Thank you, monsieur."

The door of the anteroom was just now opening. The maître d' was pulling what looked like a rack of costumes behind him.

"About the tea," she said to Monsieur Singh, but so quietly he had to lean his head to hear. "Just the leaves, if you please. Don't steep."

Monsieur Singh received the instruction as though it were a given. "Of course, mademoiselle."

And now the maître d' joined them. He had brought three pairs of shoes as well.

Chapter 14

Two More Geese

Olivier and Soter were still on the stoop to which they'd been displaced, but because the cool of night had set in, and because they had wanted to avoid the return of the old lady and her horrible terrier, they'd pulled into the recess of the doorway, and were huddled together for warmth. They could not be seen.

But they could see the man pulling the woman's wagon, and they could see it was the man who'd brought her here in the first place, and left. He passed directly by them, stopping beside the nearest lamppost to where they were, which was the nearest lamppost to the front of the maison. By the gaslight they could see his weariness, that he had come a long way, and that there was a strangely stunned look on his face as well.

They watched him set the rails down from his shoulders. They watched him take a charcoal pencil from his pouch and use it to pry loose the hubcap of the right front wheel. Then they watched him remove the wheel entirely, gaspingly, having to hold up the wagon as he slid the hub from the axle, then set the whole thing down as gently as he could. He was tired and not very big, and groaning. Maybe from thirst; he looked thirsty. He knelt awhile, and the wagon seemed to be kneeling too now, genuflecting to its paramour, the streetlamp, which was turned the other way, coyly.

But the man's work was not done. He gathered himself up, took the wheel he'd removed, and crossed to the door of the maison with it, seeming even in those twelve or so steps, and the three more up to the door, to gain in stature.

He found Madame Renée in the parlor—not alone, but playing solitaire.

"Is she asleep?"

"Oh, your girl?" She was wearing reading glasses. "She left."

"She left?"

She licked her fingers as she set down a card. "Yes."

"Where did she go?"

Another card, she shrugged. "Not everyone is cut out, you know."

He barely heard. He was already headed for Room 7, stalking down the narrow hall with the wagon wheel barking against the wall. The fat cat leapt away while the old man roused in his chair, trying to remember—what does one do with a wagon wheel again?

Michaud burst into the room, heedless of what he might find. What he did find was a single occupant standing to the side of the bureau, flush against the wall and facing it, eye level with a hole that would otherwise have been covered by the painting—Michaud's, in this case, which was down on the floor.

Unbuckled but unflustered, the man turned upon his intruder. "Room's taken," he grunted.

Michaud growled back something less articulate, surveyed, and quickly located the bowl on the bureau. Her things were inside—the *cartes de visite*, his drawing, a flower, and a card.

He took up the last, from the Café de la Paix. He read the handwritten note as well:

Ce soir . . . 10 heures?
B. Chavarin

Several times, and gropingly, his eyes retraced the simple little words, but he understood well enough.

Without a glance back at the room's current occupant, he took the card as evidence. He took the *cartes de visite* as well, and the drawing. He took his painting from the floor and left, still with the wheel clanging and cleaving down the hall. He stalked back through the parlor like a madman beggar, cussing, nearly dropping the painting as he kicked his way back out the door—the lamps and cut-glass chandeliers all shivering at his tread.

Olivier and Soter saw him storm back out withal, and stop, and glare across at the genuflecting wagon as if it were now his sworn enemy. He hurled the wheel in its direction like a giant discus; it sprang up from its landing, toppled, and toyed with a brief run before swiveling flat like a coin, all of which was just diverting enough to distract the man from his fury, expose it as the pantomime it slightly was. But he recovered his anger almost as soon as the wheel was silent. He began stalking off again before realizing that he still had the painting. He snorted and cussed his way back to the wagon, flung open the back door with a loud crack—he had to do so three times on account of the tilt; the door kept shutting on him—but finally he thrust the painting inside, then had to slam the door twice more before stalking off again, still red with rage, burning with purpose.

Olivier and Soter watched all this and did not think to follow, having no reason to believe that the woman was not still inside the maison.

§

Following one or two wrong turns and necessary backtracks, Brassard managed to retrace his path to the wicket door at the rear end of the junkman's vault.

As it turned out, getting through the wicket took just as long as finding it. The bars were sturdy and well wrought. The lock likewise. Fortunately, the willowy man had left the revolver behind, six or so feet from the gate. Too far to reach by hand, but by removing his belt, tying it to his shirt and reaching through the bar, Brassard was able to come tantalizingly close. About six inches short with a comfortable lasso toss. Closing the distance was a simple matter of jamming his shoulder through the gate, but so hard it left an imprint on his forehead. On the seventh try, he managed to hook the trigger guard and drag the gun back.

One shot later, delivered to the belly of the padlock, and Brassard was in, sitting before the cast-iron safe, which the willowy man in the Borsalino had also unaccountably left behind. Or maybe not so unaccountably. Brassard now understood the junkman's expression when he had looked inside. Here was what he found:

—a partial set of platinum flatware
—what looked like a hundred francs in coin, old and new
—some ladies' watches that appeared to be broken
—an oval brooch featuring the painting of a troubadour and his lover, on porcelain paste.

In other words, he'd squandered the evening on a goose chase of the first order. Why the little man had come for the wagon was anyone's guess, the only clue to which—maybe or maybe not—was Brassard's nagging sense that he had seen the brooch somewhere before. Something about the shape of it—palm-sized and oval, its curved line disrupted by three berry-bunch tips, one on top, and two more at roughly four and seven along the clock face. This was familiar.

He examined the back for some marking, and he did find the letters "TnT" on the casing. In a book perhaps? A magazine? He didn't strain. He was physically tired, a bit de-pressed, and he could feel the resistance in his mind, coming in the form of far too many bad guesses.

He would remember when he would remember. Until then, he pocketed the brooch and set about finding a way out of this place.

Chapter 15

The Duel

The maître d' of the Café de la Paix—who was also assistant concierge at the Grand Hotel de Paris—had nothing if not good taste. And an eye for sizes. He'd brought a rack of gowns over to the standing mirror, but passed over most of the selections quickly, briskly shoving them down the rail, muttering the reasons why: "Matronly... too many pleats... *Zzzzz* ..." He considered a more corseted look with a very narrow waist, but there was too much puff to the sleeves. He took her by the wrist, he extended her arm to judge its line, then finally settled on something more "imperial."

The chosen gown was not so different in color from the frock she'd come in. An off-white. Maybe with a bit more cream, but the texture was glossy—satin. A simple, elegant, one-piece fall, cinched in the back to allow for a small train from a high waist. Above this (and echoed at the hem) was a brocade of a much thicker golden-bronze thread. The neckline was flat—again, not so unlike the frock, but lower and more revealing, extending all the way across her breast, then squaring at the shoulder to provide for a pair of very brief box pleats. It was a gown that pleaded for high hair, up-swept and classical, but that was obviously not an option here, both because of time and because the young woman's hair hadn't sufficient body or length. Failing that, a choke necklace was chosen, of a similar golden-bronze tone to the brocade. Likewise, two pearl clips for her hair, one above each ear but set asymmetrically to frame the face, which was, the maître d' allowed, a lovely face. "The thing," he said, by which he meant the centerpiece. The moral of the story.

The maître d' presented her to Monsieur Singh when he returned from seeing about her requests. "This, yes?"

Monsieur Singh agreed. Yes, this. They agreed upon a pair of low-heeled court shoes as well. She stood before the mirror for them, and for herself. She laughed. Not loud. Not long, but enough for the maître d' to take offense and excuse himself.

"I *am* grateful," she said, and she was. She would blend now.

The first to note her entrance—or re-entrance—was Mademoiselle Eschette. She was struck by the immodesty of the choice, and thankful that she had not made a very similar one (save for the color of her gown, which was practically vermillion). Chavarin was not so troubled. Indeed, he was as impressed with his own eye as he was with his guest. Another find. He came to collect her from Monsieur Singh.

"Ah, here she is. This is better, yes?"

He looked around to offer his compliments, but the maître d' could not be found. Others turned and welcomed her to the circle—the baron, Montesquiou, and Monsieur Zidler. They were impressed as well. It was Chavarin's director, Duchamps, who gave voice to the general sentiment.

"Do you dance?"

They all laughed, because they knew what he was getting at.

"Do you?" Chavarin asked more seriously.

She said yes, of course, because who doesn't dance? She had danced at the wedding party.

"Do you sing?" asked Duchamps.

Again. *Sometimes.* She was handed a glass of champagne.

"What about acting?" he asked.

This she was not so sure about. She was acting at the moment, no?

"Of course she does," Chavarin answered for her. "You see? Everything. But look at how she carries herself. This is most important."

She sipped her champagne and immediately coughed. They laughed.

"I think the bubbles surprised her."

§

Mademoiselle Eschette was not the only person standing back and watching this in wonder—in her case, at why there should be so much fawning over a grubby girl she assumed was either an urchin or a *pute*. Probably both.

There was François Michaud as well, standing outside the café and looking in, but like a dead man almost, scrunch-shouldered, mouth agape, as if there were an invisible noose around his neck. He did not understand. Had he gone mad? Had this evening even happened? He squinted to make sure it was her. He scowled. A sister perhaps? A twin? He studied her arms, and then her hands. No, that was her. Look at the eyes.

But how? In this gown, surrounded by these men, these fakes, and this one especially. Bruno Chavarin? To see this unctuous charlatan—this gigolo—treating her this way. He was touching her back! As if she were his! *Was* she his? François Michaud could not comprehend what he was seeing, could not square it with the immensity of what he had been feeling the last—was it only four hours since he'd first seen her at the Expo? But he had killed a man! Taken his life, dumped him in the river like garbage. For this? For her, who was to be his partner in pastlessness, in futurelessness, in the eternal presence of each other?

He was, in short, a man confronting evidence of such a

fundamental misunderstanding—on his own part, that is—he might as well have been watching the ocean spill off its tray.

§

"But it's very simple," Duchamps was saying to her. "All you have to do is lie there, and try not to breathe too deeply . . . as you are trying to appear dead, you understand."

"A dreamless sleep," Chavarin clarified.

She nodded, though it wasn't clear she understood—why they were telling *her*, at any rate—and this apparent indifference to what they were suggesting, the absence of either reluctance or excitement, Chavarin took to be a sign of disappointment. Perhaps.

"It's a start," he said, and glanced the way of the Mademoiselle Eschette, who'd just joined the circle. "It's how you got yours, no?"

"Yes, and look at me."

"Do look at you," he replied. He didn't like being challenged in public. And she wasn't doing too badly now, was she?

Here again, the maître d' stepped in—with good news. Madame Parisot had, in fact, agreed to sing.

"Ah, wonderful!" said Chavarin. "Everyone, please. In the salon?"

Yes. Even now, beyond the bar, the sliding doors of the parlor room were opening to welcome them into its even more select society. Yet there was another stir coming from behind, a flicker of static on the smooth current of the evening. All heard and turned. There were raised voices as well.

"Sir, you cannot come in here."

This was the maître d', doing his best to stand between the rest of the room and the intruder, who was Michaud, of course.

"Sir, this is a private party."

But Michaud—whom everyone assumed to be drunk and probably a vagrant—shoved him aside.

"I have friends!" he was barking. "There! Her!"

He pointed at the young woman. And she saw his face, but it took her a moment to recognize him, for he too seemed to be in disguise. His eyes were wild and his face was red.

"I thought you should know . . ." he was saying, struggling overtop the maître d' again. "I keep my word! I found your wagon! I found your home!" He was howling and pointing, and now all the people were looking at her. Chavarin as well.

"Is that him," he asked. "Is he the one who brought you to Le Montyon?"

She was still trying to understand. She didn't know the name was Montyon. And this was the one, yes, but this was not the one, no.

Chavarin didn't wait. He snapped to his second, the valet. "Go find her a seat. And save one, please." Then to her, more softly: "I'll be right there, and don't worry. We're not going to hurt anyone."

With a glance, he requested the cane of his friend Montesquiou.

The café did not have a bouncer, per se, but it did have in its employ a bartender of some three hundred pounds, who was also a butcher, and who happened to be on the floor this evening. He was already moving in on Michaud to grab hold and restrain him. He did this with relative ease, in fact, which permitted Chavarin to approach the situation with his usual insouciance.

"Now what seems to be the problem?"

"Who the fuck are you?" Michaud lunged, but the butcher caught him and lifted him by the collar, and all four men, the maître d' included, wedged their way back outside and onto the street.

At Chavarin's direction, they removed themselves to the alley by the delivery entrance. Michaud might as well have been a ragdoll as the butcher shoved him up against the wall and pinned him there.

"Now, the real question," said Chavarin, gesturing freely with his friend's brass-tipped cane, "is who do you think *you* are? Because you have no business with a woman like this."

"A woman like this? And you know who she is?"

"I know who *you* are."

"Yes, and I know you!" Michaud spat, flecking Chavarin's chin among other things. "You are nothing but a whore yourself. The 'kept man'? That's how you got your money, no? You fuck old ladies for it?"

Chavarin was *almost* charmed by this, but only as the lion is charmed by a field rat. He cleaned his chin with a white kerchief, which he then handed to the butcher.

"To within an inch," he instructed.

The butcher wrapped the kerchief firmly around the knuckles of his right hand, dragged Michaud into the shadow of the alley, and commenced the beating . . .

§

The guests were all still taking their seats back in the salon, and asking one another polite and pointless questions. An elderly woman with seven strands of pearls asked the young lady if she had been at the performance this evening.

She shook her head, she didn't think so.

"You're in for a treat," the older woman said.

Monsieur Singh found her a chair in the front row and saved a seat beside her. He set down the white kerchief from his pocket.

"Is this the latest?" asked another—discreetly. Monsieur Singh shook his head, no.

Meanwhile, Mademoiselle Eschette—the *actual* latest—had found a seat for herself at the back of the room, with her friend Montesquiou on one side and an open chair on the other. Just to see.

The light dimmed. The piano rang—

§

" . . . Enough."

The beating concluded, and the butcher withdrew from the shadow, unwrapping the bloody kerchief from his knuckles.

However, as he, the maître d', and Chavarin started back for the café, a voice croaked out from the shadows.

"Hey, tuv' man," it said, through a split lip and shattered teeth. "Tuv' guy . . . Good 'fing, eh?"

Chavarin paused, but did not turn. The voice went on.

"Good 'fing you go'll your money now, hunh? Because I can zee, you're gedding a li'l thick in the middle, no? And the neck. Because tha'z all you are, you know, is a fat aging whore."

Chavarin turned and entered the shadow, cane raised high, and with a quick jabbing motion, cracked the speaker directly in the mouth, driving the metal tip through his shattered teeth and into the soft anemone of his tongue.

§

The contralto Madame Parisot stood before the room, high-chinned in her midnight-blue gown and long satin gloves. She sang an aria from the Massenet, *"Regarde-les ces yeux,"* which featured an extended passage of coloratura. How she juggled all those notes at once, the young woman—the new find, that is, sitting beside the empty seat in the front row—couldn't imagine.

She also could not focus. The notes were so many, so jumbled, and her mind was elsewhere. She was thinking of the artist and of the look in his eye as he had howled across the room at her—that demonic, outsized fury—and she knew that he had found her again. The bearded man, that is. He had followed her here, and she was more aware than ever that this dream, this interlude—whatever it was, this respite—could not go on for too much longer. She was too tired, but not so much from lack of sleep— sleep was everywhere, sleep was breathing, as far as she could tell—as from the effort required to keep at bay the raging sea of everything that came before.

When the aria ended and the assembled guests all were applauding and calling out for more—"Encore! Encore!"—the dashing Monsieur Chavarin slid into his seat beside her with a smile and nudge on the elbow.

"I think I should go to my room," she said.

He made a sorry face, but claimed to understand. She did look tired. He signaled for Monsieur Singh to come take her. "Go rest up." He patted her hand. "And we will see you in the morning, yes?"

She smiled wearily and excused herself before the music started again. Monsieur Singh received her at the sliding door, while Chavarin looked over his shoulder to see if Mademoiselle Eschette was still about.

She was not. There were two empty chairs beside his friend Montesquiou, who let him know with a glance that he should probably leave his leading lady be this evening. Chavarin understood this as well. So he enjoyed the concert in the salon, while Monsieur Singh took his guest up to his suite on the seventh floor, and while the butcher dragged the beaten, battered Michaud down to the river and deposited him there—as Monsieur Chavarin had specifically directed—in the sludge where the slaughterhouse dumped its carcasses. Chavarin did not think of following the young woman up to his suite. Well, he *thought* of it, but only to confirm that he would not think of it. Not tonight. He would go home and sleep at the mansion tonight, and he was very proud of himself for this.

§

Monsieur Chavarin's personal guest suite was on the seventh floor, and could be accessed by any one of three doors. Monsieur Singh gave the young woman as brief a tour as the space permitted, just to make sure she understood what was available to her:

A reading area, with a library and a roll-top writing desk, outfitted with stationery, pens, an envelope opener, and most notably, a pair of tortoiseshell scissors. There was an empty birdcage, a tea nook, and a vanity. The windows were several, all tall and draped. The central-most included French doors that opened to a balcony, which was also of interest; Monsieur Singh showed her the key to the lock. There was a grand piano and a bar stocked with green bottles and amber bottles and smaller bottles of ochre and russet brown. Several arrangements of seasonal flowers and fruit had been stationed throughout. Here, cherries, as well as something globed she didn't recognize; ripe, though, to the touch. There was an abundance of pillows and chaises and chairs, and textured paper on every wall—stripes and paisleys and floral designs—along with still lifes and seascapes, maps and

botanicals. The *lavatoire* had two sinks, a bidet, and a standing bathtub with soaps and salts. There were stacked towels.
She counted five. Ample.

Her frock was hanging in the walk-in closet, laundered
and dry. Her sabots were on the floor.

"I should leave the gown here?" she asked.

Monsieur Singh smiled. "I'm quite sure the gown is a gift,
mademoiselle, compliments of Monsieur Chavarin."

She proceeded to the bedroom. A life-sized panting of a
girl on a swing, and a four-poster bed with an embroidered can-
opy. Monsieur Singh showed her the braided silk rope hanging
within reach of the sleeper. If there was anything she needed,
she had only to pull this rope and someone would come.

"You?" she asked.

He answered no, though he seemed moved by the question, and humbled.

Behind him, a porter entered with what appeared to be a
tea service on a rolling table. She could see a cup and saucer, a
creamer, a sieve, a sugar bowl, and a jar of honey even, which
she had not requested.

Monsieur Singh asked, "Would the mademoiselle like to
make sure the service is to her satisfaction?"

She said, "I trust you."

He lifted the top of the tea caddy to make sure the leaves
were there and dry, which was why she trusted him. He
sniffed the oil as well, and observed: the ginger had been
sliced into paper-thin coins.

"This is acceptable?"

She nodded that this would be fine, though seeing it all
together—everything that she had asked for—caused her
heart to quicken slightly. Her breathing grew shallow.

Behind them, the bellhop had turned down the cover of
the bed. He lit the lamp now, surprising her, which Monsieur

Singh saw. He also noticed her hand was trembling.

"I am tired," she explained.

He asked one last time if there was anything else they could bring her. She told him no thank you. She believed she had everything she needed.

"Then I will come for the mademoiselle in the morning."

"I understand," she replied.

He paused—his eyes, as ever, were respectfully averted but still intent. "I will come at nine o'clock," he said clearly.

Again she said she understood. With that, he bowed and left her, following the porter out the door.

She shuddered slightly at the click. She supposed a part of her had hoped that Monsieur Singh might fail her, though she had known that he would not. And she was grateful. She even noticed now, there was a knife beside the tea dish. For luck.

She sat. The quilt here was softer than any of the blankets back at the maison. The top sheet as well. She rubbed it between her thumb and her forefinger, and she drew a deep breath. Out the window, the tower was dark in the distance, black against the night.

She let the breath go and started unmaking the bed.

Part Five

Thursday

Chapter 16

Anonymity

The first of the envelopes appeared a little before 8 A.M. The countess saw it while going through the morning mail at her letter desk—a cream-colored, handmade envelope, the oddly improvised nature of which gave her pause; it had been gift-ribboned by a coarse brown string. With a curiosity leaning on suspicion, she slipped the knot and unfolded the page.

On the backside was a handwritten message:

> *I have information in which you may be interested, regarding your husband.*

The words were ragged, faint, and teeter-totter, which the countess took to indicate that the author was uneducated. A more trained and professional eye would have quickly identified the left-handed penmanship of a right-handed person. Either way, no indication was given of what to do, or how to get the information at question. The message was "a tease," as the dramatists like to say, to which the countess replied with a reflexive sniff.

"When did this come?" she asked.

Marie, her sergeant at arms in the house, replied, "With the rest, ma'am. This morning."

"And did Sylvia get the herring?"

"She's at the markets now, ma'am."

The countess tossed the envelope directly in the wastebin.

§

Her husband was at the Folies Nouvelle. Early for him, but he had made arrangements with the young woman the night before to meet him here, and Duchamps as well, to go over the role of the Dreamless Sleeper.

And Duchamps *was* here, as was the costume man and the makeup man, and most of the rest of the players in the number. The marble slab on which the Sleeper did her sleeping was in place. Monsieur Singh was here as well.

Only the young woman was not.

"What time did you check the room?" asked Chavarin.

Monsieur Singh replied, first at nine o'clock as they had agreed, and then again just before he left the hotel for the theater.

"And there was no message at the desk?"

No, monsieur.

"Nor in the room?"

No.

They waited another fifteen minutes, long enough for Duchamps to have his third coffee. When he was done, it was decided that the part should go to a member of the chorus. At least for tonight's opening.

"We have other girls," said Duchamps, which was true. They were all surrounding them, stretching, reading— gazelles at the watering hole. "And if the young lady has been detained for some reason, you can tell her—what was her name, by the way?"

It wasn't until this moment they realized they did not even know her name. Everyone had assumed that someone else knew.

Chavarin and Singh did return to the hotel, though, just to make sure there hadn't been some miscommunication.

They went to the room to see if there was any note or clue, but it had been serviced by then. Only the gown from the night before was hanging in the closet. The court shoes were aligned underneath.

Chapter 17

The Tribunal

The conference room chosen for Brassard's probationary review was actually called "The Tribunal." That's what it said right on the door, which should have tipped him. There was nothing pro forma about this morning's meeting.

At one end of the room was a long desk, almost like a dais, with three high-backed chairs facing in. He himself had been provided one free-floating (and shorter) chair in the center of the room, backed only by the chair assigned to his sponsor, Captain Monsaingeon, who'd been his supervisor during his cadet years in Paris, and his only real advocate during the whole imbroglio in Champagne-Ardenne.

They had entered together and were made to wait a good quarter of an hour in silence, time he wished he could have used to go and freshen up. He'd had to rush to get here, having awakened late, having gotten to sleep *very* late. Why? Because in the first place it hadn't been easy finding his way out of the ruins. Then he'd had to retrieve his saddlebag. Then go confirm that Soter and the boy were *not* waiting for him at the tower. Walk all the way from there to the barracks. Wake up the provost and take the only bed available, which was in the infirmary next to a staff officer suffering from pleurisy.

So no, not much sleep. Come morning, he'd barely had time to wash his face and dress. He'd meant to clean and press his tunic, but no again, so he was not looking his best— *très déshabillé*, in his father's phrase. Even Monsaingeon had asked if he was feeling all right.

But this was not even the worst of it. When the members of the panel finally arrived, they entered from the door behind the long dais, single file. Leading the way was the director of the Parisian bureau, Lieutenant Colonel Duroq, whom Brassard knew by reputation and had no reason to fear. Next came the director general himself, Philippe Bonheur. Brassard had met him on several occasions, including when he was a boy. Formidable, but decent and admirable.

It took Brassard a moment to recognize the third officer in line. In part this was due to certain physical changes that had taken place—he looked thicker than he had the last time, or softer—but also Brassard simply hadn't been *expecting* to see him—here—which, now that he did, struck him as being so stupefyingly obvious, he wondered how he could have pictured any other outcome because of course, *of course* the final member of this morning's panel would be him.

It was Larive, the man whose damning letters he had imagined racing him, chasing him all the way here; the man who had, in fact, *initiated* the case against him back in Champagne-Ardenne; *and* who decided it; *and* who in the thirteen months since would appear to have ascended to the rank of lieutenant-colonel, at least to judge by the profusion of medals, ribbons, epaulets, and shoulder knots now decorating his tunic. Larive had done much better than to send defamatory missives from parts north. He'd seen to it that he should be here *in person*, to sit in judgment, to finish the job, and in that regard was failing miserably—now as he took the seat to the immediate left of the director general—to conceal the immense pleasure he was taking at this moment, notwithstanding the faux-solemnity of his expression, or the repugnant new mustache he was wearing, a narrow brush that barely spanned the canal of his upper lip.

It was Lieutenant Duroq, however, who began the proceeding, and who seemed to have been charged with making sure that everything-but-everything related to Brassard's suspension the year before was entered into the record. He made Brassard walk them all through the case in far greater detail than he had been expecting. Not that Brassard lacked command of such detail, but it was a tricky business treading the line he had to—between accepting due responsibility for what he had done, and not admitting to violations he certainly wasn't guilty of, while also not inculpating any other members of the department (which required some outright lying in the face of Duroq's strange persistence); and to do all of this in the presence of that slope-shouldered, long-necked weasel Larive, who knew damn well the truth of what had taken place, and therefore knew damn well the restraint that he, Brassard, had shown back at the time of his suspension, and that he was showing now again, for not pointing directly at him and saying, "Sirs, if I am dirt—which I may be—then this man here is excrement of the most vile and liquid variety."

But of course he did not say this. On the contrary, he maintained the same basic posture of nonresistance as had guided him through the farce of thirteen months prior, making no attempt to defend or explain himself, which of course Duroq took as an invitation to grind his nose a bit and lecture him. Fair enough. Brassard continued to express nothing but contrition and gratitude for lessons learned, though admittedly these declarations might have been more convincing had his appearance not been quite so undermining. He did not look the part of a penitent young officer.

It went without saying that the director general should go last, if he deigned to join in the interview at all, so it was Larive's turn next. Like Duroq, Larive seemed to be most interested in what he knew least about—meaning Tonkin, in his case. Clearly he had ideas, but these seemed to be based on the same reflexive resentment that had fueled his earlier investigation of Brassard. For let there be no mistake: There had been no incident or falling out between the two. Larive had detested Brassard from the start, with a catlike aversion that—if it must be named—boiled down to Brassard's not being "salt" enough—too aloof, too erudite to be trustworthy. And, of course, too ambitious.

"So over the course of the eleven months, you participated in how many campaigns?"

"Seven."

"You were captured in the seventh?"

"Yes."

"Do you mind discussing the circumstances?"

"No." He didn't, although this was all clearly laid out in the report. "We'd received intelligence that the insurgent group we had been tracking was holed up in one of the mountain villages, Panhou. When we got there, the village had been abandoned. It *seemed* to have been abandoned at least, which wasn't unusual. As we were leaving, one of the houses started burning. We were not able to determine why, but took action to put the fire out. I led a small unit up the hillside to release one of the water gates, and it was in that effort that we met with the ambush."

"And we are talking about the Black Flag here?"

"Well, remnants, but yes."

"And were any other members of your column captured?"

"Three."

"Where did they take you?"

"I don't know. We were wearing hoods, but it was some miles away and underground. Or in a hill. A tomb, I think."

Larive's nostrils flared slightly. "A tomb?"

"Yes." Brassard declined to explain, but they were mostly

farmers in the region. They buried their dead in the fields, but after enough years had passed, they'd come collect the bones and store them in hidden caves and ossuaries.

Larive asked., "Were you alone?"

"I was not in the presence of any other prisoners, if that's what you mean."

That *was* what he meant. He turned a page.

"And what was your understanding of how these people treated their prisoners?"

Brassard recognized that he was being examined for damages. He remained calm. "It was my understanding they did not treat their prisoners well."

"Based on?"

"Anecdote, but evidence, too. One encountered their captives from time to time in the jungle."

"Encountered them how?"

"Hanging. From hooks usually."

Larive affected disgust, souring his face just as one of the director general's personal aides entered the room to deliver what looked like another letter. The director general thanked him for it, but let it sit flat on the table in front of him.

Larive continued. "And in response to these barbaric displays, the legion has adopted certain unusual policies, as I understand."

"You're referring to what was in the Domi report."

There had been allegations some months before that certain columns were choosing to shoot their own men in the field—when they were either too injured or ill to keep up—rather than leave them behind to be tortured and killed by the enemy.

"Yes," said Larive.

"I would not call this a policy, and I never saw it implemented."

"You didn't?"

"No."

"Glad to hear that." He made a note. "But in any case, these bandits who captured you, they're the ones who took your ear?"

"Yes."

"And has it affected your hearing, by the way? It doesn't seem to have."

"No," said Brassard. "I don't *source* sounds as well, but I hear them."

"And no further complications?"

"No. The left side of my head feels sometimes colder than the right, and I was told the canal might be more prone to infection. I've not found that to be the case."

Larive made another note. Or pretended to. "And as I understand, they subjected you to other punishments as well?"

"This is true."

"If it's too difficult—"

"No. But most of this is in the report."

Larive nodded. "So then—sleep deprivation."

"Some."

"Food deprivation?"

"Yes. They fed us, but yes, not as often as they might have."

"Stress positions?"

The room seemed to fall especially silent. Duroq shifted in his chair.

"I was bound, if that's what you mean."

"For extended periods."

"Yes."

"Which can be quite painful, as I understand."

"Quite."

Duroq cut in. "If you don't mind my saying, Monsieur

Brassard, you seem awfully sanguine about all this."

"Well, in the first place, I wouldn't want to overstate my own duress, out of respect for those who suffered more. But also, I think when one enters into situations like that, one must accept certain possibilities as a given."

Larive asked, "Did you at any point feel that your life was in danger?"

"Of course."

"Did you think you were going to die?"

"At times. But there again, one becomes something of a ... fatalist."

"A *fatalist?*" said Larive.

Brassard considered and upheld the choice of words. "One begins to feel that, on some level, the final determinations have all been made, and that one is merely finding out the results."

Larive managed a smile, though clearly it was answers like this that accounted for just how much he despised Brassard; therefore lost was any suggestion that Brassard might have been referring to the present proceeding.

"I'd forgotten what a philosopher you are." He turned another page. "I guess my point, Lieutenant, is that when prisoners are subjected to the sorts of treatment you've been describing, usually it's because their captors want something in return."

"I'm not sure I agree with that, but you're speaking of intelligence?"

"Yes."

"Well, as you'll see in the report, there wasn't even a translator. Have you read the report?"

"Oh, yes." He nodded, referring back to his notes; he wasn't through. "So this lasted all of eighteen days, your captivity?"

"So I'm told."

"At the end of which there was an exchange?"

"Yes." He looked to Bonheur and explained for his sake. "Apparently the local leader wanted someone back, one of his lieutenants, whom the L.É. had been holding. We suspect this was why they set up the ambush in the first place."

"But so they did *want* something?"

"Well, yes, of course, but if you're suggesting that I—"

"Were the other two men released? The two who were captured with you?"

"At that time, no."

"Were they ever released?"

". . . I don't know. Not as of the time I left, but if the insinuation is that I disclosed anything or had any hand in negotiating the terms of my—"

"There is no insinuation. I am simply trying to figure out: If you were nothing to them but a bargaining chip, why did they see fit to"—he pretended to search for the proper phrase—"to damage you in these ways?"

Again, Brassard knew that he was being provoked, and the thought did flutter through his mind of the "damage" he would do to Larive if they met on a road someday as civilians. Yet he had the strange sense that he'd have been avenging Quan's honor more than his own. Quan had been his keeper in the tombs. Somehow he felt as if Quan was the one being insulted here. In answer, all he offered was a shrug. "Old habits, I guess."

At this, Larive sat back and closed his folder. He was finished. Brassard frankly wasn't sure who'd won the exchange. He was still standing—figuratively speaking—but Larive *had* managed to recast his Eastern tour, from being a wholly voluntary and valorous act of national service (which it hadn't been, quite) into a fruitless and even marginally costly misadventure in which his chronic self-servingness had once again been exposed (which wasn't quite true either).

Now it was the director general's turn.

Again, Brassard had always judged Bonheur to be a man of high integrity, one who understood not just the practical significance of his office, but the symbolic as well. Noble-featured like a Roman bust, he carried himself with a suitable balance of gravitas and humility. His tunic was spotless and stiff, but modestly arrayed, not a showpiece. The face had added some flesh since Brassard had last seen him, not unbecomingly, though the extra weight lent his eyes a look of added strain.

"Tell me, Monsieur Brassard," he said, and suddenly the strain looked more like disappointment. "Why are you doing this?"

Brassard wasn't sure what to say at first, the question seemed so out of the blue. For the briefest moment, he thought the director general might be referring to his pursuit of the young woman and the wagon.

"Sir?"

"Why exactly do you want to come back?" the director general said. "You're a young man. You've served well, you've sacrificed. You're still able bodied for the most part, and obviously clever. It seems to me you could make yourself useful in any number of ways."

Again, it took a moment for Brassard to adjust to the tack, though in fact he had been rehearsing his answer to this question for several weeks now. He could only stammer out the beginnings. "I suppose it's that this is what I've worked for," he said. He sat forward now, to think. He knew he had a better phrase, a better way. "My father served," he said. "He served thirteen years—"

"Yes, and your grandfather served thirty-three," said the director general. "I'm well aware. But this isn't what I'm asking. I'm asking why *you* want this."

He looked at him again with those straining eyes, but more probingly now, profoundly, yet all Brassard could feel at the moment was the quiet pleasure Larive was taking in his struggle.

The director general continued in a tone which could not have been more kind. "I hope you don't think I am insulting you when I say this, but I'm just not sure you are a man of law. This is not necessarily a flaw. Not everyone can be. But a man of law is a very particular thing. I won't bore you with platitudes, except to say that above all he must be a servant, which simply means that in his heart there must be a willingness—but more than a willingness, there must be a *preference*, an *eagerness*—to subordinate his own interests, his own desires, and yes, his own ambition—for the greater good. And for the good of the corps. He must see himself, first and foremost, as being part of something larger—something that was here before him and will be here long after— and this must be what brings him the utmost pleasure in life, and a sense of fulfillment." He stopped. He considered if there was something more to add, but on concluding that there wasn't, he sat back and looked at Brassard, or looked at his tunic, in fact. "And I'm just not sure I see that here."

Brassard had been fairly well blindsided by this—despite the setting, despite the putative purpose of the meeting. He hadn't remotely expected an affront of this type, least of all coming from Bonheur—and he'd been distracted, too, by the expression on Larive's face, who was looking across at him with all the smug delight of a successful ventriloquist.

Still, he was aware of what he might have said in reply, had he had his feet beneath him. He might have pointed out that Bonheur was right—in one respect, at least. There *were* any number of things Brassard could have done with himself in the wake of his suspension the year before. He could have worked in security for Société Générale and done quite handsomely. He could have worked for the consulate, or sold his expertise to any one of a dozen enterprises, public and private. But he hadn't even considered such things, not really. He had gone directly to serve the country again, le Tricolore. On the far side of the world, no less. Seven missions. Seven fruitless, foolish, thankless, harebrained sorties into a bug-infested jungle, to roust out the vermin, the "tunnel rats," as they liked to call them over there; to enter as predator and come out prey. What made him do this, other than the willingness—the "eagerness" as Bonheur put it— to be part of something larger, greater than himself?

And how much larger were they talking about here, by the way? How much more sacrifice did they require? He knew what they suspected, of course—what Larive had tried to get out of him. They suspected that he had broken in Panhou. He had given the Flag information—specifically, that their man Zhou was still alive, and that this was why they'd let him go. In exchange.

But did they even have the courtesy to ask? What made them think he'd even *wanted* such an exchange? Because that was the dirtiest little secret of the whole affair. They'd just assumed, so it seemed to him that the least they could do was to honor that presumption and accept his application here and now, forthwith. Count their blessings. Because that was the *other* thing that seemed to be going scandalously unsaid here, the fact that he was a *far* superior officer to anyone in Champagne-Ardenne, including the bullet-necked, pin-headed chauvinist in all the ribbons here. Brassard was *more* lawful, more knowledgeable, more dogged, more keen. Never lazy, never complacent, never cowardly, never . . . wrong. Gasp if you like, it was true, and he could prove it.

Would they could have seen him last night, or in the days to come. He was on the trail of something—he *knew* it—and he would prove it to them.

Which was part of the reason he did not actually say any of this. He could tell just by looking at Bonheur, there'd have been no point. No syllable of such an appeal, however tastefully or ardently delivered, would so much have reached the scales of this man's consideration, much less tilted them back in his favor. So Brassard held his tongue, and the director general, when he was satisfied that no answer was forthcoming, took up the envelope he'd been delivered and held it out.

"We need you to sign that," he said.

He couldn't reach. Brassard had to rise from his chair, but the aide stepped in to complete the handover.

Brassard was still confused, not knowing what the letter was—more slander from Saigon, for all he knew. Did they need him to verify the contents? Then he saw it was an official document of the Guard; it bore the insignia, and the first line included his own name. "*I, Emile Brassard, hereby agree...*"

It was a pledge, awaiting his signature.

"What you'll see," said Bonheur, "is that it prescribes the consequences for any further misconduct of the kind we've been discussing."

Brassard's eye continued to scan without really reading: "*Sixty days*" ... "*should the assignated*" ... "*a period of ten days,*" and so forth. It was a deliberately daunting and determined block of text, with subheadings and sub-subheadings setting out the various costs and contingencies: "*will result in dismissal*" ... "*and formal censure*" ... "*immediate*" ... "*but not before a period of*"—

"Take it with you," said the director general. "Read it carefully, Monsieur Brassard, and think about whether this is what you really want. If you decide it is, and that you can abide by the terms outlined there, we would like your signature by the end of tomorrow. I assume that will be enough time."

"Yes, sir. Thank you, sir."

With that, the director general stood, then Duroq, then Larive, whose eye Brassard hadn't the stomach to meet. He merely stood as well, understanding that with the transfer of this document, the meeting had effectively realized its purpose and was so adjourned.

He was about to offer his salute when he saw that the director general had paused on his way out. He was looking back at him, in fact, with the same burdened eyes, as if lit by a slightly more personal glow, now that he had risen from his official chair.

"I knew your father," he said.

"Yes, sir."

"I was at the funeral."

Brassard nodded. "I am aware, sir."

He was aware. The director general, back when he was first lieutenant to Trochu, had indeed attended. Brassard remembered his face because of how stricken it had seemed, and he had thought back then, *Does he feel this about each and every man?* He couldn't imagine. Yet here it was again— older, thicker, but the very same shade seemed to be hovering behind those eyes, as if his father's death were fresh, a crust of bread that he must chew and swallow anew every time he thought of it.

Standing there, he did swallow, and the grief gave way to the subject at hand. His eyes refocused on Brassard and pinned him square:

"But that's no reason, son."

He held him there for one more moment. He might have

held him there forever, it seemed, had Brassard not finally offered a nod—his surrender, in a way—receiving which, the old man turned and led the others from the room by the same door as they'd come; Duroq following, and then Larive, who did not look back. He didn't need to.

Brassard was still stunned when he stepped back out into the long marble hall. His legs felt numb. His throat was dry. His sense at that moment—which he was aware might be the most accurate sense he would ever have, coming newborn from the event, and before his own desires could enter in and begin to twist and re-light the significance of what had taken place in there—was that he had just been thoroughly and in no uncertain terms *discouraged* from returning to the Guard. Their reasons were several—some good, some bad—but again, what stung most was that no consideration whatever seemed to have been given to the actual *quality* of his work.

"Bad luck," said Monsaingeon, who'd accompanied him out, "drawing Larive."

"I don't think luck had much to do with it," said Brassard.

They'd been joined by one of the cadets as well. Now that Brassard's official business had concluded, he would need to be escorted from the building forthwith. They started off, the two of them abreast, leading their soft-cheeked escort; he couldn't have been more than seventeen.

"I wouldn't make too much of that business with the pledge," said Monsaingeon. "That's how Bonheur works. You sign the letter, you do good work; he's happy to eat his words. Say, 'You have proven me wrong.' It's the way he inspires."

"That's kind of you to say."

It was, and Brassard appreciated the thought, though there had always been a blustery kind of "all's well" quality about Monsaingeon. This made him a good friend, a good superior and loyal, but also difficult to take too seriously.

"It's possible they'll make you wait another round," he said. "Just for show. Just so the thing doesn't look like a done deal."

Brassard nodded, but he wasn't really listening. Their boots clicked in unison, and carried them by the Hall of Records on the left, a room Brassard knew very well, in fact. The words were painted in black and gold on the frosted glass window of the door, the same missing piece in the "R" as had been there for twenty years, since Brassard was a boy.

But now Monsaingeon was stopping them. He was indicating the next room down. "Did you want to use my office?"

To sign the letter, he meant, but Brassard was still in a haze.

"I haven't really had a chance to look it through. I think they wanted me to."

"I suppose that's right." Monsaingeon nodded, then squinted at Brassard's shoulder. "But did you not have a bag with you?"

He did. He had—his saddlebag. He'd left it back in the Tribunal. Monsaingeon asked their escort, the cadet, to go fetch it for them, leaving the two of them there. Awkwardly.

To fill the space, Brassard said, "I spent a lot of time in there, you know." He indicated the door to the Hall of Records. "My father used to leave me there when he was stationed here."

Monsaingeon smiled kindly, though it wasn't clear he'd heard.

The Hall was the central and most comprehensive library of all the case files and histories from all the divisions of the Guard, and Brassard had read them all, most of them several times over. They'd been his Hugo and Dumas—literally hundreds upon hundreds of hours he'd devoted—as result of which he probably possessed a more thorough knowledge of all the crimes committed in France between the years 1750 and 1869 than anyone in the corps—or anyone in the world for that matter. The records before 1750 hadn't been so well kept.

He remembered, too, how he used to imagine the room on fire; someone left out a cigar, or a lamp tipped over . . .

"Did I see your name on a report about some body in the woods?" asked Monsaingeon, his turn to break the silence.

"In Traconne, yes," said Brassard. "I sent a dispatch to the office in Sezanne, along with the copy I filed here . . . seeing as I couldn't really investigate."

"No, you did well . . ."

They rocked on their heels once or twice more, and now came the *cl-click cl-clack* of the young cadet's boots returning. Brassard recognized the sound as well, from those same days back when. His father wouldn't return until quite late sometimes, but young Brassard would know it was him just by the tread, then his shadow behind the glass. He'd snap his fingers, that was all, and young Brassard would return his folder to its file, the file to the drawer. Then the two of them would leave together, him straining to match his father's stride, *cl-click cl-clacking* the rest of the way down the hall and out the great red doors. No word was ever said.

Brassard was handed back his saddlebag. Time to go.

"Very good," said Monsaingeon. "Look the letter over, but as I say, this is the way they work. If you're here tomorrow, stop by. Maybe I'll take you to dinner."

Again, he was being very kind, very upbeat, but Brassard still couldn't help feeling pitied under the circumstances. Even as he thanked the captain, he looked at the door again, and again, as if by reflex, he imagined the golden orange flames behind the frosted glass, imagined all of the shelves and drawers inside, crammed with all the histories, the catalogs of dates and evidence, depositions, testimonies, letters, all of them curling up, orange and black, and billowing away—the same as he'd pictured when he was a boy, and not because he'd been a budding arsonist or anything of the kind. On the contrary, it was more a kind of tragic fantasy he entertained, because he considered it such an awful thing, the thought of so much loss, so quickly accomplished, and nothing to be done. And such an awesome thing, too, that—were such an accident to occur—then maybe the only place in all of France where the records would still be safely kept would be his own little brain.

That was the idea behind the fire, at any rate, and that is when it came to him—back in the hallway now, which was how these things tended to happen. Having set the question aside for this very reason—so that the answer would come of its own, or that some seemingly random train of thought would steer him so *near* to the answer, all it would have to do is raise its hand, clear its throat, draw the blind—whatever the signal was, it had apparently just revealed itself, because at that very moment, reminded of the notion of his prepubescent skull being the one last repository of the complete history of crime and punishment in France, Brassard realized where he had seen that brooch, the one he'd found in the cast-iron safe.

"You forget something else?" asked Monsaingeon, having apparently noticed the sudden glint in his companion's eye.

"No, no," said Brassard. "Just remembered something actually."

He was almost sure of it; so certain, in fact, he had half a mind to burst into the Records Hall right then, just to confirm.

"You have a place to stay?" Monsaingeon asked.

"What? Oh, yes. Yes, I do," said Brassard, which wasn't

true, but that was fine. He was very excited all of a sudden.

Monsaingeon told him to get some sleep then, it looked like he could use it, and Brassard thanked him one more time, but much more effusively now. He looked him in the eye, because this was *why*, after all—the *real reason* he wanted to return. *This*. And he would show them, prove it to them.

Swiftly he made his way to the great red door, an un-expected gust of wind in his sails. A moment later, he was floating back out into the glare of the day. He had to cover his eyes, the sun was facing him so directly, but right there waiting for him was the boy, with Soter beside. They were standing in the shade of the one tree on the curb, and the moment the boy he saw him, he stuck out his hand, palm up. He wanted his money.

"Ah, ah, ah," said Brassard. "Not so fast. Let's see what you've earned first."

Chapter 18

Entente

Attendees of the luncheon at the countess's included two editors of *Le Monde*, one critic for *Le Figaro*, one member of the Chambers, as well as the Madames Corot and Mieux (who was nearly deaf), *and* Monsieur Lepin, a neighbor and former head of the Treasury. Herring was served.

The topics of conversation were several and varied, but most concerned politics, which was as the countess preferred: the revolution, of course, because this was the 100th anniversary—the Exposition being the national commemoration—and because, remarkably, no one there seemed able to remember what *instigated* the storming of the Bastille. "But precisely," the countess kept having to say. "Why *that day*?" Madame Corot's repeated insistence "because it was the *fourteenth*!" served to clarify only one thing.

They discussed the recent legislative elections, in which the center-left had done very well, thank you; and Boulanger, who was a bête noire of the countess's, and whose recent legal troubles as such were extremely gratifying. "Completely unjust," as she put it, "and very well deserved." They discussed the Exposition as well, of course—and what was to become of all the exhibits now that it was over.

"Oh, it's going on tour," the columnist was saying.

"The tower?" asked Madame Mieux.

"No," chuckled Lepin. "The diamond, you meant, yes?"

"No, the *zoo*," the columnist clarified. "I think it's headed to Belgium next."

"Cold!" shivered Madame Mieux, just imagining.

The countess smiled thinly, but mostly to veil her increasing irritation. The chair at the far end of the table, her handsome husband's, was empty and would remain so through the tarte and coffee. There had been no word from him, and when the last of the guests were leaving—the two mesdames—it was still only the countess seeing them to the door, thanking them for coming (as loudly as she could), and apologizing on her husband's behalf. He has been so busy, what with the revue.

It was upon closing the door behind her that she turned back into the foyer and noticed the second of those envelopes on the mantle, just like the one that had come this morning—made of the same rough paper, folded the same way, bound by the same coarse brown string.

"And when did this arrive?"

"Not sure, ma'am," said Marie. "Must have been during the luncheon."

She opened it right there. This time, however, when the page unfolded, a card fell out.

It was a *carte de visite*, but a cheap one, the kind you could buy on the street, featuring a young woman. And again, the countess might not have looked at it twice, but that the face did seem familiar. She tried to think where she had seen this woman, and found the effort unexpectedly disturbing.

She went directly to the door and stepped outside, as if the person who had delivered it might still be there. She scanned for some sign, some stranger, but the street was empty—all but for the hasty approach of her husband.

He saw her as well, and her expression.

"So sorry. So sorry. Something came up at the theater."

She said nothing. She drew him back inside.

"Again, I tried to send word." He set his hat on the stand,

and then his scarf. "How were they? How was Lepin?"

She thrust the photograph at him. She made him take it.

He removed his gloves to do so, but as he looked down at the picture now, it wasn't clear to either of them whether he was going to pretend innocence or not.

"Where did you get this?" he asked.

"Why am I being sent it?"

His brow lifted obnoxiously. He swallowed his chin. "Surely you don't think—"

"It's the girl from the tower?"

"I don't— Who sent you this?"

"Apparently someone who thinks I might be interested." She started up the stairs.

"I don't understand." He followed her. "Did they ask for money?"

She turned abruptly and slapped him. Hard, and in a clearly disciplining way.

"These are *your affairs*. If you cannot manage them, and keep them out of mine, all of this can go away."

Blunt and to the point. She ascended the rest of the stairs, not in the manner of someone who had been hurt, but rather someone who had better things to do.

Chavarin was duly chastened. And warned. It only took a moment, though—and another glance down at the photograph—for his chagrin to turn to outrage, which is, after all, the far more pleasurable sensation.

§

The gypsy wagon was still there on the curb, just as Olivier had said, kneeling across the street from the brothel, Le Montyon, which was where the boy claimed she'd spent the night.

"You're sure?"

Olivier nodded, but Brassard did not for a moment consider the possibility that she was a prostitute.

"And you say she met this man at the Expo?"

Olivier nodded.

"Did he wear a hat?"

The boy nodded again.

"What kind of a hat?"

"Black. Kind of floppy again."

Brassard paid him a franc and asked him to wait with Soter.

He used an alley to change back into his street clothes, and moments later was in the parlor of Le Montyon, interviewing Madame Renée and a young lorette, who both confirmed that, yes, a woman answering to that description had come in last night—on the arm of one François Michaud—but they had never seen her before.

"And who is Michaud?"

A regular, they said. When he had money.

(*Not even*, said the younger one.)

"What does he do?" asked Brassard.

"He's a painter," said the young one—"Odette"—who possessed suggestive eyes, and seemed to be looking for business. Always.

The madame was more straightforward. "He's a thief," she said.

"And he tries to sell girls to model at the schools," the younger one added, adjusting her strap. "Why, is he in trouble?"

That depended, said Brassard, who'd indicated vaguely that he was in the employ of the young woman's uncle. "But you say she definitely left *before* he came back?"

"Well, yes," said the madame, as if that would have been

the point, no? To get away from him.

"What time?" asked Brassard.

"Ten?"

"And she didn't say why?"

No.

"Something must've spooked her," said Odette. "Strangest thing."

Not so strange, said the madame's eyes. "She wanted a card, but she realized she wasn't going to get one."

"What do you mean?"

"I mean our doctor had a look," she said. "He was here. With all respect to your client, his niece wasn't exactly the driven snow."

Brassard asked to see the room and they obliged. Seven. He noted the bars on the window. The candle on the bureau. The war-weary divan. They also showed him the few belongings she'd left behind, which turned out just to be the flower. Odette had thought there was more. Some photographs.

"She must've taken them."

That was as much as the two women seemed to know, but Brassard did ask them one more thing before leaving. About the brooch. He showed it to them, in fact—the front first, with the mandolin player and the young maiden.

"Sweet," said Odette, who hadn't given up on his business just yet.

He turned it over and indicated the initials. "This is who made it?"

"Correct," said the mistress.

"And you wouldn't happen to recognize the marking?"

She had to put on her glasses to see. The little gold chains did a dance.

"*Trésors du Temps*, I think," she sniffed. "For tourists."

"But they're here in Paris?"

"Third Arrondissement." The Madame let Odette see. "Rue du Temple?"

Odette thought so, yes.

Brassard thanked them again and took back the brooch. Odette asked him to say hi for her. "If you do find her." She left him with a crooked, broken-toothed smile that was admittedly becoming.

He was just on his way out when another man entered, dashingly handsome, and beaming with an almost theatrically furious expression, all gritted teeth and anviled brow. He swept right by Brassard without noticing him. His second, however—an Eastern Indian of some stripe—did offer a gentle nod in passing.

Olivier was still outside with Soter, still awaiting the balance of his pay.

"Afraid not," said Brassard.

Why? said the boy's expression.

"She did not spend the night there."

"She did, too."

"She did not. She left last night. At ten. Here. Help me."

There was a busted wine cask at the alley entrance, there to catch rainwater. Together they rolled it over and propped it underneath the wagon where the wheel was missing. The wheel was in the alley as well, but Brassard just wanted to level the floor a bit. He entered alone to inspect.

He wasn't sure what he was looking for exactly. Evidence. There was a dark smear near the door—probably blood. Probably the junkman's. He assumed the junkman had been dumped in the river at the first opportunity, not far from the Pont Neuf. He checked in the hidden compartment just to see if he might have missed something in there, a deeper section, but it was empty. There was also a painting on the floor, which hadn't been there before. Dark. A night scene, of a man on a stoop. It was signed in the bottom-right-hand corner. *Michaud.*

He took it back outside to see better in the daylight. A man with a rooster. He was either removing the metal spurs from its legs or putting them on. Probably removing them. The rooster was ragged and bloody, and there were coins on the step beside him.

"But now tell me," he said, speaking to Olivier, "did she seem to know this man?"

"Who?"

"The artist? Were they acquainted?"

Olivier shook his head with such unquestionable confidence, Brassard was tempted to toss him a coin just for that, but didn't. He was looking at the hands of the man in the painting when the door to the brothel burst open.

"You!"

It was the dashing man with the anvil brow, pointing across the way at him.

"Are you the one looking for the girl?"

This was Bruno Chavarin, of course, impresario of the lower entertainments. They convened back inside the wagon, along with Chavarin's second, the exotic valet, who stood throughout, the ceiling just barely clearing the upsweep of his luxuriously combed hair. Chavarin sat on the palette bed while Brassard examined the little photographic portrait— the one that Monsieur Chavarin's wife had received in the mail this morning. All agreed it had come from the photography exhibit at the Expo. They also agreed that it had been sent by the artist most likely, Michaud, the same who'd painted this picture here, and who'd brought the girl to the Montyon, then followed her to the café.

No mention was made of the merciless beating.

"But he didn't ask for money?" asked Brassard.

"Not yet," said Chavarin. "I don't think he's that clever. He's a pimp. He wants to be."

"Is she your mistress?"

"No."

"Then why is this man trying to blackmail you? Or whatever this is. Extort."

"I have no idea," said Chavarin, whom Brassard did not think was lying, save unto himself. "Because I paid for her room last night. Perhaps he made assumptions—but no, she's just a girl. Innocent. And I've seen this. They come here to Paris, girls like this. People take advantage."

"So when did you last see her?"

He turned up his hands, which were large and clean and extremely well manicured. "Midnight? Monsieur Singh did. She was in the hotel room."

Chavarin looked at Singh, who confirmed this with a nod.

"And since that point, no one at the hotel saw anything?"

No.

"Is it possible I could see the room?" asked Brassard.

"The maid's been," said Chavarin. "But we were thorough. Some blankets and towels may have been taken. And a knife. We think."

"What kind of knife?"

"Butter."

The Indian so confirmed.

Brassard looked back at the photograph, which hardly did her justice. She looked like a mannequin.

"So you think this man, this artist—"

"He *says* he's an artist," Chavarin cut in. "He's a pimp. Who hired you again? Her uncle?"

"... He sent me."

"But then who is she? Where did she come from?"

"I'm not at liberty to say," said Brassard. "But so, to be clear, you think this man *kidnapped* her?"

"Obviously." He paused. "Or they're setting me up. I don't know. I'm as confused as you. But he shouldn't be hard to find. We know where he lives"—he included the Indian in this—"where he drinks, all that. Which we're happy to share."

Brassard nodded as if this would be helpful.

". . . provided you let me know when you find him," said Chavarin. "I will pay you."

"That won't be necessary."

"I think it might be. Where are you staying?"

"Again, that would be confidential."

"Then I want to meet with you. Every day if that's possible. As I say, I think we need to act quickly. I have a bad feeling. I don't like to think what's happened here." He affected a suddenly stricken look. "I fear if we don't find him soon. . ." He seemed to be imagining the worst, then shook his head like a horse in bridle before reaching for his money pin. "We have to go, but here." He snapped free a bill and set it on the bench beside him. It was a fifty-franc note.

"Sir, I can't take your money."

"Then you'll have to give it back to me. Tomorrow at the Trocadéro gardens. We'll say five?"

Brassard didn't agree or disagree, but the two gentlemen left the wagon even so, the Indian with a bow of appreciation that seemed to speak for both of them.

Singh . . .

An Indian name, and complexion, but something about the jaw put him in mind of the field assistant captured with him in Panhou. Xi. Good man. Great shot.

And almost surely hanging from a hook somewhere.

Chapter 19

The Crypt

Brassard still wanted to visit that jeweler's shop on Rue Temple—Trésors du Temps—but in light of these discoveries, he agreed with Chavarin that finding François Michaud was probably the first order of business, and he had a fairly good idea of where to begin looking.

Olivier and Soter were still outside the wagon. Olivier had found a stick and was trying to engage Soter in a tug-of-war, to no avail. Brassard gave the boy the fifty-franc note.

"You have a safe spot for that? Where do you stay?"

"I have places," was all the boy said. He stuffed the bill into his left shoe, a composite of leather, rags, and rope.

"All right, but I'm going to need our friend." Soter.

The boy understood. Brassard invited him to join them at least as far as the river. A walk of a mile or so down Montmartre, the first half of which proceeded in a more or less comfortable silence. Fine by all three, but Brassard used the second half to do some more personal detecting, and by a series of direct questions that required only monosyllabic answers, was able to gather and deduce that young Olivier had never known either of his parents, and that his mother may not have known his father at all. The boy had bounced some between an orphanage, the hospices, and an "uncle" who lived near Rue St. Jean with seven children of his own. "Cousins," he called them, but that seemed hardly likely; they worked in textiles. It was from this uncle that Olivier had escaped last spring. The boy didn't know if any effort had been made to track him down. Brassard doubted it.

That brought the three of them to the river, where they parted. Olivier headed west, Brassard and Soter east.

And here Brassard's mood did grow dark, in part because of all that with the boy—how common and how damning a tale. (Brassard was himself a bastard-by-descent. His grandfather had been an orphan, the one who'd served in Belgium.) But he was also growing more pessimistic about the case, such as it was. It was another gray day. The water was all slates and blacks, and somehow just the look of it, the menace of its endless undulation—that gleeful mask of death that just kept sweeping on and swallowing all—seemed to underscore the possibility upon which Chavarin had finally focused. Time could well be running out for that young woman, if it hadn't run out already.

Brassard didn't lend much credence to the idea that she and Michaud were in league. Far too much deliberate deception required, and disguise. The modus operandi of most criminals was panic and brutality, and Michaud didn't seem like an exception there. He was on a typical run of terrible decisions, including the one to murder the junkman the night before. He was almost surely the one who'd sent the photograph to the countess, and he was most likely the reason the young woman had fled Le Montyon.

Occam's razor agreed with Chavarin, then, that Michaud was either holding her ransom, or blackmailing Chavarin, or worse. He may have bungled into taking her life already, in which case these missives to the countess were the beginnings of an attempt to shift the blame and maybe frame the impresario.

Stranger things. Stupider things, as the river would no doubt attest.

But now he and Soter had reached the island. The previous

night, he'd found an alternate route out of the underground, one that didn't require any keys to the junkman's gates, or crawling out through sewer ducts. The exit let out not far from the cathedral, and could have been mistaken for a secret back entrance to the Hotel Dieu. The only catch was that the final passage—or from this afternoon's perspective, the *opening* passage—was a thirty-foot vertical drop down a very narrow column, furnished by iron rungs bolted to the wall. A tight squeeze, particularly with Soter in arm, but he was glad to have the dog. Already he could smell the dank air again, and the must of bones. Again he could feel the strange power that pervaded, however many fathoms beneath the accepted customs and practices of the surface world, the *living* world.

When they reached the first platform, he lit his flashlight, a dark lantern, exposing the tunnel ahead in all its cruddy pale-brick and well-bottom black. He tried to give Soter another pull on the maiden's kerchief, but for all these same reasons—for having entered this kingdom of death and bones and ancient death smells—Soter was already overstimulated. He took off down the passage ahead, scampering and sniffing along the crevices and corners, smacking the walls with his tail.

Likewise—and also for the purpose of disguise—Brassard now lifted his own neckerchief and masked himself in the manner of an American train robber, as he had been taught by his Revanchist thug-friends up north. He also drew his gun, the 6-round he'd found the night before in the junkman's vault—which was also his destination at the moment. He didn't expect that Michaud would actually *be* there—more likely he was running one of his errands up top—but inasmuch as the criminal mind lacked all imagination, was drawn to the scenes of its crimes, and tended to colonize what it's plundered, the vault would almost surely have occurred to Michaud as a possible headquarters for his current enterprise, whatever it may be. Brassard was here on more of a reconnaissance mission, then, or the first step in a long process of elimination.

Yet even as they came upon the second long corridor, the lantern slashing the way with shadows and light, Soter could be seen to suddenly stop cold and turn his ears. Something had just moved up ahead. Or someone. His snout agreed.

Was it she?

For one heroic inhalation, Brassard actually thought it might be. But the tone of Soter's growl said no, as did the silence that followed, the distinctive silence of someone trying to be silent—the silence of held breath—giving way, as it nearly always did, to the squeak, the groan, or in this case, the *crunch* of the prematurely ventured footstep.

Brassard had barely gotten the second syllable out, "*Allez*," before Soter bolted, splashing gutter water behind. He was halfway down the passage when a man appeared, comically dashing leftwards in a panic. Soter turned the corner after him, barking now. Brassard followed, not nearly at pace, but he could hear the man as well, venting a string of unreservedly cowardly howls that, for their shamelessness, did faintly pluck the heart strings. Around the next turn, Soter was sounding like five dogs in the echo, and the chorus led Brassard directly to the wicket gate of the junkman's vault.

The space was as he'd left it, only with Soter now planted firmly before a recess in the left-side wall. It was like a dugout or a fireplace with a bricked-up flue, and the man was crouched inside and cowering.

Brassard approached slowly. "Quiet, Soter. Shshsh." It was definitely the same man from last night, but the face— "Look at me"—the face looked as if it had run headlong into a boat propeller. His nose was smashed and smeared to the left. He right eye was an oozing eggplant. And his mouth was a hideous splay of bursted, swollen lips, shattered teeth, and impacted blue gums. Also, he was rank. Even with the scarf over his nose, Brassard could smell—the man stank like dead flesh for some reason, which explained Soter's trembling focus. The dog was to be commended his restraint.

"You're Michaud?"

The flare of his one good eye seemed to say yes.

"And where is the woman?"

Though Brassard was holding Michaud at gunpoint, it was the captive's horror of dogs that seemed most compelling. He was petrified, sensing which Soter offered another series of low growls.

Brassard silenced him, then tried again. "Where?"

"I 'on't know," said Michaud, the injuries to his mouth preventing any clearer answer, though the notes of insolence still came through. "I 'on't." he repeated, which could have been either a lie or a confession, it seemed to Brassard, if the young woman's body was already scuffing somewhere at the bottom of the river.

"Stay," he said, as a collective command to both man and dog.

Again, he hadn't been expecting to find the suspect quite so quickly, and he certainly wasn't prepared to return to the surface with him. There was no sign of any captive on premise, but he made a brief survey just to collect his thoughts. The cracked safe was there; its contents had been squirreled away, no doubt. Michaud appeared to have made nest in one of the corners. His hat and his jacket were draped on the junkman's little chair. Brassard saw the chain as well—the wagon chain—but it wasn't until he came upon the kitchen area that any plan of action took shape. From various lootings, the junkman had put together a little *cuisinette*, complete with kettles and pans, a potbelly stove, and a very handsome oak cabinet, on the high shelf of which sat three full sacks of coffee beans, like siblings in a row.

So did the trackless shadows of the Parisian underground offer their recommendation; so did Brassard reluctantly agree.

He took down the largest of the sacks, tore it open, and dumped the contents into the nearest pot. He took the little chair. He took the chain. He took a heavy coil of manila rope as well and returned to his prisoner.

"Put that on."

He tossed him the emptied coffee sack—for his head. The prisoner complied.

"Now stand."

Michaud offered no resistance. He raised his hands, and Brassard draped the chain over his shoulder; it was so heavy, Michaud buckled slightly. Then Brassard handed him the little chair.

"All right, forward."

With Soter at his heel, and the rope and the lantern on his other arm, Brassard used the barrel of the junkman's gun to prod Michaud back through the wicket door and out into the more labyrinthine passages of the catacomb. No part of him relished what he was doing, or was about to do, but he did not resent it either. Some mysterious confederacy of forces, well beyond his power to control, had conspired to bring him here—to play this round of turnabout. Best, in that regard, to treat the coming exchange as a test, not a surrender, to see how he faired in the role of captor and inquisitor.

The coffee sack seemed to be taking the desired, pacifying effect. Michaud went meekly over the rise, down into the marsh again, stumbling here and there, but otherwise offering no sense that he was contemplating a run or anything so daring. Only once did he ask where they were going, to which Brassard replied, *de rigueur*, with a firm gun poke to the high spine. He kept his eye out for the young woman, of course. Soter did the same in his way, sniffing all the while but signaling nothing. No one here but the dead.

At length, then—and by the crooked inward spiral dug some eight hundred years before—they came to the same little room Brassard had found the prior night, the skull-and-bones crypt with the baptismal column at the center.

"Sit."

Michaud blindly set the chair down in front of him and took the seat.

Brassard proceeded then to bind Michaud to it, first using the rope. He tried to be firm, as Quan had been—more businesslike than abusive, but by that token maybe the more dangerous. He shifted the chair to face the wall of bones, while Michaud continued to accept his handling with a kind of lissome resignation—not so unlike his own back-when, accepting that this was the sort of treatment one might have expected to receive, based upon what one had been doing. Fulfillment of the scripture.

When the prisoner was secure, Brassard cut loose a final six-foot length of rope and positioned himself directly behind—just as Quan had done—but still careful to keep the scarf over his face. He removed the prisoner's hood and allowed a moment for his eyes to adjust, to take in the dimensions and the design of his situation. Those globular rows diagonally dividing the herringbone columns of human vertebrae? Zippered skull tops.

"So, where is she?"

"I 'on't know."

Brassard chucked the back of his head—a quick, two-finger strike where the occipital bone met the meat of the neck.

"When did you last see her?"

Michaud shook his head vaguely. "The café? Las' night."

"At the café or the hotel?"

"Not the hotel, no."

"Did you speak to her?"

"I don't even know who she is!"

Brassard chucked his neck again. "Did you kill her?"

"No!"

"Why did you come for the wagon last night?"

Michaud squinted. He was having trouble speaking, but he was clearly confused by how much Brassard knew. "It was hers. Who are you?"

"So you wanted to give it *back* to her. Why, because you liked her? And is this why you smashed in the junkman's skull? Romeo-Romeo?"

"Who *are* you—"

"Did you kidnap her?"

"No!"

"Then why are you sending pictures to the countess?"

"Look, I don't know who you are. I don't know what you fink you know. You can 'it me, tie me up, it don' matter . . . I don't have anyfing! Shoot me in the head—"

"I'm sorry, is this you confessing?"

"No, i'z me telling you . . . Do what you want! I don't care. I zhit you."

"You *shit* me?"

"Yes. I zhit all of you. Fugh you!"

This last bit did kindle another flare of affection in Brassard—and pity—but he kept his focus. Abruptly he took the chair from behind and jerked it back flush against the column at the center of the crypt. He took the chain and started wrapping it around Michaud and the pillar

"What are you doing?"

"You need some time to think." Brassard snaked the chain through the rungs.

"You're leaving?"

"I thought you said you didn't care."

"When are you coming back?"

"Well, that depends." He gave the chain a yank from behind. Michaud grunted. "Everyone agrees that what causes a body to rise from the bottom of . . . well, a river, say . . . is gas, yes?" He reached into his pocket for the padlock. ". . . As the flesh decays, the bacteria give off fumes. The fumes inflate the body like a balloon, and this is what makes it float up to the surface for the children to find." He hooked the finger of the padlock through two links and jammed it shut with a loud *clap!* "The dispute is over what sort of a body will rise the quickest." He retrieved the final length of manila rope. "Some say it's the little ones—you know, the most petite and delicate—for obvious reasons: The less weight the gas has to lift, the more quickly it will do so." He now extended the rope between his two fists, reached over Michaud's head, and yanked it into his mouth like a horse's bit. Michaud reeled in pain.

"There are others, though, who point out that what the bacteria like to feed on *most of all* is fat." Brassard pulled tight to tie the two ends on the far side of the pillar. "More fat, more fumes. So according to *them*, it's the big boys that rise the quickest. You know, the really obese ones . . ."

Knot firmly tied, Brassard leaned over and spoke directly into his ear:

"I'll let you know as soon as we have a winner. Sleep tight."

Then he took the only light, his lantern, and snapped for Soter to come, leaving his prisoner there alone in the blackest black imaginable.

Chapter 20

La Bijouterie

Trésors du Temps was on the Rue Charlot, as it turned out, not the Rue Temple, but they were only a block apart, and only about ten blocks northeast of the city island, in the Third Arrondissement.

As Madame Renée had warned, this was not a posh establishment, and didn't pretend. According to the sign above the door, it had been there for twenty-five years, alongside several more of the "manufacturing" jewelers in town, all of which appeared to be trading more on the city's name than the quality of their merchandise.

There didn't seem to be anyone in when Brassard first entered; Soter chose to stay outside. The main room was cluttered and dim, and absent any clear organizational principle. As Brassard made his way along the first and largest aisle, he passed shelves of figurines standing beside stacked plates standing beside flatware and necklace racks and snuffboxes. The specialty of the house seemed to be estate sales and imitation knock-offs. Statuary as well. In fact, there was an exit in back leading to a small tree-shaded plot, and it was there, just inside the door, that he finally found the proprietor. He was seated at a small work desk surrounded by knee-high garden sculptures—stone cherubs, gnomes, and woodland creatures.

For some reason, Brassard took the man to be the founder's son—perhaps for being so much older in spirit than he was in years. A long-since defeated soul. He was fixing a metal watch strap, and treated Brassard's inquiries with not much interest or patience at the outset, Brassard giving no indication that he was an officer, or a would-be officer. He was a man with a brooch, about which he had some questions.

The jeweler took it and inspected it beneath his lamp, focusing on the painting within the silver frame, of the man and a woman in a garden. The man had a mandolin and was wooing the soft fair maiden with song.

"A wedding brooch," said the proprietor. "Or engagement."

"So something a groom buys for his bride."

"Yes."

"Did you sell it?"

He turned it over to inspect the back.

"... Yes. It would seem." He didn't sound proud.

"And do you keep a ledger of accounts? Bills of sale?"

The man looked at Brassard, dead-eyed. "Yes."

"Would you be able to tell me whom you sold this to?"

The man hesitated again. "May I ask why?"

"I'm an estate broker," said Brassard.

"It's worthless."

"To you."

Very grudgingly, then, and after an extraordinary amount of fastidious rearranging—including collar and cuffs and the kerchief-cleaning and repositioning of his spectacles—the man finally got up and went back to a small office-shed out in the garden plot.

Alone again, Brassard felt his mind drift back in the direction of the cathedral, and the little man he'd chained to a pillar in the catacombs underneath. Probably not his proudest moment, even if the man *was* a murderer, and a kidnapper most likely; at the very least an extortionist. A night alone would probably do him good, though he did make a mental note—Brassard did—to bring some water in the morning. Maybe some bread.

He craned in his chair to see what was taking the clerk so long, and at just that moment a gray cat passed, casually curling its way around a crooked stack of pots, rubbing its ears and forehead against the lily-pad plate, then padding past a shelf of figurines, tail aloft as if to show: There among the porcelain shepherds, mermaids, and varnished blackamoors sat a little Buddha. Bronze, not stone, and only the size of a hand, but sitting in the manner of Quan's—cross-legged, eyes closed, medicine jar in its lap.

As much as he loathed Larive, that question he'd posed during the Tribunal—about why, if his captors had wanted nothing from him, they'd seen fit to treat him as they did—probably deserved a better answer than the one he gave.

The final day in Panhou—before Brassard had been told anything, but long after the terms of the exchange had presumably been arranged—Quan had brought him a bowl of rice. He had to unbind him, but he didn't remove his blindfold. That and hunger combined to lend the experience an unusual acuity, and poignancy. There were shavings of coconut, imagine, and vinegar in the rice. Even a thin slice of mango. In short, it was as simple and exquisite an eating experience as Emile Brassard had ever known, made even sweeter—and more bitter—by the near certainty that it should be his last. He'd had no doubt about this. He could hear Quan out in the passage, in his usual place beside the chiseled Buddha, crouched in the way the farmers there are able, with their shoulders tucked between their knees, cracking seeds and eating them from a pile he'd scattered between his feet. Waiting.

As soon the bowl was empty, he heard Quan rise and pad back in. He'd brought the block with him, and the ropes, and he bound him once again. Quan's arms were short, and soft and very nearly hairless, but his hands—which often smelled of green onions—were powerful and shaped like two crabs. He'd muttered something as he tied the ropes. Brassard had no idea what it was, but when he heard the boot knife slide from Quan's belt, he felt he understood.

He had not. Quan took his ear instead. The very last day.

But now the proprietor was back. He was wearing dark green arm sleeves and bearing two ledgers that looked to be roughly the shape and the weight of Moses' tablets.

He resumed his seat and made another sweeping show of opening the first, tilting the shade of his lamp. He ran his index finger down the line, his lips very gently sounding the names. "Limoges," they pooched, and "*Non . . . non . . . non.*" Brassard could see, not only were the purchasers all list-ed, but their provenances as well, in parentheses. The man turned the page; the sleeves glided: "*Non, non, non, , ah.*" He seemed to have found one. Or two.

"Well . . . it would either be to a Madame Leland or . . ." He turned the page and squinted, finally relocating the line. ". . . a Monsieur Dupree."

"—who lived in Fontainbleau?" asked Brassard.

"Lived?" The jeweler looked up at Brassard over his spec-tacles. He didn't make the connection at first, but then he recollected—"Oh"—as if he'd felt a twinge in his side, only to remember the pain was not his own. He subdued a mo-ment of titillation—the nasty little tickle that follows from the recognition of someone *else's* grave misfortune—and then more properly sobered. ". . . Oh."

Chapter 21

The Kliegs

Tonight was the last night of the Expo. The Paris Opera, in its temporary home at the Grand Hall, played its fiftieth and final performance of *Esclarmonde*, which Massenet had written for the fair. As had happened during the previous forty-nine performances, the third section of the overture was briefly interrupted by the distant boom, boom, *boom* of the cannon at the top of the tower, though by now the audience seemed fairly used to it. They hardly murmured, and the orchestra didn't miss a beat. The countess, attending alone, did not seem to hear at all.

Outside, the blasts were harder to ignore, if only because of how they seemed to spark the swooping lights again, as they had every night of the celebration. The kliegs at the top of the tower launched their narrow beams out into infinity or whatever came between, scissoring high, sweeping low, and revealing the fact that much of the Exposition had already been taken down. Most of the kiosks were gone, as was the photo booth, and the locomotive. What was left was being dismantled even now, piece by piece. The paintings that had been hanging in the western hall were leaning against one another, ready to be picked up and taken back to their various galleries and homes and academies. And the jewels as well, and all the machines from the Hall of Machines were returning to their makers: the clocks, the watches and phonographs, and the latest telegraph machines were safely in their crates, stacked in the back of carts and truck beds, some of which were already trundling out beneath the arches of the tower, which didn't seem to be going anywhere; Chavarin was right about that.

The klieg lights followed them across the bridge, then wheeled around and found the natives, also awaiting their removal. The Arabs and American Indians huddled under blankets while their tents were being taken down, folded up, the poles all stacked and bound. The various boulders and bushes and pillows and trunks were trolleyed off. The Pygmies played chess and smoked cigars, barely lifting their eyes as the lights swooped out into the esplanade, flicking across trees and pathways, then back along the river from bridge to bridge. They seemed to be looking for something, or someone—peering down the streets and into alleys, checking the catwalks, prodding the low-slung clouds. After all, who knew where she might be by now?

They found the gypsy wagon, standing on its cask beside the streetlamp, but dark inside.

They found the rag-and-bone man, walking the black donkey to the factory, prepared to sell. Any price.

They found the streetwalkers and the street performers and carousing bands of youths, and bands of rats as well. They found the can-can girls on the Boulevard du Crime, sent outside to drum up business. They found the Baron there—von Dorn—sampling tobaccos while he waited for another introduction. And Montesquiou at the stall of another outdoor bazaar a mile or so away, selecting the costume for his upcoming tableau, a waistcoat for his dear friend "Portia," who, like her namesake, liked to dress as a man.

They even found the former sous-lieutenant Brassard, finagling his way back inside the headquarters. He was using the envelope Bonheur had given him, explaining to the sentry at the door that he had to deliver a letter.

The white light blinkered by, unamused. The red light

followed. The search must go on. They didn't have much time, after all. Frantically they found Monsieur Singh sitting at one of the outside tables at the Café de la Paix. He was not so frantic, drinking his Darjeeling tea and thinking. He had been stationed there in case the mademoiselle might return. After all, she had left the dress behind. Who knew what else she might have stashed, or planted? They were attributing her every possible motive at this point, and role—from conspirator to victim to madwoman. If Monsieur Singh harbored an opinion on the matter—which he did—he kept it between himself and his teacup. But he did not expect that she would be returning to the hotel this evening. The only reason would have been to return the tortoiseshell scissors to the letter desk; she had taken these as well.

The kliegs flashed on by and separated, none the wiser. One found the rag-and-bone man again, trudging with his donkey friend to the paper shop now.

The other, the red, found Brassard emerging from the barracks, file in hand. How he'd gotten it, the light could not imagine. Another crafty lie. It flashed right by, headed west, and found the boy, Olivier—or his feet at any rate—poking out from the hollow of the belly of the horse at the Trocadéro gardens, the Greek soldier's steed. Olivier was not thinking about the lady in the white dress. He was thinking about the baby in the zoo, and what was to become of it if it never got to come and breathe the air? Would it have to go back? And go back where? Or would it just disappear inside the mother as if it had never been?

No answer from the kliegs. They'd long since stilted on by, still searching and still not finding. Not among the spires or the stained-glass windows. Not on the Ferris wheel or down along the river, though the water itself was giving nothing away. It just kept flowing and swelling, its endless undulations making daggers of the moon's reflection. Was that where she was hiding then? Perhaps she was too deep to see. Perhaps it was too dark down there. Again, who knew?

So finally, after all of that, the kliegs gave up, convinced that they could shed no further light. They left the further investigation to the three men.

§

To Chavarin first, who couldn't help himself. Even from the comfort of his box inside the Folies Nouvelles, he looked. When the faux marble slab took its place—center stage, for the forest number—he observed the body beneath the drape. While all the dancers preened and posed around it, he narrowed his eyes and he hoped. Maybe this had been a kind of magic trick. He held his breath while Mademoiselle Eschette descended on her wires to remove the linen cover—this was her role, as forest fairy, and she played it most suspensefully. As slowly as she could, she slid the linen down past the hairline (which was blond), and past the brow (which was similarly broad). Chavarin leaned forward in his seat to see the eyes, and see that no . . . no, he didn't know this woman. This was someone new, and he felt a strange rebuke for having hoped. He sat back in his seat, and he consoled himself with the thought that one can only do so much.

Some people just refuse to be helped.

Indeed, he looked to Mademoiselle Eschette, then, as she was looking up at him. He saw that she had seen all this—his momentary hope, his disappointment, his consolation—and the most beautiful woman in all the world smiled cunningly at him. With her eyes, she burned a hole right through the fourth wall, and he thought to himself, *Yes, and there are the other people, too, who help themselves . . .*

§

Michaud searched as well, such as he was able. He had a rough night of it, in fact—bound, gagged, and chained to the pillar in the crypt. For a time, this had seemed like just the thing—relieving his body from all responsibility to support itself. The masked man had done a nice snug job of it.

But then the spasms came, and the itches and the aches, the creep of infection, and shooting pains—in his back and down his leg. His shoulder, the nape of his neck felt like a tightening knot. He howled in pain (around the deeply dug-in gag), he raked his throat, but all the wailing and raging only chafed the corners of his mouth until they, too, were raw and bleeding, and visited him with such pounding headaches, he entered into delirium, which was probably just as well.

He heard things first. For an abandoned tomb, the ruins seemed to be awfully alive and busy, between the drips, the shifts, the scampering rats, the human footsteps—how many different footsteps did he hear? Near and far. He tried calling out, but they'd just go silent, wait, and then return, furtive ghosts. He heard the skulls in front of him turning slowly; the bones settle; the bones crack.

He wasn't measuring time very well. He believed at certain points that he was surely dead already and that duration was a thing of the past—or behind him. But there was a certain pair—of feet, that is—a lighter and more padding pair that had been making their way around the spiral, little by little, growing more and more clear as the passage wound them nearer. He moaned to these more quietly. These feet knew him.

At length he could sense that they were right behind him, in fact, and he could feel her there, looking at him, and he whimpered—pathetically, gratefully, pleadingly. He heard the shift of her dress, and he could not imagine how she'd found him. He didn't remember bringing her down here, yet he could feel her warmth. She was standing right beside him. She was wearing the white frock, and he could see it and he could see the faces of the skulls reflected in her light. They were looking out now, she'd brought them all to life. She'd given them flesh and eyes to see with, so they could watch while she released him. And some were from Rome, and some had been slaves, but some he knew. Teachers. A few of them weren't even dead. Gérôme? Gérôme wasn't dead, the bastard. Was he? She took a key from under Gérôme's tongue—the shit—and he was quite compliant actually, like an altar boy. She wiped the key dry on his hair, and Michaud was weeping, looking at her, because he wanted to tell her he'd killed a man! He'd bashed his head in for her! That man right there, in fact, beside Gérôme. The big one there, scowling at them with the jowls and the hair and the dent in his head. *I put that there!*

She understood. She moved behind him and unlocked the chain, while Michaud spoke to her, or tried to speak to her, and she forgave him silently. She seemed to anyway. He turned and already she was going. *Where?* Back into the shadows. She withdrew again, but he was free to follow her now, and free of pain. He got down on his knees and crawled in after her, into the black spiral and deeper in and through and out again onto the shushing sand and the little shack on the bank of grass, and the palm trees whispering overhead, and the beautiful blue ocean lapping, lapping, lapping at their feet, erasing each day's drawing with the tide . . .

Chapter 22

The Wagon

And finally there was Brassard.

Over by Le Montyon, long after the kliegs had given up, the gypsy wagon was still standing across the street on its peg leg. A very good dog was sleeping on the driver's seat, though there was a light on inside. This was Brassard in his little carrel for the night—the wagon being the one place he was fairly sure no one would come, unless it was she, in which case good.

He knelt on one knee with the junkman's revolver beside him, and the contents of the Dupree file splayed across the floor: press clippings, some photographs, and a police report, timelines, affidavits, and depositions. As he scanned them one to the next, reading, squinting, studying, all the dots began to connect; or to use the language of his hidden prisoner, Michaud, the sketch he had been drawing in his mind for the last three days began to deepen into a darker study. A chiaroscuro.

The initial surmise—still very much in place—had been that the young woman was responsible for the remains of the body in the woods, and had tried to bury them, but that the afternoon shower and the nosy wolves had foiled her effort, that effort having taken place a few hours before he and Soter arrived on the scene, or however long as it takes a heavy rain to fall, and the wolves to crawl out from their dens, or a donkey to haul a gypsy wagon five or so miles? And break a wheel? And stop for tea? However long that takes. The sequence was the important thing, and the sequence was not in doubt.

The questions he had been trying to answer ever since: Why she had done this? Where she was headed? And what did that have to do with the safe she was bearing in the belly of the wagon?

Truth be told, now that he was closing in on answers, he felt as if he'd known. From the moment he'd laid eyes on her, in fact, there had been a little voice inside his head telling him just exactly who she was, only a certain amount of training, a certain *kind* of integrity—as well as a certain kind of treachery—had all conspired to ensure that this voice should not be listened to until there was some evidence to substantiate it.

Here now was that evidence, the chintziest piece of which was riding high upon the breast of the otherwise dour, dead-eyed woman in the tintype photograph, Madame Dupree. This was where he had seen the brooch: in the famous family photo. The brooch in the safe had been hers. The cutlery, then, had been theirs as well. And the candlesticks.

The Duprees of Fountainbleau, whose names were known because the case was known, had received much press when the crime had first occurred, right around the time Brassard was coming under scrutiny for the work he'd been doing with the Revanchists in Champagne-Ardenne. He had been several districts away, but was aware of the case thanks to all the press and intradepartmental bulletins, not to mention the specious hay made by certain special interests in the wine-making industry.

Dupree was a tenant farmer who lived in Fountainbleau, a commune to the south of Paris. He oversaw grape vineyards. Not a rich man. Not poor. Not a particularly significant man until the bodies of his wife and two daughters were discovered, brutally slaughtered in the large stone farmhouse where they lived, a half mile from the fields where he worked.

There were no witnesses, but the consensus was that Monsieur Dupree had been the perpetrator, a theory lent substance by widespread testimony to the effect that he had been a hopeless drunk given to sporadic and increasingly frequent bouts of violence. There was also talk that he saw demons in livestock and spoke in tongues, as did his wife, who was of Bohemian descent and apparently an active member of a Moravian Church known more colloquially as "the hidden seed," which may or may not have been relevant.

The last anyone had seen Monsieur Dupree was at a bistro in the neighboring village of Samoreau. According to patrons, Monsieur Dupree had gotten quite drunk (as usual), started complaining loudly about the mud on his boots (less usual), and staggered out to his horse at around 3 P.M. It wasn't until two days later that his wife was found dead in her bed from a shotgun blast to the face. The older daughter, who was seven, was found in the doorway of her bedroom, likewise shot in the chest. The body of his two-year-old daughter, also the victim of a shotgun blast, was for some reason out in the unweeded garden, the evidence indicating that the assailant had dragged her there *after* shooting her; no one was sure why.

And there was one more victim as well, in the womb of his wife, who was apparently near full term.

Much horror, then. Much shock, amplified (and eventually diluted) by a very zealous, vintner-subsidized temperance organization called the League for the Suppression of Absinthe in France, which seized upon the incident as exhibit A in the case they had been making for several years now against the green fairy (*la fée verte*). It was the LSAF, in fact, whose own independent investigation had revealed that on the day of the murders, which occurred some time in the late afternoon, Monsieur Dupree consumed seven glasses of wine at breakfast, six glasses of cognac in the field, one brandy-and-coffee and two *crèmes de menthes* for lunch, and finally two glasses of absinthe on his way home, at the aforementioned local bistro.

It was these last two tilts, of course, that had been decisive in what happened next, at least according to the LSAF. The League saw to it that the photographs of the crime scene were widely circulated: a stone farmhouse in the French countryside, the tintype of the family (the father and his victims), as well as several shots of the scene itself, tastefully framed by splattered doorways and partition walls—enough to show Mrs. Dupree's leg, awkwardly bent, the blood on the daughter's bedsheets and on the wall. These images were, for a brief time, famous, none more poignant or upsetting than the little patch of garden where the younger daughter had been left, a black clump by the fencepost; the little duck-bill shape must have been the toes of a shoe.

But these images had been tasteful by comparison to the others that Brassard was now seeing for the first time. The mother in the master bed. The older daughter's chest. These conveyed a much starker and more graphic picture of Monsieur Dupree's malice and derangement, but really only reaffirmed what was (thanks to the LSAF) the general understanding of the case—that a lone man's fury-unto-madness had found a bottle and a gun, that he'd used the latter to blast his universe to shreds and crawl out through one of the holes.

There had been a brief manhunt. Dupree's picture was still tacked up on dozens of tavern and posthouse walls throughout the countryside—not a bad-looking fellow really, maybe a bit contemptuous for seeming so pleasant. But time being time and memory memory, all of these images had drifted from the public consciousness in their failure to be resolved. Dupree became a reason not to drink (and to outlaw absinthe in particular!), a reason to bolt the doors at night and scrub behind the ears and come home straight from school. The hope was that he'd simply disappeared, gone to Timbuktu, or maybe done himself in. That's what happened most often in cases like these. The coward's end. If he brought a gun with him—or a rope—this was almost certainly what happened . . .

So what new light was shed this evening—by the lamp in the wagon here, and by the events of the last few days? The discovery of the cache, to be sure, directly linking the wagon to the Duprees. There was that. Which didn't necessarily mean the wagon *belonged* to Dupree, or even that the body in the woods had been his. The driver could well have been an itinerant, another thief, a field worker. There was no end to the alternate possibilities one could conceive, but the simplest scenario—and therefore most likely—was that Dupree had commandeered the wagon somehow and had been living on the lam for the last year or so, on stolen chickens, hunted squirrels, rabbits, grasses, and the dwindling reserve of a modest estate locked away in that little cast-iron safe.

That, by this reckoning, had been the plan up until several days ago, which introduced the question of the young woman and how she'd been snared into this unspeakable nightmare. Again, one could imagine myriad scenarios—wherein she had been picked up along the way, seduced, nabbed by the creek side while gathering cresses.

However, there was one small detail that had rankled Brassard from the very beginning, going back to when the murders were first made public. Police reports had indicated there was no help in the home—no servants—which made sense. The Duprees were not a family of means, and were apparently "insular." However, Madame Dupree had been profoundly pregnant at the time of her death—perhaps even bedridden, which may have partially explained Dupree's anger about the condition of his boots.

Furthermore, in one of the famously published photographs of the daughter's bedroom, there could be seen the rounded end of what looked like a slat of some kind, or a bracket, just creeping in the left side of the frame. In fact, it was the armrest of a low stool; the leg was nudging in as well. A very strange shape which one would only recognize if one knew: that was a birthing stool. Brassard knew the style. His aunt had been a midwife in Amiens.

And of course it was entirely possible that the Duprees had a birthing stool of their own—with two children already—but there was something about its presence there, just peeking in the frame. It was like a sign almost, that there *had* to have been a midwife, no? If Madame Dupree was that close to delivery (and if Monsieur was out drinking himself blind in the fields all day)? And *if* there was a midwife, then most likely she'd have been living on premise, wouldn't she? That is, if the extra bed in the nursery meant anything. And if *that* were the case—if there'd been a midwife in the home— where were *her* remains? Or if somehow she'd been spared, why had she not come forward to share her story?

Why did no one ever speak of the midwife?

Again, such questions were the stuff of instinct, notions— though what is instinct, but a notion that turns out to be true? No matter, Brassard knew as he knelt there, the same voice that had whispered in his ear on the road three days ago—*She has come from the burial site. Look at the hands, look at the nails—* that voice had been speaking to him from a much more remote place. *She is the midwife.* Maybe not as clear as that, maybe too far away to hear—but the voice was speaking to him loud and clear in the wagon now. *She is. She was.* There was no doubt in his mind. And he knew this not because of any photograph, or note, or some stray pronoun in a neighbor's deposition. He knew because of the space that he was kneeling in. He could feel it in the fetidness of the air. This was where she had been his captive. Here. The evil around him was like a cloud, like a stench. She wasn't the driven snow, eh? Brassard knew why, and what the chain was for—to keep her in the rolling dungeon, another little torture chamber. Not only was there method to the man's madness. There was sentiment.

Soter began to moan outside, even in his sleep. Brassard let him stay. Better off.

He lay down on the palette shelf, not to rest; he couldn't rest, the specters were too close. He lay down there to let them in, to harden himself, and to punish himself, too, because he was angry. He knew. Wherever she was right now, that was his doing as much as anyone's—for not having intervened at the roadside, for foolishly having followed the wagon instead of her, for letting her fall into the hands of those two miscreants, Michaud and Chavarin. They may not have been as bad as Dupree, but they were still dangerous. Few things more dangerous than a man trying to prove himself.

And that went for him, too, yes?

The lamp was dying now, for want of oil, and he could feel his mind was running down as well, and beginning to swarm. He tried to stop it. He could have gone across the street, he supposed—see if "Odette" was about—except he couldn't move. He looked up at the ceiling just as she must have, at those three indifferent beams. Or were they smiling upside down? And at that crack in the paint, the soot stain there that looked like . . . Sicily. What must that have come from? Smoke? And those holes for the nails. Four. And five more over there.

Nothing helpful. Nothing revelatory. Just the grim horror of what had taken place here. His captivity? Monastic by comparison. He could smell it in the wood, hear it in the groan—the way the room shifted and swayed on its wheels. Dupree's rocking cradle.

There was just the one piece he still couldn't fit.

Her face. He had lost it for most of the day; it had become more of an idea than an image, but he could see it now as clear as if she were there in front of him, right down to the lashes, or the little pockmark riding high on her right cheek, that whisper of a smile. The image filled him with a strange kind of dread, and not just because it was so incongruous with the rest of the story he was uncovering, but because—again—he felt like he'd seen it somewhere before. She was not new to him—

And now a final flicker and a hiss and the light was gone completely. The face bloomed white before his eyes, then faded like smoke as the room flooded with darkness, all but for the pale slivers the streetlamps could slip in through the slats that boarded the windows. And with the sudden gloom, a second wave of exhaustion washed over him, and a wooziness as all the clippings and words and images seemed to be lifting from the floor, with no more light to pin them down. Up they came, to hover and spin and float into his brain, tumbling in for the night, to find new beds and rearrange.

And he knew he shouldn't even try to stop them, that they'd be back in place come morning, digested, clarified. That's how these things usually worked. But for now, the images just kept swirling and mingling—the coins and the cards and the flower she'd left behind. And the noises, too—the scratching, digging claws and the hot breath. They'd been at it the whole time, hadn't they? Burrowing closer, sniffing him out—from the moment he'd come in—and whom was it he had been talking to? Or thinking to, ever since he'd opened the folder and laid out the files? Not Monsaingeon. And not Bonheur. Quite. Someone who knew better, someone who would understand, and who could hear the paws as well. And the chain, and the coins ringing

Was it the professor? Samsa? Because yes, he would have understood—another man of hunches. Samsa was the one who had tried to protect her, after all. He had seen her face, and the wagon. He had fixed it! He knew about the Moravians, too, no doubt, and the crypt, because the tower went down underground. That's what someone said, and either way, any engineer would know the tunnels all connect. And Brassard understood he was making no sense at this point. His logic had begun to twist and to conflate, but on some level it was still true, the tunnels *do* connect, which was why he needn't feel so villainous for imprisoning poor Michaud there. Brassard had sat in that same chair—just over on the far side of the world. In Panhou. So he knew the truth, which he could have told them if they'd bothered to ask. He could have told Michaud, except that he already seemed to know.

He'd felt it from the moment they removed his hood. From the moment he saw the cell and realized he probably wouldn't make it out alive, it was as if a valve had been released somewhere inside his brain. He'd sensed it the whole time he was in there, the steady dissipation of a pressure he'd never really noticed before, and the source of which he hadn't fully understood, again, until that final day when Quan stood behind him, took his head in his hand like a coconut and held the knife to his neck. Brassard could still feel the cold breath of the blade against his skin. He'd assumed it would start *down*, of course, slice into his jugular, sweep across his throat like a cello bow. He imagined the geyser and the black shroud descending. Only not quite—or not at all, really—

as that is when the vision came (and not for the first time, mind you. He'd caught glimpses of it going all the way back to his early childhood, just never with such a religious clarity—as befit a final moment, he supposed). It was as if some impossibly well-polished lens had descended before his eyes, through which the whole world surrounding him—as well as everything he'd ever experienced leading up—or really anything that *anyone* had ever experienced . . . or thought . . . or felt . . . anything that could be held in mind in any way—was revealed to be pure figment. From the loftiest prayer, to the grubbiest coins in one's pocket, *all* was smoke. This was suddenly blazingly obvious to him, as was the corollary, hovering to the side like a white-winged seraph (or a grinning guru, as the case may be), that the whole of the glorious experiment here coming to its end—of Emile Brassard's ever having existed—had been an exercise not just in the profoundest vanity imaginable, but breathtaking absurdity as well. A quelled belch.

Yet this wasn't even the dirty little secret. The dirty secret was that in the face of this blackest and most ecclesiastical of revelations, he had felt so calm. A queer kind of ecstasy had set in. Even as Quan's blade sank in and started on its *upward* path—into and through the cardboard flesh of his left ear— Brassard had nearly laughed. Not for being spared, though, no. More for being allowed to see it finally. The folly. And sensing this—the quiet delight that his prisoner seemed to be taking at his own mutilation—Quan had finally had to yank the ear flap from his head, snap off the last sinew and start striking him with it like a dumpling noodle, again and again as if to say, *Yes, yes! You remember this!* Brassard had simply nodded, yes, of course he would, and thank you! (And no, these really weren't the sorts of secrets that one shared—not with one's superiors, at any rate—but he couldn't help it. *She* understood at least. She'd been there the whole time watching, no?...

...No?)

Oh, like a swallow it dove. Like a swallow at twilight it darted down to pluck the dragonfly from the surface of the pond. So comes the truth, and we are gaping carp beneath the surface.

In Panhou? She...?

A second time, the swallow swooped. "Yes! Yes, that's *exactly* where you saw her! Don't you remember?"

But now it was gone again, so swiftly that a moment later, not only did he not know why she looked so familiar to him, he couldn't remember *anything* about what he'd just been thinking—his ear, or Quan, or the unexpected buoy of all-pointlessness. Gone, swept away on a stiff and purposeful wind, a brick wall erected in its place.

It would come back, though. One must trust. Stay still, don't chase. Stay in the boat. Let it float. Stay in the wagon. Stay in the chair, because yes, he'd sat in that chair, too. A world away, and then again today. And had he not lied again? His father was cold. A bitter man. His father used to call him "his mother's son"—in front of others—and he wasn't being kind. He called her "the Jewess." That was the reason Brassard hadn't cried at the funeral. He wasn't being brave. His father was empty. A vicious, self-deluding—

And there it was again, the swallow, swooping through...

...Damn. And gone. Worse than gone, fleeing-flying away, and this was the problem. The revelations go and hide behind the gibberish, the false epiphanies, and then they disappear. And it was all well and good to think that the sunrise would bring them back, that the nonsense would just dissolve in the daylight, but maybe it was the other way around—

(She was nodding, yes. She *had* been there.)

—Maybe all of this, these clippings, this mess, was just another distraction like the tower, a misdirection, and maybe the swallow *was* gone forever. Whatever he'd just remembered, he would forget; he had already, and maybe *that* was how it worked. Maybe all we do is keep forgetting what's true, and remembering what's false, and that's the reason we keep having to wake up—yes?

(And she was nodding very clearly from her niche now, *yes! Good.* And look, she even had the jar in her lap! Look!)

. . . Maybe so. Maybe we prefer the tunnel in the end. We prefer the catacombs, and calling for our dogs to come save us. Because he could *still* hear them, the wolves—they hadn't let up for a moment, clawing and digging through the mud. They'd smelled him, all right, and all he could do was huddle and pray and hope that Soter would come to pull him out from behind, because they were right outside the casket now, clawing to get in, to gnash their teeth into his neck and belly; devour him, digest him and scatter him across the forest floor, just to mark their territory . . .

Part Six

Friday

Chapter 23

"Peg"

The exact time isn't known, since no one was there to see, but at some point early the following morning, down along the river and not far from the southernmost arch of the Pont Royal, the glassy surface of the water was disrupted by a sudden effervescence, a seismic furrowing that gave rise first to a series of little bubbles—*pop, pop, pop*—which served as a kind of misting drumroll to a much larger and more flatulent pair: *pop, PLOP!*

The water curdled and whirled a bit more, then settled.

§

As was custom, Monsieur Singh was notified first thing in the morning, by messenger, that Monsieur Chavarin had spent the night at the hotel. This gave him time to cab on over and see to his master's breakfast, which it was understood he should deliver in person, the more easily to review the day's agenda.

A pot of coffee. Two newspapers usually—*Le Monde* and *Le Petit Journal* today. A bowl of seasonal fruit—berries. Tartines. A poached egg, in shell. It was the number of eggs and number of coffee cups that served notice why he'd spent the night. Or not always eggs. Mademoiselle Corbin, last year's most beautiful woman, craved sardine sandwiches for breakfast. The year's before that? Kipper and tomato.

Nothing so telltale today, other than the second cup and

saucer. Singh could sense upon entering the suite, however, that the guest was still on premise—a moving shadow in the bedroom. Chavarin came out to greet him, freshly bathed and scrubbed. His shoulders and back were pink and scalded from the brush, and his mood was bright, as usual. He clapped his hands when he saw the food.

"Come in, come in!" He stole a berry from his own bowl, took up *Le Monde* first, and put up his feet. The front page featured articles about the closing of the Expo, of course, and the further fall of Boulanger and the Revanchists.

"So they're indicting him, eh?"

"Yes, monsieur."

He tsk'd twice. "I still don't understand the 'conspiracy' part."

"And treason, monsieur."

"Well, *that* I understand." He turned the page. "And by the way, I need you to deliver that."

There was an envelope on the mantel.

"To whom?" asked Monsieur Singh.

"The gentleman we met yesterday. The detective. What time did we say?"

"Five o'clock, monsieur. At the Trocadéro."

"Yes, would you?"

He glanced over to meet the valet's eye, and so to confirm: He himself would not be attending.

"Of course, monsieur. Your shoes, monsieur?"

"—are in the bedroom, yes. Sorry about that. And you can take that in as well." He indicated the *Journal*. The cover featured a cartoon of Boulanger in a prison suit.

Singh could see through the sliding door, which was half open on one side, that the bed was unmade but empty. He tucked the *Journal* beneath his arm, poured a cup of coffee, and brought it on its saucer, his eyes on the floor.

The shoes were by the bed.

"Bring it here."

The commanding voice of the countess. She was standing at the window, looking out upon the morning traffic through the narrowly parted curtains.

"Yes, Madame la Comtesse. Did you want your breakfast in here?"

"Please." She didn't turn, but by the sifted, partial light it could be seen that she was still wearing the harness beneath her robe, from the crux of which protruded the eight-inch ebony phallus, affectionately known by both the monsieur and the countess (whose Christian name, it bears reminding, was Marguerite) as "Peg."

Chapter 24

Sausages and Squab

When sleep finally did come for Brassard, it came drastically, like the blackest cloak imaginable, smothering and smuggling him away to an almost deathly place, well beyond the reach of dreams. Or wolves. It was mid-morning by the time the blade of light that carved its way between the shutter and its frame finally glided across his eye. Also Soter had been scratching at the door. Time to walk. Time to eat.

The dog was right. Once he'd gotten some bread and coffee in his stomach, Brassard started them for the river just in case, with the clear intention of checking on Michaud next. He remembered to bring bread. And water as well, in his canteen.

It occurred to him that he should also probably begin taking inventory of what he could and could not disclose in the event that his investigation should go public, as seemed to be an increasing likelihood. He used the walk to piece together as unoffending an account as he was able. In sequence: He had come across a body in the woods (true); he had reported it (true); saw the young woman on the road, which he found suspicious for reasons *x*, *y*, and *z* (all true); saw the wagon again in Paris (true); saw that it was abandoned (somewhat true) . . . but here came the tricky part. He didn't particularly want it known that he'd been crawling around the sewers and catacombs, lest it be taken as more of the same rogue behavior for which he had been suspended. But it was important that they know about the brooch and the connection to the

Duprees. He wasn't quite sure how to square all that.

He and Soter had reached the river now. Brassard was about to turn them east along the bank when he saw the small flotilla over on the far side—a police boat, a little barge, and another fishing boat poking its nose in. There were officers as well, standing in a circle on the bank.

And of course, he had predicted this—that a corpse, or maybe two, would soon appear, coughed up by the river. Still, a wave of nausea shot through him, because his first thought was that this was she. He was too late. He had failed.

His mind flashed with anger—first at the artist, then himself. He started across the bridge, moving swiftly though the traffic, but the gathering on the far bank was clustered so close around the body, he couldn't see—just that someone had brought a coal cart down. He shifted to the rail, but the buttresses kept getting in the way, and more officers. One stood back to remove his hat, and for just a moment Brassard could see inside the circle—the arm there, and the hand, the five little sausages. A stranger actually said the word "junkman," and Brassard stopped. He set his hands on his knees just to breathe, and a moment later the thumping in his chest resumed its normal, less recriminative beat. Soter sat.

"... Monsieur Brassard?"

The reprieve was short-lived. Of all people, it was Lieutenant Colonel Duroq—head of the Paris bureau, and the least barbed of the assessors yesterday. Brassard straightened, tilted, and straightened again.

"General. Good morning."

"Are you all right? You don't look well."

"I may be coming down with something." He wiped his brow, which did feel clammy.

"Captain Monsaingeon was looking for you."

"Was he? Is he at the barracks?"

"He was." With some concern, Duroq looked from So-ter to Brassard's beard, his two-days' growth. "He's at the morgue. He wanted you to meet him there."

"The morgue?" Brassard felt another poisonous surge of dread. "What's he doing at the morgue?"

Duroq shook his head, merely the messenger. "You could ask him. He's probably still there." He checked his pock-et watch then gave Brassard another glance up and down. "Is there a reason you look like you've been sleeping in the street?"

"No. As I say, I've been under the weather. Thank you, though." He saluted. "General."

§

The bridge was a fifteen-minute walk from the morgue, which was located just behind the cathedral and therefore not too far from the entrance to the underground. With So-ter keeping pace, Brassard did his best to hurry, half running, but on rubber legs. He was feeling queasy again. Did this mean she'd been found somewhere else? And how did Mon-saingeon know to summon him? Again he was scrambling to carve out some explanation—for his own actions the last few days—but his mind was a blur. Where would he leave off? And how conceal the fact that he'd been keeping a suspect in the ruins beneath their feet? He still had no good idea, even as he and Soter came bustling around the last of the side chapels to the little plaza in front of the morgue.

The captain was just leaving.

"There he is!" The great bristle-brushed grin spread across his face. "You got the message. Good. Where were you? You don't look well."

"Above a revel," said Brassard. "Nowhere I'll stay again."

"You should use the barracks. Could have been arranged."
He gave Brassard's elbow a playful tap. "Well, glad you're here
in any case. Come in." He looked down and saw Soter. "He
should probably stay outside."

Brassard had assumed as much. He showed Soter the
spot where he should wait.

"And you don't find this a hindrance?" Monsaingeon
asked.

"Soter? Heavens, no."

They entered directly to the gallery—the display case
for all the cadavers collected in the previous month or so. A
glance confirmed she wasn't here—yet—but Monsaingeon
was escorting him back into the innards of the building,
through a small amphitheater to a kind of locker room furnished with all the metal drawers in which the bodies were
refrigerated overnight. One of these was already slid open,
and draped.

Monsaingeon said, "You haven't just eaten, I hope."

Brassard shook his head, still bewildered by the captain's
bounce, but his heart dropped when he saw how small the
figure beneath the cover was, or seemed to be. Once again,
the green cloud of nausea wafted from his core.

The captain gave the nod. The attendant brusquely pulled
down the sheet, and what followed—inside Brassard—was
a strange admixture of reactions, starting with revulsion, of
course, the image before him was so primordially disgusting.
But primordially fascinating, too. The smell was not pleasant,
yet the net sum of his feelings was much closer to glee—for
the simple reason that this wasn't she. It was a man—or what
was left of a man. In fact, it was the extremely partial quality of
what was there that let him understand.

"From the woods," he said.

"Yes," Monsaingeon replied, still beaming as if the carcass were his firstborn. "Came in last night, from where you said. Or thereabouts."

They paused to admire. The head was intact, the top part of the face anyway, while most of the flesh below had been stripped by teeth and beak and whatever a maggot uses to eat with. Most of the innards were gone, the spine picked clean, as well as the rib cage right up into the collarbone. It looked like a squab after dinner.

"Won't be putting this one on display, will they?" remarked the captain. "But look at this." He removed a paper from his pocket and unfolded it. Brassard already knew what it was—one of the WANTED posters that had been in circulation the year before. There was the image of Dupree, cropped from the family portrait.

"Add the beard," he said, "and here."

He reached down and actually touched the cadaver's face, what was left of it. He brushed his thumb along the eyebrow, to indicate how the pattern and the length of this man's here matched that of the gentleman in the photograph.

"See it?"

Brassard nodded, as if this were news. "Well, what do you know."

"I know one thing," said Monsaingeon. "You're due a commendation!" He patted him on the opposite shoulder, in a semi-embrace. Brassard could smell his breath; claret with breakfast. "You see? Do what you ought, you get credit for finding the most wanted man in the country."

Brassard gave a humble shrug. "Bit late, but yes." He nodded slowly then, as if the moral applied and would require some digesting. He pointed.

"So the throat, looks like."

"Seems so, but don't you trouble yourself about all that. We've got a team there now, and those woods are crawling.

We'll find who did it. Probably a Gypsy, no? Maybe a Turk. Looks like a Turk's work."

On cue, the lab assistant re-covered the remains, and Monsaingeon let go of Brassard's shoulder with one more sturdy whack.

"So. I just wanted you to see. Are you headed back to the barracks?"

Brassard told him no, he had an appointment, and the captain didn't pry. They parted back outside, Brassard's relief providing a passable likeness for the pride and satisfaction it had been Monsaingeon's purpose to bestow.

Chapter 25
The Little Bull

To the ruins, then.

Brassard left Soter above-ground this time. He wasn't sure why, but he preferred to go alone today, down the narrow column and into the now-familiar reek of wet stone, mildew, and death. Through the maze of tunnels and puddles, he wended his way like Diogenes with lantern, down another landing and into the curious, angular spiral. As before, he had no sense of any unknown presence, or presences. As before, he could feel the shadows trying to have their way with him, invade him with their inhuman spirit.

But he could feel just as surely—and unlike his previous two visits—a kind of a glowing seed in him, of a hope he didn't dare give name, but which was there just the same, and which seemed to be fending off the darkness very well, thank you. Valorously.

When he reached the little crypt, he found Michaud right where they'd left him, chained to the column, tied to his chair, and at the moment, asleep. Brassard held the lantern to his face, and he was almost sorry to awaken him, the captive looked to be in such a preferable place. For all the bruising, the lacerations, and caked blood, the eyelids were peaceful and shining. He looked like a child almost—a murderous, blackmailing, probably syphilitic little innocent, whose body and clothes were still awaft with the stench of rotten meat.

For this reason and others, Brassard once again lifted the

neckerchief up over his nose before leaning down over the captive's shoulder.

He had already determined his play; he was not proud of it—repeating the trick the Seine had just played on him—but it had been quite revealing.

"Are you awake, little one?"

Michaud grunted, shifted, opened his eyes.

"What?" he said.

"Your friend . . . your friend showed up just now. In the river."

Michaud only groaned as the lovely dream dispersed and he began to remember, and re-poison.

"Did you hear?" Brassard leaned round to see his expression, but it was difficult to read with the gag. He dug his finger into Michaud's cheek, down under the rope, and yanked it from his mouth stiffly. It caught on his bottom teeth and tugged his whole head down before coming loose. Michaud gagged and rasped and Brassard remembered his canteen. He held it for him from behind, tilted it into his open mouth.

"Spit it first," he said, and Michaud did, while Brassard untied one of the ropes that had been binding him. Michaud bent and heaved as all the pain rushed back into his brain, and for a moment there he was aware of the two worlds equally: the one from which he'd just been snatched, with the little thatch-roof shack on the beach and the nudes in the shifting palm shade; and the world he'd just been thrust back into—of injuries and dark crypts and human bones. It was the latter, alas, that took precedence, proving itself in a dozen or so knifelike breaths to be quite real and stubborn. Brassard didn't wait.

"Don't you want to know which one?" he asked.

Michaud gasped again and swallowed. "What are you talking about?" His lips were stringing spit as he exercised his jaw.

"Which friend of yours showed up just now. In the river."

Michaud looked around at him, or he tried; the rims of his eyes, within the purple welts, were pink and wide. "I know which one."

"Do you?" came the voice. "Are you sure about that?"

As intended, the question unsettled the artist. His head started to twitch involuntarily, and his eyes began to jerk about, frantic and unseeing. "... What are you saying?"

"What *am* I saying?"

"If he did anything to her . . ."

Brassard offered only a shrug, and Michaud inferred what he would, as his gallantry preferred. His rage awakened him fully. He tried scrambling to his feet, but with his arms and ankles tied to the chair, and the chair bound to the pillar, he fell again and the chair fell with him and twisted him, which enraged him all the more. He tried getting to knees. He tried wriggling free, but he looked more like a turtle on its back than a furious lover.

The display was still convincing, though. Really, it was just a more spastic version of the panic Brassard had felt out on the bridge, when he hadn't known whose body that was below. Did it even matter, he wondered, that such passion was based upon a fiction? Imagine, killing one man out of valor, blackmailing another out of jealousy, and now this, this writhing, wild-eyed conniption on the floor, all because of an hour he'd spent with her at a fair? Was there no court somewhere in the clouds that could compensate a man his misspent fury, his fear, his sorrow? Or was a broken heart a broken heart, however delusional it may be?

"Stop," he finally said.

But Michaud was too riled, cussing and threatening what he would do if he were let go. "I will kill him with my spit!" he spat. "Hire me, whoever you are! I'll do it. I'll beat him with his own—" Again the chair tackled him from behind. He tried smashing it against the column. Brassard was concerned he might succeed and pull the ceiling down on both of them.

"Stop!" he said again. "It wasn't her."

And this did stop him—from fighting at least, though his face remained flushed with rage and pulsing blood, his neck engorged like a bull. A little bull.

"There now," said Brassard. "Calm down. It wasn't her. It was the fat man."

And Michaud did calm down, still on his side, huffing and puffing, feeling his relief exquisitely—she was not dead—only to feel it be replaced by a clearer sense of the situation at hand. It descended like a blanket onto his panting frame: The body of the man whose skull he'd bashed in two nights ago had been found, and an apparent witness to that effect was standing freely behind him.

Brassard let this settle for one more moment, then took the back of Michaud's chair and hoisted him upright. The little bull was breathing more slowly now. The world reoriented.

"So," said Brassard finally, "am I to conclude that you really never met this woman before two nights ago?"

The little bull nodded woozily.

"And she told you nothing about herself—where she was from, where she was going?"

He shook his head. Somehow it hadn't come up. He turned as if he were about to say something. He didn't, but the effort gave Brassard a clear look at his profile. The prisoner had opened his wounds again. He was bleeding from above his eye, down his cheek and jaw. Another scab was hanging loose and wavering featherlike with each exhalation. The only uninjured feature was facing him square, that strangely baroque ornament emerging from the middle—that fleshly, lobely, cartilaged beach-shell, with all its flowing contours and caverns, rendered in an even starker relief by the limited lantern light. Very odd.

He still had questions, though.

"I assume you were going to request money at some point."

Michaud seemed to allow as much. Money would have been nice.

"What was she going to pay you for? The countess, I mean."

Michaud smiled, then winced at his own best laid plans. "*She* wasn't going to pay me. He was."

"What for?"

"To stop." He tilted his head down in the direction of his breast pocket. Brassard dug in over his shoulder and found what felt like a deck of cards. He pulled them out.

It was a small stack of photographs—the *cartes de visite*—of the young woman. He fanned them in his hand, ten or so, and the outline of Michaud's plan revealed itself, such as it was.

"So you just keep sending these until a thousand francs show up in your mailbox?"

"Not the mailbox. But he'd have found a way."

That was true. Bruno Chavarin never met a problem he couldn't settle with cash. And while one would assume the countess had learned to look the other way—when it came to her husband's dalliances—there'd have been something especially disturbing about the thought of him with this woman here. Obscene. And therefore worth keeping under wraps.

"Might've worked," he said.

Michaud nodded, even more slumped in his chair now.

Brassard came around in front of him for the first time,

though he still had on his mask. "Someone will be along to collect you." He showed him the key to the lock, and set it on top of middlemost skull in the wall. Likewise, he held up the photographs. "I'll be taking these." He was about to leave, but paused. "I suppose I could spare you one."

Michaud considered, then nodded, he would appreciate that. Brassard removed the topmost from the stack and tossed it in his lap—a souvenir of his last days as a free man.

He looked at the prisoner's unmolested ear one more time. Was this the part where he lopped it off?

Apparently not. He leaned in close instead.

"But we will not mention her," he said lowly, as if someone else might hear. "Is that understood?"

Michaud offered a second nod, and Brassard made his way.

§

Soter was waiting when Brassard emerged from behind the Hotel Dieu. The dog welcomed him with a questioning look, as if there might be something his master needed to confess. Brassard conceded nothing, and the two of them made straight for the Pont Neuf.

A small police presence was beginning to gather here on the near bank, undoubtedly on its way to unlocking the gate which led to the tunnel which led to the junkman's vault.

Brassard recognized none of the officers, and for reasons previously noted, he still preferred to steer clear of the lagging investigation. He did see one familiar face, though—the *second* ragman, the wandering starets with whom the wagon thief had briefly consulted before descending underground two nights ago. He was sifting through a heap of ashes that had been dumped from a nearby window, and he seemed a bit more lunatic in the daylight, perhaps because his white hair was free of its hood, perhaps because he was talking to himself.

For Brassard's present purposes, this wasn't necessarily a bad thing. He approached in a suitably roundabout and loitering way, finally positioning himself with his back to the same wall, two strides from where the ragman was picking through the remains of a chicken dinner. He proceeded much as if the meeting had been planned.

"So? Did they take him away already?"

The ragman ignored him at first. Brassard tried again.

"The junkman. Did they take him?"

The ragman this time replied with a screw-eyed glance, which Brassard took as his invitation. He slid a half-step closer and lowered his voice. "If I say there might be profit in it, would you answer me one or two questions?"

The ragman wiped a bone on his smock, but he was listening.

"Are you familiar with the tunnels beneath the island, and the various tombs?"

The ragman allowed as much, but did his best to seem indifferent.

"Then do you know of one?" Brassard followed. "Apparently it's very small, round, with a column in the middle. And the walls are all skulls—"

The ragman nodded most assuredly. "The crypt," he said.

"That's the one. Would you know how to find it on your own? If someone were to ask you?"

Here the ragman finally looked at him square, his interest piqued; his self-interest piqued even more. "What for?"

"Well, I can't say too much, obviously." Brassard tilted his head in the direction of the river, the apparent dumping grounds of all the city's villainy. "But just between you and me, there's word the police are already looking for someone. There's also word they'll find him in this . . . 'crypt,' as you call it." He leaned in even closer now. "And I'd wager they'll pay for any help that leads them to their man."

"What, with money?"

"Well, yes. If money was what one wanted."

The ragman pondered this, bagged another bone, but was confused. "So then what's stopping *you* from showing them?"

"Well, I would," said Brassard. "The problem is, I don't know the way."

The ragman paused again, unsure if he was being drafted into some impromptu partnership. He clearly did not like this idea. He also seemed to understand, by instinct, that he enjoyed some advantage here, he just needed a moment to think how he might take it. He drew back, squinting with one eye as if to consider the board between them, then finally chose his move.

"Well, neither do I," he said.

"Really? It seemed like you were fairly clear before."

The ragman stood firm. "Sorry."

Brassard deflated, as though to receive the blow of having been so cleverly outplayed. "Oh, well."

That was all. The ragman, finding nothing more of value among the ashes, and having picked this last exchange of its best bones, moved along to the next heap down, the better to conceal his further intentions.

Brassard made his way as well, uncertain only as to whether he should inform the nearest officer that the wild-haired vagabond over there might have some useful information regarding the death of the junkman. To be safe, he concluded that he should, and presently did, in the apparent spirit of selfless civic duty.

Soter observed all this from the height of his master's knee, and offered no overt objection while the two performances played out, but as the pair of them now headed east toward the tower, he did seem a little disappointed.

"What?" said Brassard. "I'm very hungry."

Chapter 26

"Tathagata"

Their next stop was the Trocadéro gardens, and they would be early, but that was fine. Brassard *was* hungry, notwithstanding the still lingering image of Dupree's carcass. He bought a sausage sandwich from a vendor, and an éclair, and he sat out at one of the blue tile tables—painted with sailboats—with Soter at his feet. He had an espresso as well, and permitted himself, at least for the moment, just to taste, to savor, let the day happen around him. Watch the pigeons coo and seek their alms.

The strange thing was that he felt oddly uplifted by the day's developments—first the discovery of the junkman's body, then the identification of Dupree, which settled the fact that the young woman had been with *him* and not some Gypsy vagrant; had been his captive most likely, at least to judge by the lengths she'd had to go to free herself.

Yet she had. That was the thought that Brassard kept coming back to: She'd gotten away from Dupree. She had gotten away from the professor. She'd gotten away from Michaud. So who was to say she hadn't also slipped through Chavarin's fingers, recognized him as being one more in a long line of men who'd treated her as their own personal chance for redemption. Each had failed. Each had let her get away, and maybe that's what happened here again. One might argue that this was cause for concern as well—it was—the thought that she was out there now somewhere, at large, vulnerable to the needs of some *other* self-justifying man. Still, the coffee tasted sweet for some reason, and he could hear the trees and the river.

He took the letter from his pocket—the one from the director general that he was supposed to sign as condition of his reinstatement. He still couldn't bring himself to read it—too many words—but that was beside the point. The point was to commit regardless of contingencies—to show his good faith—and maybe it was better to do so without her; without pulling some rabbit from a hat.

He took out his pen and unscrewed the top. He let the tip hover above the signature line, let gravity tempt it to the page. Not that he was resisting. This was more like that moment's pause before the kiss; there was a pleasure in the space-between that almost exceeded the touch.

Yet into that sweet interval wedged the thought of Chavarin again—Chavarin's ongoing interest, that is—and whether this required another moment's pause. He hadn't even decided whether he should tell Chavarin about Michaud. Probably not. The greater concern was what Chavarin might tell *him* now. Might he have turned up some lead? Some information? Brassard frankly hoped he hadn't. He was far more at ease with the thought of her on some train somewhere, or in some carriage, looking out the window with that undiscriminating gaze. Just the idea humbled him in a very pleasing way, and deepened his resolve to sign the document beneath his pen. Admit defeat, admit her victory, and let this be his last mistake. Let his signature mark the turning of a new leaf—

"Detective."

And he'd been just about to—commit the tip to paper—when the voice intruded, and he saw the pair of polished two-toned wing-tip shoes standing there beside him.

It was his appointment—or half of it at any rate. Chavarin's valet, the Indian, was tilting down toward him, smiling solicitously in his high collar, his three-quarter coat and lush black hair.

"Oh. Hello." Brassard's tone expressed the pleasantness of his surprise. He preferred the valet, in fact. "Is Monsieur Chavarin not coming?" He offered a seat, but the valet chose to remain standing. He produced yet another envelope.

"Unfortunately, monsieur, no," he said. "He has sent me to deliver this, and to inform you he will no longer be requiring your service."

Brassard hesitated; he wasn't aware he'd offered Chavarin his service.

"Did you find her?"

"No," said the valet, "but Monsieur Chavarin has determined that the young woman is no longer a concern of his. He is aware there was no formal arrangement between the two of you, but he would like you to have this, both as token of his appreciation, and to compensate you for any trouble you might have gone to."

He set the envelope on the table. The going rate for silence presumably.

"We wish you and your employer well," he said. Then he offered a slight bow and turned to make his way.

Now, this had all happened so quickly, and caught Brassard so off-guard, he hadn't known quite how to react.

"Wait," he said, though as yet he wasn't sure what for.

The valet did turn and look at him—patiently, openly, encouragingly even—while Brassard worked to muster up some good question. Had he not just been presented with the clean break he'd wanted? He had, but only if she really was on that carriage, that train, that steamer. And he did not know this, after all.

"But what about you?" he finally asked.

"Monsieur?"

"What about you? Did *you* speak to her at all?"

The Indian clearly hadn't expected this line of inquiry either, but welcomed it. "Only a few words, monsieur."

"Did she say anything that might be helpful?"

"About what, monsieur?"

"About where she might be going. Who might be waiting for her. Or following her. Anything like that?"

The valet pondered this, generously but dubiously. "You said you work for the uncle, monsieur?"

Brassard nodded, he had said that.

The valet smiled, and his eyes seemed to widen. "...I did not speak to his niece."

Brassard would normally have chafed at this—evasion wrapped in sophistry—except that the man's expression was so brimming with glee.

"...What do you mean?" he asked. "Whom did you speak to, then?"

Now the valet turned his eyes away—a modest fraction—as if it would have been too bold, or too intimate, to keep them there for what he was about to say.

"You are familiar with Lord Buddha, monsieur?"

"Of course," said Brassard, though with somewhat more assurance than was warranted.

Monsieur Singh continued: "Lord Buddha said that he who sees only with his eyes, and hears only with his ears, is on a wayward path and will never truly see Tathagata."

"I don't know what this is, 'Tagathata.'"

"Tathagata."

"*Tathagata*. I don't know what this is."

The valet smiled again, and now his eyes re-met Brassard's directly. "But this is who I spoke to!" he said, and they delighted again, so much so Brassard could not help delighting as well, seeing which the valet dipped his head for one clearly final bow.

"Good day, Monsieur le detective."

And away he went, the black flame of hair posed perfectly on his head.

A moment passed before Brassard thought that he should make a note of this word, the long one, but when he looked down, he saw that the tip of his pen was now resting on the director general's letter, and blotting the bottom margin with a franc-sized ink stain.

"Shoot."

Chapter 27

Mon Jésu

He capped his pen and lifted up the page. The black puddle swerved and swirled, and a stream of it spilled over the edge and down onto the table, which was inlayed with blue and white tiles. The black ink used the grouting as canals, but before it reached the edge, Brassard dabbed it with his napkin and began blowing on the page as well—not quite frantically, but the image was still comical enough, the sudden juggling act, that he could see himself—which was when he realized he was being watched. Soter stood up from underneath the table.

It was Olivier this time, whose eye was not on him or his attempt to corral the ink, but rather on his uneaten éclair.

"Oh. Hello." Brassard lay down his page to let it finish drying. "Did you want this? I'm full." This wasn't entirely true, but he'd bought the éclair for the boy, suspecting he'd come around.

The boy nodded and reached for it directly.

"You can have that as well." Brassard indicated the envelope on the table, the one the Indian had given him.

The boy took this and, without looking inside, slid it into the breast pocket of his coat. His hands were filthy.

"Do you want to come?" he asked.

"Where?"

With his éclair, he pointed in the direction of the tower. "Zoo's leaving."

"Who?"

"Zoo people. It's supposed to be happening right now."

Brassard hadn't been all that aware of the zoo, but decided he could use the walk, if only to digest some more. Soter, too, seemed restless, so he folded the director general's letter into its envelope—blotted, dry, but still unsigned—tucked this into *his* inside breast pocket, and the three of them proceeded, Olivier with éclair in hand.

News of the zoo's departure apparently wasn't widespread. The Pont d'Iéna was empty of traffic now that the Expo had closed, and it was turning into a raw evening.

Brassard was trying to collect his thoughts around Chavarin and what was to be made of this sudden withdrawal of interest. The hope was that he had come to a similar conclusion as Brassard, that the young woman might have simply slipped away, and that in the long run this might be best for all parties.

Of course, the likelier implication was that Chavarin had discovered something potentially incriminating and didn't want the matter pursued any further. That pointed the finger at his wife perhaps, the formidable countess. No doubt she had strings she could have pulled if she felt sufficiently provoked. Brassard darkened at the thought, and conceded he should probably pay a visit to the Grand Hotel as well, just to have a look around; and better soon; and better in the evening if he wanted to interview the night staff—

"They say she had the baby, too," said Olivier, apparently having a very different conversation in his head.

"Excuse me?" asked Brassard. "Who?"

"The African lady. There was a pregnant one, but the baby wasn't coming . . ." He examined the middle of the éclair with slightly crossed eyes, then dove in for another bite. "It finally did."

"Oh," said Brassard. "That's good, I guess. But you should keep your mouth closed when you're eating."

On the far side of the bridge, they could see there was more of a buzz beneath the tower. A small crowd was gathered, which seemed to be paying especially close attention to the wagons coming through, though these two here, turning left and headed up the Quai d'Orsay, were piled high with nothing but crates.

Olivier hurried along. Another cartload was parting the people, and this one had passengers standing on the bed. Brassard assumed they were workers at first, but then he heard the people saying "Arabs! The Arabs!" and one of the riders was waving.

"The sultan," said Olivier. "I think. You can't really tell without the turban."

He pointed again. Here came another wagonful, and this bunch was easier to identify. The Pygmies, wearing little tweed suits. The Parisians all squealed and waved. The Pygmies waved back. More squeals until one of the little men smiled and showed his teeth, which looked like a baby shark's. The Parisians fell silent, and all there was was the sound of the wheels trundling by.

"Where do they get the suits?" Olivier asked.

Brassard shrugged. "Tailor."

The crowd turned again, and seemed to thicken as another large wagon came staggering through the gate of the zoo, which had been relieved of its wrought-iron sign—happily, as this one appeared to be a double decker. The second level was unroofed, but the passengers were nearly impossible to see, what with the nightfall, the fog rolling in, and the fact that they were so dark.

"The Africans," said Olivier. "The Malawi! They're the ones that had the baby."

He'd only meant for Brassard to hear, but someone else replied, "Did they? Is that true?" And the nods all around seemed to say that yes, that's what they were here for obviously. "A boy," said another. "Yesterday morning." And they craned and strained to see as the bus swung around toward them and entered under the stanchion lights of the tower.

The Malawi were much more visible now—matte-haired, gleaming-skinned, and all bundled up in patterned robes and scarves, smartly folded, tucked, and tied; the air was cooling. Some were smiling back, though most appeared to be ignoring the Parisians below, even as the pushing and the shoving began in earnest. The guards had been trying to keep the path clear with ropes. It was no use. The crowd closed in and was blocking the way. The driver had to pull the horses to a stop, causing the Parisians all to arch up onto their toes, the young and old alike, to get a better look at the departing players, maybe even catch a glimpse of the one they'd all been waiting for.

Brassard's eye was on the lower level of the omnibus, the interior, which was difficult to read—so thick with bodies, he couldn't even tell if they were sitting or standing. There was one man, though, with his back to the window, and a woman's head on his shoulder. She was wearing a light-colored head wrap. He couldn't see her features, but as the bus stopped, her eyes drifted open briefly, then closed again. Then she resettled her head against his neck. It was possible he was carrying her.

"There!"

Someone was pointing to the open end of the bus, where a narrow set of spiral stairs joined the two levels. Halfway up, a much older woman, low and sturdy, was leaning against the rail. She had a coral-colored wrap around her shoulder, and inside the wrap—nestled against her breast—was the distinctive orb of a little human head.

There was a sudden frenzy as the whole crowd shifted. The children all scampered around the outside of the pack and wormed their way in for a closer view—"*La grandmère! La mémé!*" they said, and they began squealing and ooh-ing and aww-ing, though all anyone could see was swaddling.

Obligingly, the older woman descended just one stair, which turned her more to face them, and she was smiling now—she had no teeth in front—but she folded down the little blanket from the head. Brassard had to shoo aside a man who'd stepped in front of Olivier, but now they all could see the infant's face. He seemed to be looking back at them—which couldn't be. He couldn't see at all, but he was wearing a very serious expression just the same, the kind of overly severe frown that only babies and great statesman can achieve, and which, if it didn't necessarily reflect what he was feeling at the moment, still stood as evidence of an expression he would use to great effect someday.

And looking at him there—the forward thrust of his gleaming brown forehead—Brassard felt his estimation change. He had begun from a place of pity. He pitied all of them, the life that lay ahead—the dispossession, the exposure, the indignity. But as this child looked back at him (or so it felt) with that self-same and still very serious frown, Brassard wondered who was he to pity this one? This one least of all, for behind those scowling eyes there did seem to be an equally emphatic determination—and this was no echo from the future; this was there, in fact—the same desire as had compelled him yesterday, and every day before that. To live. To breathe. To join and see and maybe even testify. Brassard didn't pity that at all.

But now the bus was lurching forward. The driver was starting the horses again, and the people were clearing the way to let them through. The grandmother covered over the newborn and leaned his head against her so as not to strain the little neck. She waved again, her hand like a heavy leaf in the rain, and the people replied in kind, but Brassard had noticed something else now.

Soter's nose was turned the other way, back in the direction of the zoo. While everyone around them smiled and clapped their hands and waved good-bye—"*Bonsoir*, little one." *Mon mignon. Mon petit. Mon Jésu*—

"What is it, boy?" asked Brassard, leaning down.

Soter replied with two strides in that same direction, and then a stop.

"Go ahead."

And Soter started through the people, like a sleek fish through seaweed. The crowd's attention drifted along after the bus—even Olivier's—trying in vain to keep the newborn in view. And while they shared smiles and said how beautiful—"*They really are*"—Brassard followed Soter, who was trotting now, back into the grounds where the human zoo had been.

Chapter 28

The River

Only a few remnants of the habitats remained. The tents were gone, and most of the fences. All that could be seen were the workers sweeping up, carrying away potted palms and other exotic plants. But the grotto was still there, and that was where Soter was headed directly, tail wagging.

Brassard already knew why. He might not have said so, because to say . . . perhaps he was being silly, but Soter wasn't being silly. He trotted up to the opening among the boulders, stopped and sat just outside, pointing with his nose. *Woof.*

Brassard caught up, and he was certain now. As sure as he'd felt her absence down in the crypt, he felt her presence here. He crept up to the opening and peered inside.

She was sitting in the dark, almost as if she were invisible and not the farthest thing from. She was in her white frock again with a hotel blanket draped across her lap—pale blue. A pile of soiled sheets and towels was lumped in the corner, and there was a strong smell of some foreign musk, something sweet, and a sting of oil as well. Castor, maybe.

He had not seen her in two days. Not since the roadside really had he looked her in the eye, but she didn't seem at all surprised by his appearance there, or by the dog's. She stood, and he could see the frock was stained as well, smeared along the front with a grayish brown—presumably some blood, but mostly afterbirth.

There was, both in her body and expression, a clear desire for sleep. Her eyes were wrung, and she had appeared almost forlorn at first, but now as she looked at him directly, she seemed to dispel this with a shake of the head—as a matter of courtesy. The faint smile again.

Strange, though, because from the moment he'd met her on the roadside, he had made it his purpose to track her down, figure out who she was, what she had done, where she was going. Having found her now, he could say that he had succeeded on nearly every count. The body in the woods had been identified. Here stood the digger of the grave. Here stood the killer, the captive, and the midwife: Behold the infant less than one day old. Behold the smudges on the frock.

So yes, he would appear to have solved the case quite brilliantly. Yet as he looked at her now, and beheld again the disarming serenity of her gaze, all of that seemed oddly irrelevant, so much so he wasn't quite sure what to do next. It was she who preceded him out of the cave, back into the misting night, with all the lampposts lit.

The Chaillot station was just across the river. He supposed he could take her there; he wasn't really thinking that far ahead. He started them around the outside of the tower. He didn't want to walk her through the crowd, though Olivier had seen them now. The bus with the Malawi was long gone, and the boy was wandering back in their direction in a kind of loose-ankled way. Brassard gestured for him to stay away. He sent Soter, in fact.

"Call him," he said, and Olivier obliged—*Here, boy*— Soter trotted over. Olivier took his collar, and the two of them watched while Brassard continued on, just him and the young woman.

They were on a path headed north to the river, through a little park and bound for the next bridge along the way, the Pont de L'Alma, she apparently in his custody, even if it didn't feel that way. He was walking at her pace and a stride behind, and as they passed through the trees and guarded flowerbeds, he felt a kind of fog lifting—though in fact the fog was setting in more thickly, in a roiling, tumbling way that seemed to muffle sounds as well.

Yet in his mind a clarity was descending. He had been aware of it for several days now, hovering at the periphery of his view, waiting for his full and waking attention. The only reason he hadn't given it was because, in the first place, he'd been investigating a crime, but also because the last time he'd felt this way was in Panhou, of course, which was still no easy thing to admit: that during what should have been his most dark and terrifying moment—while his enemy-captor carved away at the side of his head—he'd never felt more at peace.

It was that same feeling now, with her, and the thickening fog only seemed to enhance the effect, dissolving all the edges, flattening the trees and the lamplight and the tower with all its iron girders, laying bare the permeability of this and that. The leaves and the sky. The bridge and the river. Blots each. Blots all, and co-creationists of each other, including him and her and the velvety pavement beneath their feet. He felt no anger toward Bruno Chavarin. Or Michaud. Or even himself anymore. For Dupree? Pity. It was true. Bless his children. Bless his steely wife. But he felt no regret or malice toward anything that had happened. Who was he to question the mysterious, multifarious exercise of human being? Or to find it wanting in some way—either "fortunate" or "unfortunate"? What, and tell that child back there he *shouldn't* have been born?

He looked at her, at the soft-rounded line of her three-quarters profile, how evenly it moved forward along the path, like a maidenhead on a glassy bay, and for the first time it occurred to him that maybe Monsieur Singh was on to something. Maybe this *wasn't* anyone's niece. Or daughter. Or captive even. The mind is a clever thing, and among its wisest devices is to box up the most brutal collisions when they happen. Store them away until it's safe again. Take sanctuary in the here and the now, even if it means forgetting everything else.

That would certainly explain the clumsiness of his pursuit the last three days. He'd been operating on all the wrong assumptions: that she was fleeing someone, or meeting someone, delivering some cache. Maybe she was simply here *to be*, as the professor's son might say, because that was the only way. And all that gave her away in the end was the one memory—or the one instinct—that refused to be denied. Serve the mother. Serve the child. Even if that meant remembering.

They'd crossed the Quai d'Orsay and were approaching the foot of the bridge. There was no one else around that he could see, or there didn't seem to be, to an almost eerie extent. Again it was she who started them across, but so distinct and enveloping was his sense of equanimity, he hadn't really considered until now—now that they were actually *on* the bridge—what was waiting for them on the other side; the significance, that is, of all those hazy lights and lines once they resumed their usual definition. The streets. The courts. The lawyers. Depositions. Accusations. Exoneration, maybe. Who knows?

But something in him reared at this idea. Something seemed to pull at him from behind. He looked to her to see if she might be feeling the same. They were nearing the midpoint now, along the left-side walkway—and she did appear to be slowing slightly, like a marble on a track that might or might not make it to the crest.

"Wait," he said, surprising himself more than her. An arm's length from the balustrade, she had only to reach out with her left hand and touch the soft white stone. He stopped as well, and they stood a moment, there at the intersection of two clear and conflicting compulsions. Out ahead, the narrow lane descended to the far bank and everything that waited there, while beneath them the river flowed, sweeping silently and massively to the left.

Brassard removed the cigarette case from his breast pocket. He thought of offering one, just to be polite, but she'd already turned to the river. Her eyes were closed, and her head was tilted slightly upward as if to drink in all the light—which was of a strangely muted and pervasive quality, having traveled all those millions and millions of miles, to bounce off that silver plate up there and be suspended down here in a million tiny droplets, illuminating her face like a million tiny bulbs. She glowed.

On this image, he turned his back as though to shield the wind, though there was hardly a breath of it. He struck his match, but with his fingers trembling, he had to strike it two more times before it finally caught. The flame flickered and flashed in the cup of his hand—a coquette, playfully resisting the draw of his breath—this way and that before finally diving in, glowing orange at the tip and crawling down toward his lips.

Even as he watched it burn, he thought to himself, *This is the letter in my pocket. This is everything I thought I wanted.* He felt the smoke fill his lungs, and he released it, a blue-jet plume into the mist. It seemed to touch the sky and to splay as if it hit a pane of glass. At that same moment, a sudden rush of blood roared in his ears to accompany the mingling of the smoke and the mist, and the disappearance of the one into the other.

Then all was quiet again. His heart began to slow, and his hands were as calm as two stones. He did turn briefly just to make sure. The bridge lane was empty. No one was there, but he could still sense the water sliding underneath, smooth and black, and he could hear horse hooves as well, and wheels somewhere; he couldn't tell where. He'd hardly have known which way was which except for the great ghost of the tower looming overhead.

A good thing. He dropped his cigarette and ground it with his heel. Then he tucked his head against the cold and started back the way he'd come, to go find the boy and the dog, whom he knew would be waiting.

Acknowledgments

As ever, my thanks to everyone who had a hand in the making of this book, but especially my agent, Janet Silver, for her continuing faith and persistence; Lori Milken, for her devotion to the word; my trusted readers—Peter Arango, Kate Phillips, and McCormick Templeman—for their kindness and honesty; Cate School, for balance and understanding; to everyone at Delphinium and at HarperCollins, but in particular Joan Matthews and Colin Dockrill, for their care, their forbearance, and taste; to Elizabeth Shreve for her energy; and finally to my editor, Joe Olshan, whose expert stewardship in turning my manuscript into a novel could not have been more clear throughout, more generous, or more sage.

About the Author

Brooks Hansen is a novelist, screenwriter, illustrator, and teacher. His novels—*The Monsters of St. Helena, Perlman's Ordeal, The Chess Garden,* and *Boone* (co-authored with Nick Davis) were all *New York Times* Notable Books. *The Chess Garden* was also selected as a *Publishers Weekly* Best Book of the Year. He has written two books for young readers, both of which he illustrated. He received a John Simon Guggenheim Fellowship in 2005.